NATIONAL

Ralph (
Western Classic

Sabio's Redemption

Author's Work Select Edition

Formerly ***Guns on the Border***

"One of the best Western writers today."
...*Western Horseman*

Ralph Cotton's
Western Classic
Sabio's Redemption

Author's Work Select Edition

Copyright © 2016 by Ralph Cotton
All Rights Reserved.
No part of this book may be reproduced or transmitted in any form or by any electronic or mechanical means, including photocopying, recording, scanning, or by any information storage and retrieval system, except in the case of brief quotations embodied in critical articles or reviews, without written permission from the author.

He may be reached at **www.ralphcotton.com**
or **ralphcotton@yahoo.com**

Front cover photographs from **123RF.com**

Cover design & book layout by Laura Ashton
laura@gitflorida.com

Author's photo, p 279, by Shay Morton

ISBN: 978-1533453754

Printed in the United States of America

Some Reviews by Amazon Readers

*by Will W. −**Five Stars***
   They don't write 'em like Cotton writes them.

*by Lynn Martene −**Another great book by Ralph Cotton***

This is the second book I read by this author. Like the first book it is full of action, suspense and everything a book needs to grab my attention and keep it. I especailly like these characters, the old priest and how he copes with his problems. The innocent young village girl who the old priest knoews he cannot trust himself with. The author is awesome. I plan on reading all of his books. Keep up the good work Ralph. You have made an old-west fan out of me!

*by Danny F. Pelto -**Good Book***

I enjoyed reading this Book, have read a number of Ralph Cotton Books, I'm sure you will like reading this Book. If you like Reading Westerns, then this book is for you.

Millions Of Ralph Cotton Novels In Print Worldwide

For Mary Lynn ... *of course*

PROLOGUE

Gray smoke curled from the barrel of Ranger Sam Burrack's big Colt as his eyes scanned the shadowed alleyways along the dusty street of San Miguel. The street lay empty save for the single riderless horse that only moments ago had come charging at him with Dallas Fadden hunched low in the saddle, firing a pair of double-action Colt Thunderers as fast as his fingers could pull the triggers.

Upon seeing Fadden come bolting forward, the ranger had dropped from his saddle and slapped the rump of his Appaloosa stallion, sending it out of the way. *Jumping from atop the stallion might have made the difference*, he told himself, always reflecting back as soon as he could on a fight, considering what he'd done right, what he might have done differently. He could fight in or out of the saddle, whichever he had to, but out was always better, given the choice, he reminded himself.

As the ranger's eyes searched, his hands deftly opened the Colt, dropped the one empty cartridge to the dirt, replaced it and snapped the chamber shut.

He slipped the Colt into his tied-down holster, but loosely, knowing that he might suddenly require its use again. *Some parts of hell even the devil didn't travel alone*, he told himself. His gaze moved warily outward, through the raging swirl of white heat surrounding the town, out across the harsh Mexican badlands.

But this is not hell. These were poor and struggling people, no different from many of his own people on the other side of the border. In fact, was it not one of his own that had brought him here? *All right, I'll give you that*, he sighed, silently replying to the voice inside him.

After a moment he took the folded piece of paper from inside his riding duster and opened it as he kept an eye on the empty dusty street. From between two adobe buildings a skinny hound slunk out through the dust, picked up something from the dirt and raced away with it.

"Dallas Fadden, you're marked off," the ranger murmured to himself under his breath. He looked at the list of names on the paper—thieves, rapists, arsonists, assassins, wanton murderers, degenerates *all—the worst of the worst*, his captain had proclaimed them. With a pencil stub that he pulled from under the brim of his pearl-gray sombrero, he drew a straight line through Fadden's name.

On the ground at his feet, Fadden lay at the end of a long streak of bloody dirt where his trail of lawlessness had ended. A bullet hole gaped in the center of his back. The thumb of his right hand had been clipped off by the same single bullet before it bored through his heart. Seeing the bloody stub, Sam looked off in the direction the skinny hound had taken, and realized what had caused the animal to venture out before the smoke and dust had even settled. Sam folded the paper and put it away.

Thirty yards up the dusty street, an old man stepped out of a doorway, his thin arms raised high in a show of peace. "I bring you the *caballo, par favor, guardabosques?*" he said in a mix of Spanish and broken English. He stepped sideways in worn sandals toward the horse in the middle of the street.

"Sí, gracias. Pero tau lenlamente, señor," the ranger replied in stiff Spanish, thanking him for his help and at the same time cautioning him to move slowly. Hell or no hell, Sam knew that in his job, death could strike just as swiftly from beneath a faded serape as it could from a holster, or a business vest, or a lady's handbag. Death observed no borders

and no age, and it gave no warning. But enough of that. Death had just come and gone, for now anyway—he hoped.

Stepping toward him with the horse's reins in hand, the old man offered a thin, cautious smile and said with a slight shrug, *"Lenlamente, señor?* How else can an old man like me move, except slowly?"

"Gracias," Sam said, taking the reins as the old man held them out to him. His eyes moved up and down the man, seeing a battered tin star pinned onto his *serape*, but no sign of a gun butt protruding at his thin waist, and more important, there was no sign of ill intent in the time-weathered eyes. "You are the town sheriff, the *guardia?"* he asked the old man, nodding for him to lower his hands.

"Sí, I am *Guardia* Ramond Rayos." His right hand brushed against the badge.

"Then I think I owe you an apology, *Guardia* Rayos," Sam said. "I didn't know there was a lawman in San Miguel, else I would have come to you first thing, in respect for your office." He paused, then said, "I should have asked around first."

"If you did not know, you did not know." The Mexican lawman shrugged, resolving the matter. "I have been a lawman for all of my life, but I have been *guardia* for only a short time."

But Sam knew that his show of respect did matter. They were both lawmen; each owed the other respect. "I'm glad to see San Miguel finally has someone to uphold the law," he said. "Do you know this man?" He nodded at the body on the ground.

"No, *Guardabosques*— I mean, Ranger," he replied, turning his words from Spanish to English for the ranger's sake. "Should you ask if I or anyone in San Miguel would seek to avenge his death, I must tell you no." He shook his head slowly as he spoke, looking down at the body in the dirt. "And we will miss neither him nor his money, which he threw around so loosely these days he spent here." He paused and then, as if reconsidering, said, "Well, perhaps we will miss his money—but not him." He looked back up at the ranger and asked, as if already knowing the answer, "He is a bad one, no? A man wanted for breaking the law in your country?"

"*Sí*, he was a bad one," Sam answered. "He robbed and murdered a young couple back east, then fled west, robbing and killing many more before he crossed the border."

The old Mexican lawman shook his head slowly. "And he brings himself here as if God has forgiven him and he can start his life anew."

"Something like that, I suppose," said Sam. "But it wouldn't be long before he'd be back up to his old ways, if he hadn't started already."

"Here in San Miguel, he has been quiet and has kept to himself. Had he not been so I would have chased him from among us."

Sam looked at him closer, deciding that the old man still had some iron in him.

Seeing the ranger's appraising gaze, Rayos said, "He would not be the first man I chased away—or shot, if I had to." He nodded at Fadden's body. "This one made no trouble. He drank much wine and mescal in the cantina. He spent time with womenfolk, who have befriended him only for his money. Yet always, he has appeared to be a lonely and haunted man."

"Yep," said Sam, "his kind often appear that way when called upon to show some restraint. They don't feel natural unless they're killing and plundering and running wild."

"I have heard of you," the old man said, as if recognition had just come to him. He touched a long, knobby finger to his temple. "You are the ranger who rides the badlands—who killed the outlaw they called Junior Lake. You killed him and his gang."

"That was a long time ago," Sam replied. "It seems like it anyway."

The old Mexican lawman studied the ranger's eyes,

then said, "And you have killed many more since then. Am I correct?"

"Yes, you are," Sam said flatly. "I have killed many more, too many as far as I'm concerned." As he spoke, he checked the cinch on Fadden's horse and tested the saddle by jerking it back and forth.

The old Mexican lawman shrugged his bony shoulders and said, "But killing is part of our jobs, men like you and me, *sí?*"

"Yeah," said Sam, not wanting to talk about it. He touched a hand to the scar along his cheek in dark reflection. Killing had become more than a part of his job. Across the badlands and along the border, killing had become the job itself.

With a slight hesitancy, the old lawman said, "There are those who say the same as you, that you have done too much killing." Pausing for a second to see how the ranger took his words, the old man continued cautiously. "There are even those who say that all the killing has made you a little. . .*loco?*" He seemed to hold his breath, awaiting the ranger's response.

"I have heard that," said the ranger. Bending and taking a firm grip on the back of Fadden's damp shirt collar, he dragged the corpse almost to its feet and leaned it limply against the side of the horse. "What man, truly crazy, would admit to being so?" He offered only a trace of a wizened smile, as if having thought about the matter at great length.

"*Sí*, that is so," the old Mexican lawman agreed, his voice sounding relieved. He stepped forward, seeing what the ranger was about to do.

Holding the animal's reins in his free hand, Sam moved his grip from the shirt collar to Fadden's belt and, with the old man's help, shoved upward until the body slid over the saddle. "*Gracias* again, *señor*," Sam said, the corpse's arms dangling down the other side of the horse.

"You are most welcome, Ranger," the old man said. He stepped back, a bit winded from exerting himself in the heat of the day. Leveling his straw sombrero, he said, "It is not usual that someone kills someone in my country and takes the corpse away with them. We in San Miguel are grateful for not having to bury him. That is why I bring you the horse, even though keeping the horse here would give value to our town in some small way."

"I see," said the ranger, getting the message.

He took a gold coin from his vest pocket and handed it to the old lawman. In doing so he noted the tight look of humiliation on the old man's face. Yet the old man accepted the coin all the same, the ranger also noted as he took a coiled lariat from Fadden's saddle horn and shook it out.

"The money is not for me, Ranger," Rayos said humbly. "It will go to feed the people of San Miguel when our crops have failed, as they always do."

"I understand," said the ranger as he tied Fadden's corpse firmly to the saddle. Dark blood dripped in a long string from the bullet hole in Fadden's chest. Nearby, two ragged-backed cats had slipped forward as if from out of nowhere. They sat staring intently at the bloody dirt.

Changing the subject, Rayos gestured at the ranger's duster lapel and asked, "Was that *the list* I saw in your hands? The list I heard so much about from the bad ones who you hunt?"

"It's easier for me to keep a list than it is to have to keep running these lowlifes' names through my mind," Sam replied. He ran the length of leftover lariat forward, slipped the horse's bit from its mouth and looped the lariat around its muzzle, fashioning a lead rope. "When I finish what I've done, one way or the other, I mark off the name, fold the list and put it away. I don't think about who's next or what I'll have to do until the time comes."

"Ah, I see," said the old Mexican lawman. He gave a thin, tired smile. "Then you are not so crazy as some might think, eh?"

"I sure hope I'm not, Sheriff Rayos," Sam replied. He pulled on his left trail glove. Then, stopping before pulling on his right glove, he asked solemnly, "Are we squared with one another?"

"Squared?" Rayos asked, his bony arms hanging loosely at his sides.

"I'm asking, is there anything else we need to talk about, or get settled between us?" Sam said.

"No. We are squared," said Rayos.

"Good," Sam said with a nod. "Then I would be much obliged if you'd lift that pistol from the back of your trousers and sport it frontward while I ride out. It's the guns I can't see that concern me the most."

"Of course, Ranger!" Rayos' smile widened. He looked surprised. "I must beg your pardon. I did not know who you were when I put it back here." As he talked he reached behind his back beneath the long hanging serape and slowly pulled out a battered older-model army Colt by its butt with his thumb and finger.

"I would have done the same thing, Sheriff Rayos," said Sam, stepping over to Black Pot, his Appaloosa stallion, and leading Fadden's horse by the rope.

"Oh? Then lawmen like you and I must think alike, eh, Ranger?" said Rayos, sounding proud to associate himself with the ranger, and with lawmen in general.

"Yes, I would say so, Sheriff Rayos," Sam replied. He pulled himself atop the Appaloosa and adjusted his sombrero against the blazing sun. On the ground the two ragged-backed cats slipped forward and low-ered their muzzles to the fresh blood in the dirt.

"And you must come back to visit San Miguel someday," said Rayos as the ranger turned both horses to the dusty street, heading them east. Seeing the ranger look back with a dubious expression, Rayos called out, "I mean return only for a visit. So you can see San Miguel in a different light, not just as a place to carry out your job."

The ranger nodded, touching the brim of his sombrero. "Obliged, Sheriff. I might take you up on that offer."

"*Adios* until then," Rayos called out, raising a thin flat palm to the ranger and waving it back and forth slowly, even though the ranger's gaze had already turned toward the trail ahead.

PART I

CHAPTER 1

The half-breed, Caridad, had seen trouble brewing between the two men for days. But like the rest of the people in the small town of Esperanza, she had remained silent and distanced herself from them. *"Estos son hombres peligrosos, Caridad,"* the defrocked monk, Sabio Tonto Montero, had whispered under his breath to her the day the band of *Americano* mercenaries rode in from the east.

But the former holy man did not have to tell her that these were dangerous men. Danger and evil showed in them the way hunger showed in wolves. Their caged eyes, although as indiscernible as a serpent's, moved endlessly across their surroundings, appraising any and all things of immediate value to them. Things of no value or use to them their eyes discarded quickly and continued on as they drank and cursed and laughed.

The men seemed to not even see Caridad as they tossed back mescal, whiskey and tequila, all laced with cocaine, and snorted peyote cactus powder up their noses. She felt relieved that these men saw her as of no use or pleasure to them. *Not yet anyway*, she reminded herself. And what would these or any men see in her? she wondered—a gangly young half-breed scrub girl with a bucket and brush always in hand.

Standing at the rear door of the cantina, she watched them, noting how their hands never strayed far from the guns holstered on their bellies and hips, even as they twirled the cantina whores and bounced them roughly on their knees. They awaited *Capitán* Luis Murella, who had sent for them to come work for him in the procuring of American-made firearms and explosives. Caridad hoped they would not have to wait much longer.

During their short wait in Esperanza, two of the twelve whores that the *capitán* had sent from Mexico City to keep the mercenaries entertained until his arrival had died. A farmer's milk cow that had wandered into town had been lassoed, slaughtered and cooked over a raging fire in the center of the town square. One of the mercenaries had climbed to an outstretched limb near the top of an ancient oak, tied a lariat around his neck and hurled himself from the limb.

"When these men run out of things to kill they begin to kill themselves and one another," the defrocked monk had whispered to Caridad. "Stay away from *estos hombres*, and as always do not forget to pray for help and protection from the saints and from the Blessed Virgin Mother." Which she did, unquestioningly, even though her instruction had come from a man the holy church had denounced as unfit and cast from its fold.

But when the trouble erupted between the two mercenaries, it came about so quickly, she had no time to pray for help or protection.

At the bar, Desmond Prew, the leader of the mercenaries, stood talking to his new second in command, Hubbard White, when through the open cantina doorway walked Cherokee Jake Slattery, one of the two men destined to run afoul of each other. At a table sat the other man, Clarence Sibbs, an assassin for hire and former gang member from the wild lawless slums of New York.

"Hold it, White," Prew said, stopping White's conversation in a lowered tone upon seeing Cherokee Jake and Sibbs give one another dark looks. "I think we're about to see who's packing the biggest rocks in their basket." From his spot near the bar, an accordion player brought his song to an anxious stop.

Prew and White turned toward where Slattery stood, six feet away from Sibbs' table. Slattery opened his black linen suit coat and idly hiked up his baggy trousers. In doing so he let Sibbs and the whole cantina see that he wasn't wearing his gun belt.

"Here we go," Prew whispered to White. Beside the rear door, Caridad watched transfixed, unable to pull herself away.

From the center of the floor, Cherokee Jake Slattery said to everyone in the cantina, "I want all of yas to hear what I've got to say. You've all seen tension between Sibbs and me over something untoward I might have said these past few days."

Between himself and White, Prew said, "Don't buy it for a second."

Slattery continued, saying respectfully, "Well, I'm here to apologize. We're going to be all working together, making ourselves rich!" He beamed, raising a fist in the air and shaking it in a hooray. "So I want to clear the air between me and Sibbs—sort of let bygones be bygones and get ready for action together!" He turned toward Sibbs' table, clapping his hands together. "What say you, Sibbs? Can we patch things up? Be amigos, eh? As they say down here."

Sibbs stared at him and said flatly, his hand resting on his gun butt, "I ain't forgot what you called me. But I'm willing if you are. Only don't ever try telling anybody in front of me again that you caught Little Walk Pierce unawares and gutted him before he knew what hit him. I knew Little Walk Pierce and that was not likely to have happened."

Humbling himself, Slattery said, "I know you're calling me a damn liar in front of all these men. But I expect I deserve it for calling you what I did." He took a deep breath and said, "For the sake of our working together, I'm going to take this bitter medicine and swallow it down, painful though it is."

"There it is," called a drunken voice from the bar.

Slattery spread his arms and made a sweeping gesture toward the rest of the men and the whores standing and sitting with them beneath a looming cloud of cigar smoke.

The crowd murmured and shook their heads. "Water under the bridge," a voice called out, raising a shot glass as if in a toast.

"Can I do any more than that?" Slattery ended his appeal to the crowd with his hand extended in friendship toward Sibbs.

Sibbs considered the hand extended toward him. Taking his time, he stood up and reached out with his right hand, his left hand relaxed at his side, close to another holster on his left hip. "What the hell? I was drinking. Maybe I provoked you into calling me a sonsa—"

"Shhh. Hush now," said Slattery, cutting him off. "I was at fault, and I admit it." He shook Sibbs' hand vigorously. When he started to turn loose, Sibbs held on for a second.

"Where you was at fault is when you tried to say you caught Little Walk unawares. He would never have allowed himself to be set up that way." As soon as he'd spoken, he tried to turn loose of the handshake, but now it was Slattery who held on.

"Is that a fact?" Slattery said in a soft but resolved voice, holding Sibbs' hand even more firmly. He stepped in closer. A sinking feeling swept over Sibbs' face, as he stared into Slattery's cold, dark eyes. "You mean like this?"

A cunning grin crept onto Slattery's lips. The knife came from behind his back; the long sharp-pointed blade sank into Sibbs' abdomen before he saw it. He bowed forward with a gasp, seeing only the knife handle against the V of his sternum, blood spilling around its hilt. "Now you look as surprised as Little Walk," said Slattery. He pulled the knife blade out just enough to get a good slicing grip and jerked it sideways in a harsh, long half-moon pattern, opening Sibbs' stomach.

Sibbs saw a glimpse of Slattery's gold-capped tooth, up close, before Slattery yanked the knife out and stepped back, letting blood run from its blade.

Instinctively, Sibbs' left hand clutched his spilled intestines, cupping them up onto his forearm like squirming newborn puppies. But even as his insides continued to slip away from him, his blood-slick right hand tried to draw his Colt, only to fumble and drop it, causing it to explode as it hit the dirt floor.

"So long, tub of guts," said Slattery. "Tell Little Walk I said howdy." He jabbed the blade back into the open gash on Sibbs' chest and stabbed it sidelong into his heart.

"What did I tell you?" Desmond Prew said quietly to Hubbard White. He sipped his whiskey and watched Slattery guide Sibbs backward into his chair and once again jerk the knife blade out of him.

"What's this going to do to us, being a man short?" White asked. He picked up his drink and sipped it.

"Shouldn't matter much," said Prew, unconcerned, watching Slattery pull a handkerchief from Sibbs' lapel pocket and attentively wipe his knife blade clean. "We'll pick up a man or two if need be."

The other men stood watching, equally unconcerned, their arms looped around whores, bottles and beer mugs dangling from their hands. Slattery turned to them, still wiping the handkerchief along the knife blade. "Gentlemen, you have to admit, he had it coming." He grinned toward Prew and White. "Anybody arrogant enough to question my knife-handling skills."

On a different matter, a Texas gunman named Thomas Russell called out, "Damn, he's shot! That misfire got him!" He stood pointing at a young man sitting at Sibbs' table, and at the gun lying smoking on the dirt floor. The young man's face had turned ashen and pasty beneath a heavy layer of sweat. He held a bloody hand up under his armpit, squeezing hard to slow the bleeding.

"I'm all right," he said in a thick dreamlike tone of voice.

"Like hell he is," said Russell to the other men, whose

attention had swung mildly from Slattery to the wounded man.

"Kid," said Prew, "how'd you manage to get shot up there?" He walked toward him from the bar, seeing the blood flow freely down the side of the young man's green woolsey shirt.

"I'm all right, I told you," the young man repeated, trying to keep his voice sounding natural. "Just took a nick."

"Yeah, I'll say you did," said Prew, looking at the heavy flow of blood. "Nicked a big vessel is what it looks like to me." He stooped slightly and looked into the young man's eyes. "Get it looked at," he said with cool indifference.

"I will," the young man nodded, as if he'd see to the matter right away. Yet he made no effort to rise from the chair.

From the open doorway came the sound of the town church bell. As the men turned toward it, one of the lookout men Prew had posted at the edge of town came running in and said, "Prew, they're here!"

"Well, all right then, Harkens!" Prew said to the lookout man, seeing the rest of his men getting excited about the *capitán's* arrival. "Let's go greet him." Before turning to the doorway he looked down at the young man and said, "Kid, in this game, if you can't ride, you're not much 'count. You know we can't leave a man behind."

"I know it," the young man said, his voice sounding more shaky. "But I can ride—just point me—"

"Good for you, lad," said Prew, cutting him off, already dismissing him as he patted the wounded man's shoulder roughly and walked away toward the sound of horse hooves pounding along the dirt street. The rest of the men followed, their arms still looped around the whores, their bottles still in hand.

"So long, kid," one of them said in passing, as if he never expected to see the young man again.

Hearing the silence of the cantina close in around him once the last of the mercenaries had left, the wounded young man turned a pale bleary-eyed gaze to the accordion player and said flatly, "Play something."

But the accordion player and the barkeeper gave one another a look and approached the young man the way they might approach a wounded mountain cat. "Hear me? Play something," he tried to demand, his hand still squeezing against the flow of blood, but weakening in its effort.

Hector, the cantina owner, looked to Caridad, who remained against the rear wall where she'd crouched in fear when the gunshot exploded. "*Prisa, muchacha!* Go bring Sabio! This man is dying!"

"No, I'm not," the young man said, his hand having a hard time keeping pressure on his wound.

Caridad had started toward the rear door, but she stopped at the sound of the young man's voice until Hector said, "Go quickly, Caridad! This one does not know what he is saying!"

Outside in the dirt street, *Capitán* Luis Murella brought his small column of men to halt with a raised hand, followed by a verbal command from the thin sergeant who rode three steps behind him. Turning slightly in his saddle, the *capitán* sat looking at the body of the mercenary hanging from the high oak branch thirty feet off the ground. Two buzzards clung to the corpse's shoulder, picking at its dark swollen face, causing it to jerk and quiver in a grotesque manner.

"Good day to you, *Capitán*," Prew called out as he and his men stood in the dirt street facing the column of mounted soldiers. "Pay no mind to him," he added, looking up with the capitán at the corpse.

"He is one of yours?" the capitán asked, turning his attention to Prew.

"Yeah," said Prew, "he was one of the new men."

"And you hanged him?" The captain looked confused.

"No, no, *Capitán*," said Prew. "He hanged himself, the poor bastard."

"He hanged *himself?*" The Mexican captain looked back

up at the corpse almost in disbelief.

"Yep. You might say his heart wasn't in his work," Prew said, a trace of a wry smile coming to his leathery face.

The serious captain saw no humor in it, wry or otherwise. He looked the men over and asked, "How many men have you here?"

"About a dozen, *Capitán*," Prew said, not liking the idea of him standing down in the dirt street having to look up into the sun to speak to a Mexican.

"*About* a dozen?" the captain asked, pressing him. "Do you not know your numbers?"

Prew's thin smile went away. His voice took on a harsh edge. "We had a little misunderstanding and just lost a man back there, maybe two." He gestured a nod back toward the cantina.

"I see," said the captain. "So that explains the gunshot we heard moments ago?"

"Yes it would, if I felt it required explaining," said Prew, the harshness still in his voice. He continued, saying, "But even so, there's eleven of us still on our feet—enough for us to turn hell into a tent meeting if we needed to." He made no effort to conceal his appraising gaze as he cast it across the mounted soldiers.

"Eleven, eh?" The captain ignored the veiled threat, yet he seemed to consider something for a moment. Then, as if dismissing the matter, he looked at the women and asked, "These are the *putas* I sent to make you and your men welcome?"

"Yes they are, *Capitán*," said Prew, "and a fine bunch they are at that. We are obliged for your thoughtfulness." He swept an arm toward the cantina. "Why don't we get out of the street and have ourselves a drink, cut the dust from your gullets?"

"*Sí*, you go. I will join you inside," the captain replied, "as soon as I have a word with my *sargento*."

"*Gracias* then," said Prew, touching his fingers to his

hat brim. "We'll be waiting." Turning, he walked back to the cantina, White right beside him. In a lowered voice, mocking the captain, he said, *"Do you not know your numbers?"* He gave a dark, contemptuous chuckle and shook his head. "What the hell's he think he is, my schoolmaster?"

CHAPTER 2

Inside the cantina, Prew motioned for the owner to clear away the bloody table and chair and make ready for the captain. But when the captain and his men arrived, after hitching their horses, the owner was still busily throwing fresh dirt over the soft puddle of blood on the floor. As the captain and his men walked through the open doorway, Prew asked Hubbard White, "What do you suppose happened to the kid?"

White's eyes followed the blood trail across the dirt to the rear door. "If I had to guess, I'd say he's crawled off somewhere and bled out."

"A guess won't get it," Prew said just between the two of them. "He knows too much. Go find him. Make sure he's able to ride—or else make sure he's dead."

"You've got it, Prew," White said, slipping away from the bar and out the rear door as the captain walked to the bar, slapping dust from his tunic with his gloves.

Looking at the blood trail, and at the rear door closing behind Hubbard White, the captain asked Prew, "Where is he going?"

Gesturing toward the blood trail, Prew said with a shrug, "To check on our wounded man, *Capitán*."

"Is this wounded man going to be able to keep up with the others?" the captain asked suspiciously.

"That's what I sent him to find out," said Prew. "Now what will you have to drink?"

But the captain persisted, asking even as the cantina owner stood waiting, "How much does this wounded man know about what we are going to be doing?"

"Not much, *Capitán*," said Prew. "Relax," he added with a stiff smile. "Hell, I don't even know what it is we'll be doing."

But the captain wouldn't let it go. "If he cannot ride, we can't leave him here alive," he insisted.

"That's the same thing I told White," said Prew. "I told him to go make sure the man's able to ride, or else see to things. . . ." He let his words trail to an end, giving the captain a knowing look. "We're not newcomers, White or me. Now relax and drink up."

The captain nodded, seeming satisfied. He motioned for his sergeant and his men to come forward to the bar. They did so eagerly.

Prew turned and grabbed two clean glasses and set them in front of the captain and himself. In broken Spanish he said to the barkeeper, "Whiskey *para nosotros ambos*."

"Whiskey for you both?" the barkeeper said, as if uncertain of Prew's words. He held the bottle half tilted, ready to pour.

"You know damn well that's what I said," Prew growled, snatching the bottle from his hand. "Take care of these soldiers. I'll pour for the *capitán* and me." He filled the captain's glass, then his own.

Out back of the cantina, White walked along, his head bowed, following the dark blood trail until he spotted one of the mercenaries, Riley Hallit, leaning against an adobe building. The man was half-conscious, a bottle of mescal hanging from his hand. "Hallit, wake up!" White said, stepping ever closer to the drunken man. "Did you see the kid go by here?"

"Kid?" Hallit raised his eyelids only a little and said in a groggy voice, "I ain't seen nothing go by here but pretty flowers and dancing animals."

Seeing the greenish-yellow peyote powder in Hallit's gray mustache, White shook him and said, "Damn it, man! You're too old for snorting Mexican dope. Get your head cleared. The captain is here! He's in the cantina!"

"Captain who?" Hallit said unsteadily, his head bobbing as he spoke.

"Come on, sober your ass up!" White grabbed him firmly by the front of his sweat-dampened shirt. "You're coming with me. What are you doing out here anyway?"

"Looking for myself a woman," Hallit said in a drunken stupor.

"The whores are all inside," said White.

"I don't want a whore!" said Hallit. "I want a good pretty woman. One that looks like my ma."

"Whoa, that sounds unnatural to me." Hubbard White glared at him dubiously as he dragged him along the small alleyway.

"What's unnatural to one is natural as an egg to others," Hallit replied mindlessly, staggering along. "I loved my ma."

"Jesus, it sounds like you did," said White, pulling him along beside him, following the dark dots of blood, which had grown smaller now. "I don't know what's happened to you. You used to be a hell of a gunman. Now you're turning into a drunken dope-eating bummer."

"Watch your language," Hallit said groggily. He tried to straighten himself up and act sober, but it was of no use. The peyote and mescal had the world spinning before his eyes. His feet could hardly feel the ground beneath him.

From a crack in a doorway thirty yards ahead of them, Sabio Tonto watched the two draw closer, their footsteps sending a flock of chickens and pigeons flurrying aside in their wake. "Hurry, Louisa!" he said over his shoulder. "They are looking for him. Is he going to live?"

Behind him, a stout, little woman hurriedly tied a rough squared chunk of wood firmly up under the wounded young man's arm. Half-conscious, his head bowed, the young man murmured repeatedly, "*Gracias*, ma'am . . . *gracias*, ma'am . . ."

"Be quiet," the stout woman whispered to him as she began quickly wrapping strips of cloth around him, lashing his upper arm against his side. She called out to the former monk in Spanish, shaking her head. "This will slow the bleeding, but he has lost so much blood, I don't know if he will live." She crossed herself and added, "Only God knows."

"Forget about *God*. He only teases us," said the defrocked monk. "I have seen how these sort of men treat their own. If they find he cannot ride, they will kill him."

Stepping in through the side door, Caridad hurried over to the wounded man as she said under her breath, "I have a donkey cart. Hurry!"

"Good work, my child," said Sabio. He rushed to help the two women raise the man to his feet. They led him out through the door to the awaiting two-wheeled hay cart.

Once the man was inside the small cart, Sabio threw hay over him and said to Caridad, "Take him up to the old mission. I will join you there as soon as I can. I cannot let Louisa face these men. She gets frightened too easily."

Hearing him, Louisa quickly imagined the terrible things the *Americano* mercenaries might do to her. "Why are we doing all this, risking our lives for this stranger? A man we know nothing about?"

"Shhh," said Sabio, quieting her, hearing her voice grow louder as she spoke. "We do this because this is what the day has cast upon us. A moment ago you said to submit to God's will. Yet now you question the very task that God lays before us. No wonder God thinks of us as fools." He gestured with his hand, a look of disdain on his face. "Go back inside and keep silent."

Louisa shook her head and looked down in shame, then hurried back inside. Sabio took Caridad by her forearm and guided her to the donkey. He picked up the donkey's lead rope and placed it in her hand.

"But why have you not stopped the bleeding with your hands, Sabio?" Caridad asked.

"Because sometimes I do not have God's power to

perform such miracles. Do you understand?" Sabio replied in a sharp tone of voice. "Now go. Hurry!"

"*Sí*, I go," said Caridad, sounding disappointed. "But I do not understand."

Seeing the pleading look in her eyes even as she began leading the cart away along the narrow dirt street, Sabio called out in a guarded tone, "All right. I will try to heal him when I arrive."

As Caridad led the donkey cart around the corner of the street, toward the trail leading to the old mission ruins, the two mercenaries walked past her with no more than a glance. Relieved, she led the cart on and looked back for only a moment, in time to see the front door of the adobe swing open. She turned away and continued on as Sabio stared out at the two men and said in calm English, "Yes, what is it you want?"

"We're looking for one of our men. He's wounded," said White. "We followed his blood to your rear door. Is he in there?" Even as he asked, he pressed closer. Sabio held his ground at the partly open door.

"There is no one here but me and the woman. We heard someone knock at the rear door. But it is bad luck to use the back door at this time of day, so we did not answer."

White gave Hallit a look and muttered, "Damn superstitious peasants." Hallit only weaved drunkenly in place.

"I need to come inside and take a look around," said White, eyeing the stout woman who bustled about beyond Sabio. Louisa had already gathered the bloody rags and swept the drops of blood onto the dirt floor.

Sabio resisted the slight shove of White's hand on the door. "Of course you can look around but, *señor*, I beg of you, be quick. The woman's husband might return at any moment.... He does not know about me." He gave White a worried look and stepped back, letting the two men inside.

"Oh, I see," said White, with a dark chuckle. "Well, we

don't give a damn about her husband, *or* you." Yet, looking all around the one large room and seeing no sign of the young man having been there, he turned and said to Hallit, "Let's go. Hell, I can't stand the smell in here."

When the two stepped back outside and had walked away, Sabio leaned against the door and sighed in relief. Seeing the dubious look on Louisa's face, he asked, "What is it?"

"You lied," she said, her voice bitter with disappointment. "A man who took a sacred oath, and yet you lie to have things go your way."

"I took a sacred oath, but the men I made that oath to took it back from me when they cast me out," he said.

"But your oath was to God, not to those men," Louisa countered.

Sabin gave a thin wry smile and said, "A man who vows not to lie has broken his vow in its making. Listen to me, my precious." He grabbed her by her thick wrist and drew her against him. "All—men—are—liars," he said, staring into her dark eyes, his lips only inches from hers. He pronounced each word separately and distinctly as if to make certain she heard and understood.

"But for a holy man lying should not come so easily," she responded, feeling his warm breath on her lips.

"I lied to save a man's life," Sabio whispered. "What good is truth if it causes violence and death? How sinful is a lie if it prevents these things?"

"But you used my dead husband in your lie," said Louisa, feeling passion well behind her breasts. She crossed herself instinctively upon the mention of her deceased husband.

"Yes," said Sabio, "and who among the dead has ever felt wronged in being used to prevent more death?" He shrugged and added wryly, "None that I ever heard from." He drew her tighter against him, making certain she felt the hardness below his waist.

"Oh, my!" Louisa said, feigning embarrassment as she

shoved herself away a few inches. "I see what all this excitement has done for you."

"Yes," said Sabio. "Lying, saving a man's life, defending my morals to you. These things have aroused my animal urges. Now you must relieve me—take this terrible lustful aching from my belly."

Louisa held him at bay with a hand against his bony chest. "You forget that I am still in mourning?"

"Forget it? How can I forget it?" said Sabio, still holding her wrist. "I walk around as stiff as a gate handle, desiring you! If I had forgotten your mourning, I would have been mounted upon you and we would have refused to go participate in the game God had planned for us this day."

"Always, you twist God's will to suit your own thinking," said Louisa. "How can you think of such a thing in the midst of all this? A man is hurt, perhaps dying."

"Thrusting myself inside you is always on my mind, for I am a real and normal man," said Sabio. "It does not matter what human intrigue is afoot. A man who is a man thinks always of thrusting himself inside a woman and riding her like some fine hot mare in season." He cupped the front of his trousers and whispered as if in pain, "Ah, *mi amigo duro*, she is killing you!"

"Your hard friend is no concern of mine!" Louisa jerked her wrist free of him and stepped back, adjusting her clothes and dusting herself as if being against him had left her disheveled and dirty. "Do not think you can talk coarsely to me, especially while I am still mourning my blessed husband."

Sabio studied her expression, seeing that she was not yet ready for him, but also seeing, as he had after each such encounter over the past few weeks, that her defenses were weakening with every new advance. *Paciencia*, he reminded himself. *Yes, be patient*. She wants you too. He took a deep breath and said, "I am sorry, my precious Louisa. It is just that I burn so deeply for you, and I know that somewhere inside you, you burn deeply for me, as you always have."

She stood in silence for a moment, then said, "What would Caridad think if she heard you talk this way?"

"I apologize," Sabio said humbly.

But Louisa wasn't through. "What if she saw the front of your trousers bulged out like some billy goat's horn?"

"I apologize," Sabio repeated. "To Caridad I will always be a monk—a holy man. But she must understand that I am now a man like any other, no longer bound by vows I made with the mother church."

"With God," Louisa reminded him again.

"All right, as you wish. *With God!*" Sabio said, giving in to her for the moment. "Now I must go see about the wounded man. Maybe I can save his life *again*."

"So my denying you will send you off to do something good in this game God has made for you this day?" She planted a hand on her stocky hip as if in victory.

"There would have been time for me to do both," Sabio said, hoping for the last word on the matter.

"Yes, but through me, God has willed otherwise this day," Louisa said, not giving an inch.

Sabio murmured under his breath and turned to the door. He was not going to ask why she had given herself to him with abandon while her husband was alive and while he himself was so bound to the holy mother church. Yet, now, the two of them both free to do their own choosing, she denied him. "God forgive us all our craziness," he said under his breath, checking and smoothing down the front of his trousers before stepping out into the street.

CHAPTER 3

From within a long tangle of wild tamarinds, magnolia, and Jacaratia trees lining the trail, Caridad had stopped the donkey cart long enough to look down on Esperanza. "Still they come," she whispered to herself, seeing the two *Americanos* walk past the last small adobe at the edge of town and look up across the meandering hills. For a moment it appeared as if they stared right into her eyes. But she shook off her fear, knowing better, and watched until she saw them turn back toward the dusty street, as if they might be giving up. Yet, deep inside herself, she knew better.

"Come, donkey," she said, tugging on the animal's lead rope. "We are still at the task Sabio has given us."

Below, at the edge of Esperanza, Hallit wiped a hand across his sweaty forehead, still drunk on mescal, high on cocaine and mildly hallucinating on the peyote. "We gave it our best though, eh?" He looked sidelong at White, batting his eyes to get them into focus. White's solemn face appeared to change from one dark glowing color to another beneath his hat brim.

"We're not through, Hallit," White said, walking with determination toward a faded sign that read ESTACION DEL LIVERY, a long row of public livery stables where their horses were billeted out of the sun.

Hallit's drunken heart sank. "Hey, if we can't find him, we can't find him. Good riddance, I say. I never cared much for the sonof—"

"Damn it, Riley," said White, cutting him off in disgust.

"You have no idea *who* we're looking for or *why*, do you?"

"To be honest, no, I don't," Hallit admitted, looking ashamed of himself. "I'm trying to sober up and catch on as we go, all right? I mean, a man can get caught drunk and unawares, can't he?"

White relented a bit. "I expect so. But now it's time you get yourself straightened out and into a saddle. Prew said take care of that kid and that's what we're going to do."

"Do you suppose you can not tell Prew what a shape I was in when we met up?" Hallit asked, almost pleading, his eyes still aswirl with dope and mescal.

"Do your part, and I promise you Prew will never know a thing," said White, the two of them turning a corner toward the livery stables.

"I'm obliged," said Halitt, "and if I wasn't sorely attempting to get myself sober, I'd buy you a drink right now." As he spoke, he looked all around for another cantina, other than the one where Prew and the men were.

"Hold it!" said White, planting a hand firmly on his damp chest.

"I was joking!" said Hallit. "Can't a man make a little joke about—"

"That's not what I mean," said White. He stared straight ahead, watching Sabio slip along the edge of the narrow street thirty yards in front of them. "Isn't that the little weasel we called upon?"

"I—I can't say for sure," said Hallit, struggling with it, the dope and mescal not letting go of his senses easily.

"Yep, it sure is," said White, answering himself. "I've got a hunch that tricky little sumbitch knows more than he was telling. I'm going to follow him." He gave Hallit a shove toward the livery stables. "Get our horses and catch up to me."

"Get our horses . . ." Hallit murmured to himself, as if getting his instructions clear in his foggy mind.

"If you screw this up, Hallit, you'll wish to God you'd

never heard my name," White threatened. "Now get your drunken ass going!" As he spoke he'd already begun slipping away toward where he'd seen Sabio's bald head disappear into a crumbling adobe building with a weathered sign above the door that read COMERCIO E INTERCAMBIO DEL FRANCES (French Trade and Exchange).

"This might be easier than I thought," White whispered to himself, drawing his pistol as he reached the front of the building. "You're going to tell me something this time, you little weasel," he said as if Sabio were able to hear him.

Yet once White was inside the open doorway of the abandoned building, all he saw was the windowless, doorless rear wall. "What the hell?" He looked all around, but saw no place where a man, even a small man like Sabio, could have hidden.

The crumbling building had been stripped of furnishings and gutted of any interior walls. In streams of sunlight through missing roof thatch, White stared bewildered at a few sticks of furniture remnants and broken wooden crates, all covered with a coating of pigeon droppings and undisturbed dust and cobwebs. Along a broken and sagging roof rafter a line of pigeons sat cooing peacefully.

"Hell, he couldn't have ducked inside here," White growled, shoving his pistol back into his holster. Backing out the door, he saw a thin footpath leading around the side of the building. He could have sworn the man had gone into the building, but upon seeing the path he rethought himself and said, "All right, tricky little weasel. I see what you did."

"White, here they are!" Hallit called out, riding up on his horse, leading a big fine bay by its reins.

Stopping at the entrance of the darkened path, White looked at the horse beside Hallit and said, "Damn it, man, that's not my horse. That's Prew's!"

"Aw, hell!" Hallit cursed. "I'm still too doped and drunk to know what I'm doing." He started to turn back toward the livery stables, but White stopped him.

"I'm not letting this weasel get away," he said, taking the reins to Prew's horse from Hallit's hand. "Prew will understand. He'll have to if he wants me to take care of the kid."

"I know I'm blind drunk," said Hallit, "but why are you so convinced this man can tell us anything?"

White took a breath, considered it, then said, "All right, it was just a hunch at first. But now I can tell he wanted to give us the slip. He acted like he went into this building, but then he cut around this way."

He nodded toward the path as he swung himself up atop Prew's bay and nudged it forward. But fifteen feet along the path, White stopped abruptly and sat staring at another adobe wall.

Behind him Hallit sat atop his horse, batting his blurry eyes in bewilderment. "He didn't come this way unless he can climb like a squirrel." The wall reached twenty feet straight up with nothing lying around to be used in scaling it. Along the upper edge sat more pigeons, cooing peacefully.

"Come on, damn it!" White cursed. "He gave us the slip somehow, but I know damn well I saw him come this way." He jerked the horse around and headed back out onto the street. "I'll take Prew's horse back and get my own. We'll ride every street, alley and mudhole."

"So we're gonna keep looking?" Hallit asked, riding right behind him.

"Hell yes!" said White. "Prew said find the kid and take care of him, and that's what we're going to do."

Hallit cursed under his breath but stayed right behind White until they had ridden to the livery stables and started inside. But he stopped when White all of a sudden said, "Hey, look who's going there. It's that damn accordion player. Looks like he's sneaking around, up to something too."

"Him too, huh?" Hallit gave White a questioning look.

"You're not starting to think everybody here has a hand in hiding the kid from us, are you?"

White gigged the horse forward without answering. Hallit hurried his horse along behind him. When they turned a corner and saw the accordion player look back at them and start to run, White sped up, came alongside the man and gave him a sidelong kick that sent him sprawling in the dirt. A large grass sack rolled from under the accordion player's arm.

"You're not going anywhere, *amigo*," White shouted, coming down from the saddle and grabbing the man by the back of his shirt as the man gained his footing, grabbed the bag and tried to make a run for it.

"Please, mister! Let me go!" the accordion player pleaded in better than average English. "I have done nothing! I have no money!"

"Money, ha!" said White. He shook him by the nap of his shirt. "Are you saying we look like a couple of thieves?" He gave Hallit a knowing grin.

"No, mister, I am not saying that. I am only saying please do not harm me. I have done—"

"Shut up," White growled, cutting him off with another hard shake. "I heard you the first time." As he held the man, he knocked the grass sack from his hands and opened it with the toe of his boot, enough to look inside at the folded accordion.

"It is only my music instrument, mister," said the frightened musician. "It has no value, except to me. It is the only way I have to make a living. Please do not take it."

"I see what it is," said White. Knowing the man wasn't about to leave his instrument behind, he turned him loose and gave him a rough pat on his back. "Don't worry, *amigo,* we're not going to take your squeeze-box. Are we, Riley?" He looked up at Hallit with a grin.

"I guess not," Hallit shrugged, starting to feel the shaky aftereffects of the waning drugs and mescal.

"No sirree," said White to the Mexican. "What we want to

know is where the *Americano* is who got shot in the cantina. You were there when we all left, so don't try lying to me."

"Yes, mister, I was there," said the musician with a curious look. "Why would I lie?"

"Hey, *hombre!*" White slapped him roughly on his thin shoulder. "I ask all the questions—you give the answers."

"Yes, of course," said the Mexican. "I saw the man who was shot leave with the young scrubwoman, Caridad. I do not know where she took him."

White slapped him again, this time on the cheek instead of the shoulder. "Don't make me wear you out, *hombre*," he said. "I want to know where the *Americano* is. You *will* tell me."

The musician shook his head. "I do not know, mister," he said.

"All right, *hombre*," said White. "Let's do this another way." He drew his pistol from his holster, cocked it and aimed it at the grass sack on the ground. "Every time you give me an answer I don't want to hear, I'll put one more bullet hole in your squeezer. Now where the hell is the *Americano?*"

"Please, mister, don't shoot," said the musician, breaking down at the sight of a gun pointed at his accordion. "Caridad would have only taken him to one person—the holy man, Sabio."

"Where will we find this holy man?" White asked, looking pleased with himself, his pistol aimed loosely at the accordion.

"Sabio is everywhere," said the musician. "He is like the wind."

"That kind of talk will get your little friend here killed," said White. His grip tightened on the gun pointed toward the accordion.

"No, please, mister!" said the musician. "I am telling you what you ask. Sabio *is* everywhere, or so it seems. The elderly of Esperanza say he was touched by a *brujo*. By a witch, *señor.*"

"I know what a *brujo* is, *hombre*," said White, his pistol still cocked and pointed. "Keep talking."

"Others say he was not touched by a *brujo*, but that he himself is a *mago* . . . a wizard, *señor*."

"A witch-man," White said, considering it with a disbelieving grin. He already had a hunch who it was they were talking about. "What does he look like, this mysterious Sabio the *mago?*"

"He is a small, hairless man," said the Mexican. "I call him *'el sin pelo.'* The hairless one. But never where he might hear me," he added in a lowered voice.

"Yeah. *'El sin pelo,'* eh?" White grinned, making the connection.

"You have seen him, *señor?*" the Mexican asked.

"Oh yes, I've seen the hairless one all right, that little bald-headed mud-dauber."

"Please, *señor*," the musician said, looking around nervously, not knowing how bad a name "mud-dauber" might be. "Do not curse him or speak ill of him. He has power that we do not understand." As the musician spoke he crossed himself quickly, and his voice began to take on more of his native tongue. "Some say he is a blasphemer who has offended God Almighty with his unnatural powers. Others say his powers come from God's own hand."

White took on a curious expression. "When you say he's everywhere, does that mean sometimes you see him going somewhere, but when you get there you find out he's not there at all?"

The accordion player gave him a puzzled glance; so did Hallit.

"Never mind, damn it," said White, looking a little embarrassed. "Where would this hairless one, *'el sin pelo,'* have taken the wounded *Americano?*"

"I do not know, *señor*," said the musician, "but if I were looking for him and did not want to wait for him to appear before my eyes, I would go up there to the old mission." He nodded up the trail to the thick brush and foliage surrounding the peak of a hilltop in a long line of taller hilltops.

"That figures," Hallit said with an exhausted puff of breath, looking at the long climb before them.

"The hairless one lives way up there, eh?" White asked. He watched the Mexican's eyes for any sign of guile or deception.

"Some say he lives up there—some say he lives everywhere, like the—"

"Don't start with that," said White, cutting him off again. He holstered his pistol, reached down, picked up the grass sack and climbed back into his saddle.

The Mexican looked up at him and said, "*Señor*, I have been forthright with you. Please give me my accordion, I beg of you."

"Oh, I'm going to give it to you all right, *amigo*," said White. "Just as soon as we're all three standing atop that hill looking at the hairless one's domicile." He gave Hallit a smug grin and nudged his horse forward.

Hallit shook his aching head and followed.

"But, *señor*," said the Mexican, with his thin arms spread, "it is a long hard climb up the hillside. I cannot keep up to your horses."

White looked down and spoke to the grass sack on his lap, "Hear that, little friend? It sounds like he just told you *adios*." He patted the grass sack. "Now we'll just ride up to the top of this hill and see if you can fly." He grinned cruelly at the grass sack as if it were a living thing.

"No, wait. I am coming, please!" said the accordion player. He trotted up quickly alongside White's horse, staring nervously at the grass sack.

CHAPTER 4

The ranger stopped his horse and lifted the battered army telescope from his lap and raised it to his eyes. He gazed out across a deep valley at the roofless, vine-covered ruins of the old Spanish mission. The outcropping on which he and the two horses stood sat higher than the mission, giving him an inside view of the overgrown courtyards and empty stone chambers. In an open courtyard he saw the same young woman he had seen earlier as he'd looked down on the winding trail. She had been leading the donkey cart, tugging on the rope, hurrying it forward. Now this.

"You are a busy girl today," he murmured to her as he adjusted the telescope and brought her image in closer.

In the circle of vision, he watched her swipe a hand at a fallen strand of dark hair and hurry back across the dirt floor of the courtyard to where the young man sat slumped against the wheel of the donkey cart. *An American from his clothes and features*, Sam surmised. Ten feet away the donkey grazed on a patch of wild grass growing up through a low tangle of rich red and green mountain orchid. Sam studied the young man's bloody shirt, the bloody bandaging, and the fresh blood running steadily down his side.

Seeing the young man's condition, Sam lowered the lens and looked down the trail, judging the fastest route across the valley and up the other hillside. In the far distance below, at the end of the winding trail, he saw the thatched rooftops in Esperanza; nearing the top of the steep trail were two riders and a man on foot struggling to stay a few steps ahead of

42

them. Looking back at the young man and woman in the old mission, Sam sensed a connection as he backed his horse and put the telescope away. With luck, he should arrive at the mission ruins not long after the two men on horseback.

In the courtyard, Caridad had looked up for a moment and caught a glimpse of the two horses' rumps as the animals turned away and moved out of sight. "Up there? How can this be?" she asked under her breath. But she had no time to think about it. The *Americano's* condition had worsened. The bleeding had increased instead of lessening. "Wake up, *par favor!*" she pleaded, stooping, taking him by his other shoulder and shaking him.

"Please let him awaken," she prayed quietly in her native tongue, making the sign of the cross. "And please bring Sabio quickly," she added.

She squatted down in front of the wounded American and studied him closely, seeing only the slightest rise and fall in his chest as she tore the hem out of her peasant's skirt and ripped strip after strip of cloth for fresh bandaging. "Look at me. Now I have ruined my only skirt for you," she said. "Please wake up!"

As if suddenly enraged by him and his gunshot wound and her entanglement in his situation, she reached out and slapped his cheek, hard. His face rocked back and forth; his eyes opened halfway. "Why . . . did you do that?" he asked in a weak whisper.

Caridad looked stunned. "To awaken you. You must stay awake!" she said, realizing there was more to the slap than she wanted to tell him. She watched him try to hold his eyes open as his head drooped sidelong onto his shoulder. She shook him. "Please stay awake! What is your name? Tell me who you are—where are you from?" She asked to keep his mind occupied.

"I'm William"—his voice trailed off for a moment, then came back—"William Jefferies . . ."

"That is good, William!" Caridad said, surprised that what she'd done seemed to help. "Now tell me more," she said, looking at the stream of fresh blood down his side. Had it stopped, or at least slowed down? She couldn't tell.

"Let me look at you," she whispered more to herself than to him. She leaned in closer and started to peep down behind the blood-soaked bandage. But upon seeing a shadow fall over her from behind, she jerked her head around and looked up into Sabio's dark eyes.

"Yes, go ahead, loosen his bandage," said the former monk, standing with his hands raised and spread, the sleeves of his frayed robe pulled back on his bony forearms. Caridad saw the sunlight behind him glisten and shine above his smooth hairless head.

"Thank God you are here," she said. "I am preparing bandages to—"

"Take off the bandages." Cutting her off, Sabio stared at her, his dark eyes grave and intent. "Take off the bandage and remove the block of wood."

"You—you are going to heal him?" Caridad asked in an awestricken tone.

Without answering her, Sabio repeated, "Take off the bandage and remove the block of wood."

"But he has bled so much," said Caridad. "If I remove the bandage and block of wood, he could die quickly if what you do does not—"

"Shhh," said Sabio. "Do not question what I do. Do not question God's work."

"I—I am sorry," Caridad said submissively. "Of course I will remove the bandage." She lowered her eyes away from Sabio and slowly removed the blood-soaked bandage and the chunk of wood from under the young man's arm.

The young man stirred into consciousness and asked in a weak shallow voice, "Wha-what are . . . you doing?"

Caridad brushed his hand away from the bandage and said

quietly, "He is a holy man. He does God's work on earth. Lie still. He is going to stop the bleeding."

"Holy man?" Even in his weakened state, the young American stiffened at Caridad's words. His eyes opened, looking worried. "Please . . . don't kill me," he said. "Is there a doctor . . . ?"

"Silence," Sabio said in a firm tone, stepping forward and leaning down over him. When Caridad removed the chunk of wood from under the wounded man's arm, a fountain of fresh blood gushed from the wound. But Sabio seemed not even to notice it as he placed the widespread fingertips of his left hand on the young man's head.

"Oh, God," the man moaned. He swooned from the sudden rush of blood from his already depleted system.

"Ahhh," Sabio moaned. He jammed his right hand roughly up into the young man's armpit, causing the flowing blood to spread in all directions, but then to come to a halt.

Caridad sat staring transfixed as Sabio's right hand probed and poked and suddenly stopped as his finger found the bullet hole and jammed into it. "Ahhh . . . ahhh," the holy man muttered in discovery, his fingers seeming to have disappeared into the young man's chest.

Caridad watched Sabio's thin frame tremble beneath his robe as his fingertips delved farther up into the young man's shoulder, the fingertips of his left hand bearing down. *Was he reaching inside the man's brain? No, of course not*, she told herself. And yet . . . She blinked her eyes, knowing they were playing tricks on her.

"Ahh, there!" the holy man said intently, his body nearly collapsing from his efforts. His hand came out from under the young man's arm with a long thick string of blood swinging from his fingertips. "There is the demon who did this!" He slung his hand toward the ground. "I cast you out, demon!" he shouted. A bloody lead bullet plopped onto the soft earth.

"Sante Madre!" Caridad said in a hushed tone, seeing the

bullet as some living thing. She stepped back farther away from it, hiking up her already shortened and tattered skirt.

Sabio plunged his bloody cupped hand back up under the young man's arm and breathed in and out deeply and slowly. Caridad watched in silent awe for over ten minutes until Sabio seemed to come out of a trancelike state and declare in an exhausted tone, "It is done."

"Praise God, and the blessed Holy Mother!" Caridad gasped, again crossing herself.

This time, as Sabio removed his hand from the man's armpit, he did so carefully as if not to upset what he had accomplished under there. Caridad gasped again upon noting that the bleeding had stopped, as if Sabio's fingers had closed a valve inside the young man. Sabio kept his fingertips on the young American's head as he slumped forward and muttered what Caridad considered words of prayer, under his breath.

"Yes, it is done," he repeated, straightening and stepping back. He folded his forearms and shoved his bloody hands into the loose baggy sleeves. He stood in silence, his head bowed as if in meditation.

Caridad scooted around wide of him, watching him warily until she reached the side of the wounded American. She bent over his lap and looked up under his arm, seeing no flow of blood from the wound. "It *has* stopped!" she exclaimed in her native tongue, sounding surprised, as if having dispelled any slightest lingering doubt.

Without raising his head or opening his eyes, Sabio replied to her in Spanish, calmly saying, "Of course it has stopped, by God's will. Is this not what I said I would do?"

"Yes," said Caridad, "it is what you said. But in Esperanza in Louisa's home, you said you did not always have God's power to do these things."

Sabio lifted his face and opened his eyes patiently. He stared at her in silence for a moment, then said, "And before you left I told you I would come here and try, did I not?"

"*Sí*, you did," said Caridad.

"All right." Sabio gave her a curt nod. "I came, I tried, and now it is done." He gestured a hand toward the American. "As God would have it done."

Already the young man appeared to have strengthened. He opened his eyes halfway and raised a hand to the wound up under his arm. "It . . . stopped," he murmured.

"Yes, it stopped," said Sabio. "Now poke at it with your fingers until you cause it to start again." He shook his head as if cross and impatient with the wounded young man.

"Sorry," the young man said, letting his hand fall to his lap. "I—I feel better." He sounded surprised at the sudden upward change in his condition. "Is that . . . normal?"

"Talking too much is not normal," Sabio said with a sharp snap in his voice. "So why don't you lie there and keep quiet?"

Caridad gave Sabio a curious look. "Why are you being so rude with him? He has done nothing."

Sabio let out a tense breath, then turned and said to the young man, "I apologize. It is not your fault you were shot. You did not go looking for trouble. An accident fell down from the sky and landed on your back."

"Listen, Preacher, you owe me no apology," said the young man, his voice sounding stronger. "You saved my life." He looked confused for a second, then said, "Didn't you?"

Sabio looked at Caridad, then back at the young man and smiled faintly. "Yes, I laid hands upon you and stopped the bleeding. God acted through me to save your life. Now you must ask yourself, did God and I do the right thing? Is your life worth saving? If it was not, will you now make it so?"

"Sabio, please," said Caridad. Then she said to the young man apologetically, "It is something he always asks after doing God's work."

"It is something I ask, because I want to know if performing a miracle has any value other than to prove that a miracle has been performed," Sabio said bluntly. "Does saving your life mean I have participated in taking the life of another somewhere in the future? I saw the kind of men you ride with. So I ask you this—"

"Whoa," said Hubbard White, cutting him off, pushing the accordion player into the open courtyard. "There you go, talking about us behind our backs."

Sabio and Caridad both turned quickly toward the two gunmen who stood inside the open stone doorway, Hallit holding the reins to both horses in his hand. White held his pistol out, cocked and pointed. The accordion player fell to the ground in exhaustion. "You want to save somebody's life, you might want to give ole *box-squeezer* here some water," White said, waving his gun barrel toward the panting musician.

"Help . . . me," the man gasped hoarsely in the dirt.

"He tuckers plumb out on an uphill run, and that's the truth of it." White chuckled. He took the grass sack from under his arm and tossed it carelessly to the ground. The musician crawled quickly to it and cradled it to his heaving chest.

"What have you done to him?" Sabio asked. He picked up a water gourd, hurrying to the musician and stooping down to him. "Here, drink, Artesano."

White shrugged. "We didn't do nothing to him, just kept him mindful of what can happen to an unattended musical instrument out here in the wilds of *Mejico*."

"You pigs," Sabio said under his breath. He tipped the water gourd for the musician to drink.

"What do you say, kid?" White asked, looking past Sabio and Artesano to the wounded American while Artesano gulped steadily from the water gourd. "You look a hell of lot better than the last time I saw you."

"Yeah, I'm all right," the young man replied. "This fellow fixed me up, good as new!" He tried to sound far better than he felt. Yet, when he tried to stand, he faltered and sank back to the ground, fooling no one. "I—I just need a hand up," he said. His expression turned worried. Seeing it, Caridad hurried over to him and helped him finish seating himself.

"William needs rest," she said quickly, putting herself between him and the two men.

"*William*, is it?" White chuckled. He gave Hallit a grin and said, "Look like Kid Jefferies' kid ain't done bad for himself. Maybe you shoulda stayed sober and got yourself shot under the arm. Womenfolk like that sort of thing, you think?"

"I don't know what womenfolk like," Hallit offered, feeling worse by the minute, his dope and alcohol leaving him flat.

White turned back to the young man. "Kid, you know as well as we do why we're here. It's not that we don't like you." He stepped forward as Sabio stood up from beside the musician. "We just can't leave you behind."

"Move aside, ma'am, please," William Jefferies said to Caridad. "I don't want you getting hurt over me."

"No, I am staying right here," Caridad said with determination.

"You are not going to kill him," Sabio said, his voice growing strong with the two gunmen even though he himself stood facing them unarmed. "I did not save his life so he could die by your hands."

"You can die too, Hairless One," said White, grinning, turning his pistol toward Sabio.

"No," said Sabio. "I will not die and he will not die. But if you try to kill me, you will die in your own blood. This I see, and this I promise you." He pointed two thin fingers at White and shook them as if casting a spell.

"I'm through talking," said White. He pointed the cocked gun and took aim.

From the crumbling stone doorway, the ranger said in a calm voice, "Lower the gun or you'll die just like he said you would."

White froze, but kept his Colt pointed and said over his shoulder to Hallit, "Who's back there, Riley? Tell me something."

"It's a lawman," Hallit said, half turning toward the ranger, raising his hands chest high. "An Arizona Ranger, from his badge."

"A ranger," said White. His smug grin returned. "Well, Mr. Ranger, you've got no say-so here. This is Mexico, in case you didn't check the sign along the trail."

"Drop the gun," Sam said coolly.

"Or what, Ranger?" White asked in a confident tone. "I told you, you've got no jurisdiction here! If I come around, I come around firing!"

"One," Sam said flatly.

"What's he doing, Riley?" White asked, not turning, keeping his gun pointed at young William Jefferies.

"He's counting," Hallit said.

"Yeah, but what else is he doing?" White asked.

"Two," Sam said in the same tone of voice. He reached his gloved hand out and shoved the big Appaloosa away from him. The horse with Fadden's body on it followed, its lead rope wrapped around the Appaloosa's saddle horn.

"He's shoved his horses out of the way," said Hallit. "One's got a dead man tied across the saddle." He swallowed a knot in his throat and added, "I believe he's getting set to shoot the hell out of you, Hubbard!" There was something familiar about this ranger, his gray sombrero, the big Appaloosa. Hallit's dulled senses couldn't put it together.

"Thr—"

"Wait!" White called out, before Sam could finish his count. He lowered the pistol and eased down the hammer, then dropped it. "All right, I'm unarmed. But I'm telling you right now, what you're doing is *wrong!* No lawman comes down here shoving folks around."

Sam looked at Hallit and said, "Lift yours and drop it too."

Hallit did as he was told. White grew more mouthy and said, turning around, "You won't get away with this. We've got friends waiting for us in town. Soon as we get there and tell them, we'll all be storming straight up your back! You can count on it."

"Then you better get started, if you're going to tell them before dark," Sam said. As he spoke he reached over and took both horses' reins from Hallit's hand.

"Hold it, Ranger, damn it!" White said. "You can't set us afoot! It's a long hard walk down to Esperanza!"

"Any longer or harder than it was for this man walking up?" Sam asked, glancing at the accordion player, who still sat sweating on the ground. Then he gave White a dark lowered gaze. "Now start walking."

White hesitated, a worried look on his face. "Ranger," he said, "I can't return to Esperanza without that horse. It's not mine."

"Saying you stole it?" Sam asked coolly.

"Hell no, I didn't steal it!" White said. "It belongs to a man I would not want to steal a horse from."

"Then you better explain all this to him real careful like," Sam said. "I'm sure he'll understand."

"Damn it, Ranger, he won't!" said White.

"Start walking, mister," the ranger said, letting the barrel of his Colt tip down toward White's boot. "Before I clip one off."

White argued even as he backed away slowly. "Shoot me in the foot! What kind of lawman would shoot an unarmed man in the foot?"

"One that's trying to keep himself from shooting that same unarmed man in the head," Sam replied, tipping the barrel back up toward White's face.

"Come on, Hubbard. He ain't fooling," said Hallit, his impaired senses finally recognizing the ranger. "This is the one who carries a list of names of men he's going to kill. Remember him?"

White stared, stunned by Hallit's information. "Is my name on that list?" he asked.

"Want me to check?" Sam asked.

White backed off another step, turned with his hands chest high and walked away. Hallit took one last look at Fadden's canvas-wrapped corpse and followed close behind.

CHAPTER 5

The ranger stood watching as the two slipped through the stone doorway and out through the ruins toward the narrow path leading down to the steep trail. When he was satisfied they were gone, Sam turned to Sabio, the girl and the young American. "It's going to take them a good while to get back to Esperanza, but I wouldn't waste any time getting out of here."

"Thank God you are here!" said Sabio. "But where did you come from? How did you know?"

Seeing the curiosity in their faces, Sam said as he slipped the Colt into its holster, "I saw what was about to happen from up there." He nodded toward the higher nearby hilltop.

"I am Sabio Tonto Montero, Ranger," said the former monk, not forgetting his manners. "This is Caridad." He gestured a hand toward the dark-haired young woman, then toward the exhausted musician. "This poor man is Artesano Dello." He gestured toward the young American.

"I'm Jefferies, William Jefferies. Much obliged, Ranger," he said.

"Yes, thank you for coming to our aid," said Sabio. "Men like those defile the very ground they walk across." As he spoke his eyes went to the canvas-wrapped body. "But I see I can tell you nothing that you do not already know about such men."

"I know more about them than I sometimes care to," the ranger said, touching his hat brim in courteousness. "I'm Ranger Sam Burrack." He studied Sabio's name for a moment, then said, "Sabio Tonto—a wise man and a fool?"

53

"Yes, I am afraid so," said Sabio, unabashed by the meaning of his name. "At one time I was simply Sabio Montero. But after years of foolish behavior that neither God nor I could correct, I decided I must name myself after that which best represents me." He took a slight humble bow, saying, "Sabio Tonto, the wise fool, at your service."

"I'm sure you're being hard on yourself, *Señor* Montero," Sam said politely.

"Sadly, I am not, Ranger Burrack," said the former monk, with another humble bow. "But please call me Sabio." He gave a tired smile and gestured again toward Caridad and said, "This one is to me the daughter I never had." He again gestured his blood-crusted hand toward William Jefferies. "*Señor* Jefferies we do not know, only that he was shot by the very men he accompanied to Esperanza." With a dismissing toss of his hand he added, "He may be a criminal for all we know."

"Please, Sabio," said Caridad. "He is no criminal. Are you?" She looked into Jefferies' eyes. As soon as the two gunmen were gone, she had begun wrapping strips of her torn skirt around Jefferies' shoulder, carefully drawing it up snug under his armpit. Now, finishing, she patted his bandaged shoulder gently.

Jefferies returned her gaze for only a second, then looked away as if unable to face her and said to the ranger, "I'm no criminal. But I have to admit, these men I rode here with are not the most law-abiding I've ever seen."

"So I see. . . ." Sabio nodded his lowered head as if telling himself he'd been correct in his assessment of the young man. "That answers my question about saving your life, and how many people's lives I have ended by doing so."

"Wait. Hear me out," said Jefferies, struggling to his feet and this time making it, with Caridad's help. "You didn't do wrong by saving my life. I came along with my uncle. We both thought we came down here to fight on the side of right, to help free these people." He looked at the ranger. "True, we were doing it for pay, but so what? Nobody else is doing it at all."

"Who did you come here with?" Sam asked, getting a picture he didn't like.

"Desmond Prew and a group he recruited from here and there. Some of them he knew, some he hired through a newspaper advertisement in St. Louis, and Springfield, like the one my uncle responded to."

Sam eyed him closer and asked as if in disbelief, "You and your uncle came here with *Desmond Prew?*" He shook his head. "William Jefferies, if that is your real name, there's some things you need to know about the man you're riding with."

"It is my real name," said Jefferies. "And I know what you're going to say, Ranger—that Prew is a no-good crook. And you're right. But we didn't know it at the time, and when we found it out, it was too late. We were already here and saw no way to turn back."

"There's always a way to turn back, if you haven't stepped out past the law and done something that will get you and your uncle hanged," said Sam.

Jefferies stared down for a moment with regret. Then he looked back up and said, "I'm afraid it is too late for my uncle. He saw what a mistake he'd made and hanged himself. His body is still hanging from a tree in Esperanza, if nobody's cut him down yet."

"Hanged himself over making the mistake of riding with Prew and his mercenaries?" Sam asked.

"Yes," said Jefferies. "I know that sounds unlikely, but I believe joining Prew was just his last try at chasing rainbows. He told me he couldn't stand to take another letdown." He shook his head. "I thought he was just getting it off his chest. I never thought he'd kill himself over it. I think the dope and whiskey had a lot to do with it." He shrugged sadly with his good shoulder. "Anyway, he's dead now. Nothing's going to change that."

"What about you, young man?" the ranger asked. "Once you're able, are you going back to Prew and his bunch?"

"He sent those two men to kill me," said Jefferies. "I don't know how welcome I'd be if I went back now." His gaze went to Caridad for a moment. "Maybe I could hang around Esperanza for a while after they leave."

Before Caridad could say something in response, Sabio saw the look on her face and cut in quickly. "No! It is not good for you to stay there. Esperanza does not need your kind."

"Sabio!" said Caridad. "Do not be so rude. It is our way to make strangers welcome. Is that not what you taught people when you were—"

Sabio stopped her short, saying to the ranger, "I was once a monk, Ranger, but I am no longer." He cast Caridad a look of reproach. "I tell you this not because it is something I wish to have people know, but because it is something a foolish girl cannot keep herself from telling everyone." He took a breath and added, "Please do not ask why I am no longer a monk, for I am certain she would tell you without giving it a second thought."

"I won't," said the ranger. He quickly changed the subject, looking back at William Jefferies. "Prew must be up to something big if he'd kill you before he'd leave you behind."

"I heard rumors of all sorts among the men," said Jefferies, "but to be honest, I don't know what we were getting ready to do over here. I know we were awaiting the Mexican army—a fellow named Captain Murella."

"I've heard of Murella," said the ranger. "He's nothing more than a thieving murderer in uniform."

"I sort of figured that out from some of the stories I heard about him among Prew's regulars."

"Prew's *regulars?*" Sam asked, almost shaking his head at the irony of Desmond Prew's mercenaries being referred to as soldiers. "And who might they be?"

"White and Hallit—the two you chased away," said Jefferies. "There's Thomas Russell, Cherokee Jake Slattery, Braden Kerr, Meade Loden . . ." His voice trailed off as he thought of others. "There's supposed to be more coming any day." He considered it for a second and added, "There was a fellow named Sibbs, but he's dead now. Jake Slattery gutted him."

Sam shook his head, thinking of the list of names in his pocket. "'Hemp Knot' Tommy Russell and 'Cur Dog' Braden Kerr," he said, as if in dark contemplation of the two outlaws.

"You know these men?" Jefferies asked, looking surprised.

"You heard what that one said a while ago," said the ranger, nodding toward the path that White and Hallit had taken. "I've got Tommy Russell and Braden Kerr on a list I carry. They disappeared over the border two years back. Nobody has seen them since. I had hopes they'd met their end down here." He added wryly, "But we don't always get what we hope for."

"Yes, I heard what White said about you carrying a list," said Jefferies. "I also heard Kerr and Russell both talking about a ranger who's been dogging them. They said he had their names on his list." He looked closer at Sam. "So that's you?"

"Might be," said Sam. "I doubt if I'm the only lawman carrying their names around. Those two have cut a wide and vicious trail."

"If you're the one who killed Junior Lake and his gang, you're the one," said Jefferies. "You also killed a friend of theirs by the name of Ned Sorrels?"

Without answering the question, Sam said, "You heard them talking about the law looking for them and you didn't realize what kind of men they were?"

"This was after we saw what we'd gotten ourselves into," said Jefferies. He shrugged his good shoulder. "My uncle had already warned me not to expect a bunch of church deacons, riding with hired-gun mercenaries. But neither one of us was prepared for this bunch of cutthroats."

"What do you suppose they were up to—Prew and the captain?" Sam asked.

Jefferies hesitated for a moment, then said, "Ranger, it feels wrong, me informing on the men I was riding with, even if they were on the wrong side of the law."

"Suit yourself," he said, as if dismissing the matter. "I'm on the wrong side of the border to do anything about it anyway. Prew is Mexico's problem until he crosses back into my territory."

Jefferies nodded toward the canvas-wrapped corpse. "*He* was in Mexico, wasn't he?"

"That he was," said Sam. "But I was on him for what he did before he left my territory. Except for Kerr and Russell, I've got nothing on Prew and his men."

"I see ..." Jefferies paused in thought for a second, then said, "All right, Ranger. The captain wants explosives, is what I heard from the others. Prew and his men are planning to provide him all he needs—right off the army trains that run along the American side of the border."

"I see." The ranger thought it over for a moment. "If they let you know this kind of information, no wonder they didn't want to leave you behind to tell somebody."

"Like I said, Ranger, me and my uncle didn't know." The young man looked remorseful. "If we had, we never would have joined up with these fellows." He looked at Caridad as if offering her an apology. "I hope you believe me," he said in a softer tone.

"*Sí*, I do believe you, William," she replied in the same tone.

"I'm glad. Now if only there was some way I could prove myself to you, Sabio . . . and you, Ranger," he said, still looking into Caridad's warm dark eyes.

"There is," Sam said. "You can go home and keep yourself out of trouble for the rest of your life."

"That's not what I meant," said Jefferies. "I mean, I'd like to make up for things some way. I'd like to show Sabio here that my life is worth saving."

"You need prove nothing to me," Sabio cut in, having seen the way the young American and Caridad looked at one another. "Do as the ranger has suggested—go home and sin no more. Only then will I feel I have saved a life *worth* saving."

"I want to do more than that," said Jefferies, his eyes staying on Caridad as he spoke. "I want to stay here and make sure you're both safe. If I thought Prew or his men harmed you for helping me, how could I ever live with myself?"

Sam cut in, saying to Sabio, "I'll escort you and the young lady to wherever you feel safe, before I head back across the border."

"Many thanks, Ranger, but do not worry about us," said Sabio. "I will hide us both at the mission until these wolves are out of Esperanza. No one will see us again until we choose to be seen, eh, Caridad?"

"This is true," Caridad said. "Sabio knows places to hide like no one I have ever seen. He can disappear into the very wind, as if by magic."

"Yes," said Sabio, "and where Caridad and I go, no one else is welcome." He gave Jefferies a firm gaze.

"So there you have it," Sam said to Jefferies. "I have a feeling Sabio Tonto knows more hiding places in this land than a fox."

"You are correct, Ranger," Sabio tossed in. To Jeffries he said, "You must find your own way. We have done all we can for you. If you stay here you will die. It is that simple."

Caridad, realizing that Sabio was right, only stood silent with a sad look on her face.

"I'll go then," said Jefferies, speaking to Sabio but keeping his eyes on Caridad. "But when things settle, I'm coming back to Esperanza. I promise you." Turning to Sam, he asked, "Can I ride back with you, Ranger? You know this country lots better than I do."

"Yes, as far as the border," said Sam. "Then you're on your own." He nodded toward the two horses he'd made the gunmen leave behind and asked Jeffries, "Which one of the horses belongs to Desmond Prew?"

"The big bay," said Jefferies.

"That figures," Sam said, looking at the difference between the big muscular bay and the seedy dun standing beside it. "You take the dun." He turned to the musician and asked, "Artesano, are you rested enough to ride?"

"*Sí*, if that is what you need me to do, Ranger," said the musician, hurrying over and stopping in front of Sam like some soldier awaiting an order.

"You're giving him Prew's horse?" Jefferies said, astonished. "Riding that horse will get him killed if Prew ever sees him on it!"

"I'm not giving him Prew's horse," Sam said. "I'm sending Prew's horse back to him." He said to the musician, "Is that all right with you, Artesano? It could be risky."

"I will take the horse to him, but he will not see me until I arrive. He will know that my intentions are honorable." Artesano grinned. "Is that how you want me to do it?"

"Yes, that's it exactly, *mi amigo*," said Sam. "Now listen closely to what I want you to tell him."

CHAPTER 6

Halfway down the hill on their way back to Esperanza, White stopped and looked out across the jagged hilltops to the north. "Damn that ranger's bones!" he said to Hallit, who stopped beside him and plopped down onto a rock. "There's got to be a trail across there."

"There don't have to be a trail anywhere," Hallit replied in an exhausted hangover voice. He plopped down onto a rock, his face, shirt and upper trousers soaked with sweat. "These Mexicans travel like elk up and down these damn hillsides."

But White wouldn't be disheartened. His eyes searched the rugged land. "Naw, there's a place somewhere out there where a man can steal a horse or a donkey or something fit to ride. We've just got to find it." He wiped a hand across his sweaty forehead and slumped his shoulders. "If this heat doesn't kill us first."

"What are you saying?" Hallit asked. "Ain't you going back to Esperanza with me?"

White squatted down in front of him and stared into his sweating face. "Are you sober enough to understand anything yet? Because if you're not, don't make me waste my breath."

"Yeah, I'm sober," said Hallit. "My dope wore off an hour ago."

"Good," said White. "Now listen to me and let this sink in." He continued clearly and distinctly. "I am not going back to Esperanza, on foot, my holster empty, and tell Prew I lost his horse to a damn Arizona Ranger who's not even supposed to be on this side of the border. Can you understand why I don't want to do that?"

Hallit looked down and shook his head. Then he forced himself up onto his feet and looked out across the jagged hills. "There's got to be something out there, a village, something. . . ." He paused, then said, "I guess we ought to make a try at it."

"No, not here." White dismissed the hillsides facing them with the wave of a hand. "A man couldn't hack his way through there with an ax." As he spoke a black bird with a yellow and red beak rose up from a nearby treetop and seemed to jeer at them as it took flight. "Laugh, you son of a bitch," he growled. "If I had a gun I'd turn you into supper."

"Where, then?" Hallit asked.

"Farther down I recall a path leading out in that direction," said White. "Let's get moving. It'll start turning dark in another couple of hours."

The two walked on down the winding hillside for the next few minutes until they came to a turn in the trail and heard a menacing voice call out from behind a stand of plush juniper. "Hold it right there—the next one moves is a dead sonsabitch!"

"Whoa," said White in surprise, the two of them throwing their hands in the air. "We've got no money, if that's your game!"

"My game is to cut your hearts out and feed them to you!" the voice growled. But the growl turned to a deep chuckle as two horsemen stepped their animals into sight. One of them twirled his pistol on his finger before holstering it.

White let out a tense breath and said, "That's real damn smart of yas, Sonny!" He looked from one rider to the other. "You too, Koch," he said. "What if we had started shooting without giving you a chance to identify yourselves?" No sooner than he'd said it, White realized neither he nor Hallit had a gun. His face reddened.

"That would have been a good trick," said Sonny Nix,

a big ruddy-faced Californian. He stepped his horse forward with a wide grin. "We saw you've both been left shy of any shooting gear."

"Damn right we have," said White, not yet knowing what sort of story to offer, having been caught off guard. He and Hallit both lowered their raised hands. "What brings you two up this way?" He hoped to change the subject long enough to work up a believable story that didn't make him look like a fool.

"You two," said the burly Californian, pointing at White with a gloved finger. He had one eye closed as if taking aim at him. "No sooner than we got to Esperanza, Prew sent us looking for you."

"How'd you find us?" White asked.

Sonny shrugged his broad shoulders; so did Robert Koch, a thin Texan with a scar across the bridge of his crooked nose. "We come upon two sets of hooves leading out of the stables," said Robert Koch. "Figured we'd best follow them for a ways, since one of them started from Prew's empty stall." He stared at White with a flat mirthless grin.

White felt sick. "Jesus, Sonny, you've got to help me out," he said, looking up at the big Californian with an expression that pleaded for mercy. "I've lost Prew's horse."

Sonny's grin widened. He looked at Koch and said, "See? What did I tell you?"

"You damn sure did," said Koch, with his same mirthless grin. He turned a glare to White and said, "As soon as we saw yas, Sonny said, 'Damn, those boys have lost Prew's big bay!'"

"Uh-uh," Hallit said quickly. "I didn't lose the bay. He did." He pointed at White, sounding more sober than he'd sounded all day.

"Whoa, now!" said White. "You're the one who brought it to me! Don't blame me!"

"I'm also the one who told you we ought to take it back to

the stable and get yours!" said Hallit.

"Both of you stop it," said Sonny. "It's too hot to argue. Save it for when you get to Esperanza." He gave White a narrowed gaze and asked, "You were headed back to Esperanza, weren't yas?"

"Hell yes," White lied. "Where else do you think we'd be headed?"

Koch gave a dark chuckle. "To the deepest jungle of Africa, if I was you," he said. "I can't imagine what you was thinking, taking off with the man's horse that way."

"Yeah," said Sonny. "Hell, you're supposed to be his new right-hand man. Seems like you'd recall what happened to his last right-hand man and know better than something like this. Ole Hugh died a mean violent death, I was told."

"This was all a mistake," said White, getting a mental image of Hugh Elberry falling backward beneath a long spray of blood. "Is he sure I took it?" He wondered if he might somehow deny the whole unfortunate incident.

"His stall is empty. Your horse is there. We followed your trail here," said Sonny Nix. "Now what do you think?"

"I think we're dead," White murmured.

"Yep, that's sort of what I thought too," said Sonny. Beside him Koch nodded grimly.

"What if you let me cut out of here, say, out across these hills?" White asked, a shakiness in his voice. "You'd never see my face again."

"What?" said Koch. "And miss hearing you explain all this to Prew?"

"I don't think so," said Sonny.

"I've got nothing to explain," said Hallit, talking fast. "I was too drunk to know anything. I was minding my own business. He dragged me along knowing I was doped up and drunk. That's the damn truth."

"Well, whatever the case," Sonny said, gesturing them forward down the trail, "let's get on to Esperanza. Me and

Koch have fallen way behind on our drinking because of yas."

In Esperanza, hours after the captain and his men had left town, Desmond Prew sat in a thronelike chair his men had dragged from the church and set up for him in front of the cantina. He ate from a rack of steaming pork ribs one of the whores held for him in a clean white cloth. She sat on one of the wide arms of the large hand-carved chair, naked from the waist up. Close beside her another whore sat quietly washing herself from a pan of water.

Twenty feet away, in the middle of the square, a cook fire made up of mesquite kindling and broken furniture from the cantina raged. Half of the blackened pig lay sizzling on the edge of the flames. In the west, red sunlight simmered on the horizon.

"Prew. Here comes Sonny and Koch," Sway Loden called out from his guard post in the bell tower of the adobe church across the dirt street. "White and Hallit are both on foot. No sign of your bay."

Prew shook his head and took a long swig from the bottle of whiskey he kept standing between his thighs. He pushed the whore's hand holding the ribs away from his face and wiped his mouth on his shirt sleeve. He stood up enough to lift the heavy chair beneath him and turn it facing the direction of the hill trail. Reseated, he corked the whiskey bottle and set it on the ground beside his chair. Drawing his big Colt Dragoon, he laid it across his lap. "This better be damn good," he growled under his breath.

Around the fire, some of his men stood up and stared toward the far end of town with him. Inside the cantina, others had heard Loden's voice and straggled out one and two at a time to stand nearby, leaving an empty street in front of their leader.

"This is bad luck for White," said Cherokee Jake Slattery, keeping his voice down. He hiked his gun belt and leaned against a rough cedar pole.

Beside him stood Thomas "Hemp Knot" Russell and Braden "Cur Dog" Kerr. Russell replied, "Yeah, as far as being the second in command, he didn't last as long as a fart in a whirlwind."

The two men snickered. Cherokee Jake gave them a look, straightened from his leaning post and moved away from them.

"What's gotten into him all of a sudden?" asked Russell, carefully keeping his lowered voice from being heard by Slattery.

"Must figure once White's dead and gone, he'll just take over as the next new *segundo*," said Kerr.

"Yeah?" Russell sidestepped and leaned against the post Cherokee Jake had given up. "Being the second in charge in this bunch don't strike me as the most secure position a man might take upon himself." He spit and stared toward the two approaching riders and the two men afoot walking in front of them.

"Being *segundo* gets paid more than the rest of us," Kerr tossed in.

"Yep, it damn sure does," said Russell. He nodded toward White and Hallit. "Watch real close and we'll both see how much." Again they snickered among themselves. From his new spot, Cherokee Jake glanced at them, then turned his face away with a look of disgust.

When White and Hallit stopped in front of Prew's chair, Sonny and Koch moved their horses to one side and remained in their saddles.

"Obliged," Prew said flatly to them, without yet giving White and Hallit so much as a look.

Sonny nodded and touched his hat brim toward Prew, then crossed his wrists on his saddle horn and watched in silence. Koch followed suit.

Seeing the big Dragoon lying on his lap glistening in the firelight, White blurted out, "Prew! You've got to believe me,

I never meant to steal your—"

Prew silenced him with a raised hand. He took the corked whiskey bottle by its neck and pitched it to him. White caught it and stared at Prew with a stunned expression. Hallit's eyes riveted on the bottle in White's trembling hands.

"Take a drink, Hubbard," Prew said in a mild controlled voice. "You look like you need one."

White didn't trust the cordiality, but he wasn't about to say anything. He pulled the cork and raised the bottle in a long deep swig. When he started to lower it, he considered his dire straits and raised it again for another deep drink. Prew sat watching poker-faced.

"What about me?" Hallit ventured, seeing the level of whiskey in the bottle getting shorter.

Prew gave White a nod; White passed the bottle to Hallit's reaching hand. Hallit raised the bottle and drank deeply. A thin trickle of whiskey ran down his beard stubble and dripped from his chin.

"Start talking," Prew said to White as Hallit lowered the bottle and let out a deep whiskey sigh.

"Prew, I swear to God, I didn't steal your bay!" White said. "I know I never should have rode out of here on it, but so help me—"

"Why did you?" Prew's hand lay idly on the big Dragoon.

"I sent Hallit to get the horse while I kept an eye on the fellow who'd taken the kid in," said White. "He brought your bay by mistake."

Prew's eyes cut over to Hallit.

"I was doped and drunk," Hallit offered humbly, spreading his hands, the bottle dangling from his fingertips.

"Things got in a hurry on us and I ended up riding the bay instead of taking it back to the stables and getting my own horse," said White as Prew's eyes left Hallit and came back to him.

"See," White explained, "we found out the cleaning girl

from the cantina is taking care of the kid—her and that little hairless fellow who slips around here like a ghost. We made the accordion player lead us to them, up there in the old ruins." He nodded toward the hillside.

"Did you kill the kid?" Prew asked, appearing detached as he looked back and forth between the two.

"No, we didn't," White admitted. "We didn't get a chance to. There's an Arizona Ranger guarding him. It's that ranger who carries the list of names. The one who killed Junior Lake and his gang."

Hearing White mention the ranger, Russell and Kerr gave one another a troubled look.

"Oh, I see," said Prew, in a calm, understanding tone of voice. "I sent you to kill the kid so he can't tell anybody what we're up to. But instead of killing him you leave him and my horse with that damn ranger who pokes his nose into everybody's business?" He paused and sucked a tooth as if in contemplation, then shook his head, lifted the Dragoon and said, "You understand why I've got to kill you, don't you?"

"Prew, for God sakes! Please give me another chance!" White pleaded.

"Yeah, me too," said Hallit. He backed a step as if on the verge of turning to run.

"Stand still, Hallit!" Prew cocked the Dragoon toward White. "I'm not killing you."

"You're not?" White asked, looking both terrified and outraged. "Why not? He brought me your horse!"

"Because he was drunk and doped," said Prew.

"Jesus, Prew!" said White. "You're killing me, but not him, because he was drunk? That's not fair! Not fair at all!"

"I can see why you might feel that way." Prew took aim.

Before he could pull the trigger, Sway Loden, who'd been watching from the bell tower, called out, "We've got another rider coming. He's riding in fast."

Prew let the Dragoon slump in his hand. "It's not the

ranger, is it?" he called out to the bell tower.

Loden studied the approaching figure and said, "No. It's the accordion player from the cantina. He's—he's riding your bay."

Prew lowered the gun more and rose from his chair. "Well, now, this is starting to get interesting."

Artesano stopped the bay at the edge of town and looked ahead at the men gathered near the fire in the waning evening light. They moved forward slowly, staring at him as he called, "I come to bring the *Señor* Prew's horse to him. Do not harm me, *por favor.*"

"You better pray my horse hasn't been harmed, music man," Prew called out in reply.

"*Señor* Prew, the horse is fine," said Artesano. "I would not have brought him back to you otherwise." He paused and looked at the line the men had formed on either side of Prew's big chair. "May I bring him to you without fear of harm, *señor?*"

Prew slipped the Dragoon down behind his belt and called out, "Nobody's going to hurt you, music man, unless you keep stalling around. Now bring my horse to me, *ahora!*" He stood in front of the big chair like a king before his throne.

With trepidation Artesano touched his bare heels to the bay's sides and put it forward in a walk toward Prew, feeling the cold eyes of the men as he moved past them slowly. These were the same men who had thrown coins to him and bought him drinks for entertaining them with his music. Yet, now, theirs were the eyes of wolves and vultures, he told himself, knowing that with the slightest toss of Desmond Prew's hand his life would be snuffed out as easily as a candle flame.

CHAPTER 7

White and Hallit stood staring at the ground while the Mexican musician gave Prew the account of White holding his accordion hostage and the two forcing him to trot up the hill to the mission and take them to Sabio and Caridad. He told of how the ranger had appeared out of nowhere and gotten the drop on them and sent them away on foot without a shot fired. While Artesano related the incident, Prew listened. But at the same time he inspected the bay closely.

"And did you get your squeeze-box back unharmed?" Prew asked when he had finished studying each of the bay's legs and hooves in turn.

"*Sí*, I left it hidden outside of town on my way here. But I did get it back unharmed," said Artesano. "For that I am grateful."

"Grateful?" Prew shook his head. "You've got some guts, music man. I admire that." He grinned, satisfied that his horse had been returned in good condition. Turning a gaze to Hubbard White, he said with a dark chuckle, "You run this poor sumbitch up the mountain? In the heat of the day?"

White only nodded without answering.

"I wouldn't call it a mountain," Hallit cut in. "It's more like a—"

"Shut up, Hallit," Prew said harshly. Turning back to Artesano, he patted the big Dragoon and said, "Would you like to borrow my gun and shoot White's head off?"

"Oh, no!" Artesano raised his hands as if to ward the gun off should Prew try handing it to him. "I am not a violent man. Nor am I a man who seeks vengeance for himself when someone has wronged him. I am a simple musician. I only want to please everyone."

Prew looked the musician up and down and decided to believe him. "Too bad," he said, tapping his fingers on the Dragoon's handle as he gave White a dark stare, considering his fate. "Do you believe every man deserves a second chance?" he asked Artesano.

"Oh, I do. *Sí*, I do!" Artesano said quickly. "I not only believe in a second chance, I believe in a third chance, a fourth, a fifth—!"

"Enough," Prew said, cutting him off sharply. To White he said, "It looks like the man you nearly run to death has just saved your life, Hubbard. Good thing you didn't kill him, huh? Or else you'd be laying there dead right now. What do you think of that?"

White only stared at the ground, relieved for the moment but knowing he wasn't all the way off the hook. Hallit also looked relieved and took a testing step sideways toward the nearest man holding a bottle of whiskey.

Prew turned away from White and Hallit. Facing Artesano, he asked with an expectant look, "I suppose the ranger has something he'd like for you to tell me?"

"*Sí*, he does," said Artesano, feeling more confident and less in fear for his life now that Prew knew his horse was all right and that nobody had been shot.

"I thought he might." Prew rubbed the bay's soft muzzle as he spoke. He gave a knowing grin toward the men who had broken from two lines and drawn closer around the front of the big chair. "All of yas listen up," he said. "Let's hear what the ranger has to say."

Artesano looked around cautiously, then said to Prew, "His very words were, 'Tell Prew that I give him what belongs to him. When the time is right he must give *me* what belongs to me.'"

"Whoa," said Prew, feigning a mysterious look. "Now whatever might the ranger mean by that?" He looked all around at the men. Rubbing the bay's muzzle he said, "We see what he had that belonged to me—but what do I have that belongs to him?"

A deep contemplative silence fell over the men for a moment until finally Thomas Russell stepped forward and said with a worried look on his face, "Come on, Prew, we all know what he wants. He's dogged me and Kerr all the way out of Arizona Territory. Now he's right up our shirts again. He's wanting you to hand us over to him. He's got to be crazy, thinking you'd do that."

"Yeah, that murdering sonsabitch!" Kerr joined in, stepping forward beside Russell. "Him and his damned list of names!"

"I say we all go kill him!" Russell called out, hoping for a show of support.

"Take it easy, Hemp Knot," said Prew, almost in a mocking tone. "Don't expect everybody here to go after the ranger." He grinned. "Not if the only ones he's after are you and Cur Dog. Why would all of us do that?"

Russell spread his hands. "Because we're all together. We look out for one another's interest, don't we?"

"I don't know—do we? We're mercenaries," said Prew. "We all do what's best for ourselves." He motioned for Cherokee Jake to take the bay's reins from him as he stepped closer to Russell and Kerr. "You two showed up here with the law on your tails? Do you call that looking out for one another's interest?" His expression turned dark. "Now we've got a ranger poking around, wondering what we're up to here."

"I meant nothing by it, Prew," said Russell. "We never thought the ranger would come after us down here." He looked at the other men, then back at Prew and said in a quieter tone, "There's not a man here who hasn't had some kind of run-in with the law." He lowered his voice even more and asked,

"You wouldn't turn us over to him, would you?"

Prew purposely let the question hang for a moment while he seemed to consider it. Finally, without answering it, he said, "Maybe he's not even talking about you two. Think about that." He tapped a finger to his temple. "There might be something else I've got that he thinks belongs to him." He looked around. "Anybody here holding something that belongs to Ranger Sam Burrack?"

The men shook their heads, murmured among themselves and milled uncomfortably.

"Any of yas got your name on the ranger's list, or any-damn-body else's list?" Prew asked, giving Russell and Kerr a look that could be read different ways, none of which the two found pleasant. "If you do, you better speak up right now. I don't want no more surprises!"

When no reply came from the men Prew said to Russell and Kerr, "See? Nobody else brought the law down here looking for them."

"I promise," said Russell, "when we get our hands on the ranger, nobody will have to back us up. Right, Cur Dog?"

"Damn right, that's right," said Kerr. "For two cents I'd run him down tonight and be done with it." He made a gesture as if ready to go get his horse and ride out.

"Nobody's going anywhere tonight," said Prew. "All of yas are staying put here until we're ready to go do what we came here to do. Is that clear to everybody?" He looked all around, then at Kerr for an answer.

"Yeah, that's clear," Kerr said grudgingly, as if he regretted not going after the ranger.

"All right then," said Prew to everyone. "The kid is gone. I can't help what he might've told the ranger, but luckily he didn't know the captain's full plan." Giving White another cold stare, he added, "I've got my horse back!" He raised a hand as if to celebrate the bay's return. "Everybody enjoy themselves tonight!" He waved them back toward the cantina, where the women lounged in the doorway awaiting them.

"If we're through for the night," said Sonny Nix, who had stepped down from his horse and started toward a hitch rail, "I believe I'll have some of everything there."

"Hold up a minute, Sonny," said Prew, stopping him and Koch. "We're not through yet. I got something else I need you to do."

"Damn it," said Sonny. "Why us again?"

"Because you're the best scout in this whole damn bunch," said Prew.

Turning to Koch, Nix said, "Why did you have to tell him I once scouted Apache for the army?"

"Sorry, Sonny," Koch said drily.

"I still want the kid dead," Prew said.

"They'll be gone," said Sonny.

"I know they will," said Prew. "Take some food and whiskey with you. Ride back up there. Follow their tracks and finish the kid off. I told the captain he'd be taken care of, and I meant it. It's bad business, this kid just riding off like this. It's a loose end that needs tying down."

"And the ranger?" Sonny asked with a thin but confident smile. "Want me to tie his loose end down? Even after him giving you your horse back?"

"I don't trust that ranger as far as I can spit," said Prew. "He gave me the bay for his own reasons. I'm hoping he's dead before I find out what those reasons are."

"I figure he said that about something belonging to him just to get some heads worrying—try getting some suspicion started among the men, them thinking you'd turn them in."

"Yeah, that's what I think he was doing," said Prew. "Look how worried it made Russell and Kerr already."

"Well, we have to admit, the less men still alive and kicking at the end of this job, the more money it is for the rest of us, eh?" Sonny gave a slight grin. Koch followed suit.

Prew ignored the comment. "If the ranger's still there, kill him too. There'll be an extra *cut* for both of you when we finish this job. Nothing else needs to be said about who's still alive and kicking at the end of the job."

"We hear you, Prew," Sonny said in a cool tone.

In spite of the dense trees and foliage engulfing the hills behind them, Jefferies had spent most of the afternoon looking back, as if Sabio and Caridad might appear at any moment. Even when he knew he and the ranger had traveled too far and the night had grown too dark, he continued to glance back now and then in the direction of the old mission ruins. When they stopped for the night and made a small fire for food and coffee, Jefferies stared into the darkness as he spoke.

"Ranger Burrack," he asked, "do you think she will really be there when I return for her?"

Sam poured them each a tin cup of coffee and set one steaming cup over on the ground beside Jefferies. "Did *you* really mean it, that you would be coming back to her someday?"

"Oh, yes, I meant it," said Jefferies. "I'll come back for her, just as soon as I can."

"Then I expect she meant what she said, too," Sam replied. "As far as her being there, I'm sure she will. These village girls usually spend their lives where they started out, unless something big happens that forces the whole village to leave."

"But somebody else might come along before I get back," said Jefferies.

"I'll wager she's not the kind of woman who'd tell you she'll wait and not mean it," said Sam. "I suppose any woman could run out of faith after so long. But these hill country women are true to their word." He offered a trace of a smile. "You've got time. I'm sure she'll wait for you."

"I believe you, Ranger. But as soon as Prew and his men are cleared out of here, I'm coming right back," Jefferies said. "That is, as soon as I raise the money for supplies." He looked troubled and added, "I suppose that could take a while, the way my luck seems to be running."

"Your luck doesn't appear too bad to me," Sam said, raising his hot cup of coffee with his gloved hand and blowing on it before taking a sip. "You've met a young woman you care a lot for. Sabio Tonto saved your life. You've managed to break away from a gang of thieves and killers before they got you in too deep—or killed you, the way they had planned." He looked into his coffee cup. "Some would say you're on a pretty strong *run of good luck*."

"I didn't mean to complain, Ranger," said Jefferies. "I know everything you're saying is true. I realize how lucky I am to be alive. I guess I've gotten so used to expecting bad luck lately, it's hard to recognize good luck right away."

"I understand," said the ranger. He paused and sipped his coffee in silence.

They ate hardtack biscuits and jerked elk from Sam's saddlebags and washed the sparse meal down with hot coffee before killing the fire and turning in for the night. Sam dozed lightly, leaning back against the rough trunk of a large pine tree with a blanket thrown around his shoulders. He'd deliberately positioned himself facing Jefferies across the blackened campfire, his rifle out of his saddle boot and lying on his lap.

Before dawn, while the hillside lay streaked with a silver mist, they drank strong tepid coffee left over from the night before. From a small canvas bag Sam pulled out two more hardtack biscuits and pitched one to Jefferies. They ate dutifully. When they'd finished, Sam wiped his hands and carefully pulled down the bandage from under Jefferies' wounded arm.

"How's it looking?" the young man asked, unable to bend either his neck or his sore shoulder enough to see for himself.

"Good enough, for today," said Sam, pulling the bloodstained strips of cloth back into place. "Leave it be today, to make sure it doesn't start bleeding again. But tonight you'll need to wash it clean and change this bandage."

"He made it stop bleeding by just laying his hands on it," Jefferies remarked.

"So you said," Sam replied, recalling a conversation they'd had the day before on their way up a hillside trail.

Jefferies gave him a questioning look. "You don't believe he really did that, do you?"

"The bleeding stopped," Sam replied, gathering the cups and coffeepot. "It doesn't matter how it happened, so long as it happened." He stood and raked his boot back and forth in the bed of cold ashes from last night's fire.

"Yes," said Jefferies, "but I'd like to know what you think. Did he stop the bleeding by laying his hands on me, or not?"

"It doesn't matter what I think about it," said the ranger. "It's your wound. It's what you think that counts."

"I suppose I'm asking because I want to believe he's a holy man like Caridad thinks he is," said Jefferies. "But what if he's not? What if he's a phony?" He looked worried. "What if he's the kind of man who would take advantage of her?"

"I can see it's going to be hard traveling with you, Jefferies," Sam said. He stopped and took a deep, patient breath, realizing that in spite of his size and demeanor, William Jefferies wasn't much more than an overgrown kid.

"All right, here's what I think," Sam said, stooping down as he spoke. "I believe there's things in this world that are bigger than my understanding. Sabio said he used to be a holy man. I can only take his word for it. You went to him bleeding to death, and he stopped it. Are you sorry he did?"

"I'm most grateful," said Jefferies, "but that's not the point."

"It was while the blood was flowing out of you," Sam said. "Sometimes it's best not to question things too close."

"Is Caridad going to be all right with him?" Jefferies asked.

"She seems to be," Sam replied. "He's as protective of

her as a father. It appears they've been together for a while."

Jefferies considered it. "Yeah, you're right. I'm making something out of nothing." He rose to his feet and swayed sideways before catching himself.

Sam caught his forearm and steadied him. "Are you all right?"

"Yeah . . . still a little dizzy from yesterday," Jefferies said, his voice having gone weak for a moment.

"Are you going to be all right?" Sam asked again.

"Oh yeah. Once I get a saddle under me I'll be just fine." His voice was already coming back stronger.

"You wait here. I'll get your horse," Sam said. "First village we come to, we're going to get a good full meal into your belly, help get your strength back."

"Yes, that's all I need," said Jefferies, recovering quickly. He watched Sam walk away toward the horses.

CHAPTER 8

At midmorning the ranger and William Jefferies had ridden the meandering high trail across another stretch of hills until they stopped and looked down on a small detachment of Mexican soldiers who'd made camp outside a village alongside the trail leading toward the border.

"The town of Sol de Oro," Sam said. "It means 'golden sun' in English." He nodded along the trail winding past the village until it disappeared into a flat stretch of rocky sand. "This road will take you home," he added. "More than likely it's the same trail you and your uncle rode in on."

"Yes, I believe it is," said Jefferies, sitting a bit slumped in his saddle.

He'd had no more dizziness since they'd broke camp at early morning, yet Sam looked him up and down closely, then said, "Here's the meal I promised—and a clean bandage for you."

"What about these soldiers?" Jefferies asked.

"We'll swing wide around them," said Sam, "but only because they might get nosy about Fadden's body." He jerked his head toward the canvas-wrapped corpse in tow. "Otherwise they would pay little mind to a couple of gringos traipsing across the badlands."

They touched heels to their horses and followed a thinner trail that led down and into Sol de Oro without crossing alongside the army encampment. When they had reached the outskirts of the village, Sam veered off the trail and led the horse carrying Fadden's body into a thick stand of cedar

79

saplings. "Wait here. I'll be right back," he said over his shoulder, seeing Jefferies start to follow him.

Jefferies did as he was told and in a moment Sam stepped his horse out of the cedar thicket, brushing twigs and briars from his duster sleeve. "I left Fadden hidden in the shade. It's easier than explaining him to the soldiers if we come upon some of them in town."

They rode on, and as they put their horses onto a partially stone-paved street, they saw ahead six soldiers filling water bladders at the large town well in the center of the square. As the soldiers watched them riding by, Jefferies said in a lowered voice, "Good idea about leaving the body out of town."

Sam reached up and closed his duster over his ranger badge. He could feel the soldiers' eyes on him and Jefferies, most specifically on Jefferies' wounded shoulder. "It didn't help," Sam said. "It looks like they're going to stop us anyway."

No sooner had he spoken than an older sergeant called out in stiff but understandable English, "Eh, you! You two horsemen! Stop where you are."

"Usted dos jinetes, parada!" another soldier called out, saying much the same thing in Spanish.

"Yep, just like I suspected," Sam murmured. "You keep quiet, Jefferies. Let me talk for both of us."

"Sure thing," Jefferies replied under his breath.

"Yes, you!" the sergeant called out gruffly as Sam stopped his horse in the middle of the street and turned in his saddle facing the soldier. "What are you two doing here?"

"We're speculating cattle," Sam said, realizing he was not a good liar.

"Cattle?" The sergeant looked puzzled and amused. "You come from the *Tejas* or the *Californias*, to speculate cattle *here*, in my poor country?"

Sam cursed his mistake. "That was my way of saying it's none of your business," he said bluntly.

"Oh no, meester, that will not do," said the sergeant, wagging a finger. "It is my business." His hand rested on the closed flap of his sidearm holster. He gestured toward Jefferies' bandaged shoulder. "Now tell me what you two are really doing here, and what happened to this one?"

"He was shot by a misfire," Sam said, already wondering what to say next. "He was—"

Jefferies cut in. "I was shot accidentally by one of Desmond Prew's men. We ride for Desmond Prew." He stopped talking and sat with a calm gaze on his face while the Mexican sergeant let his words sink in.

"Desmond Prew. Ah!" The sergeant's stern expression turned from confused to elated. "Then you two are some of the men who supplied our weapons, eh?"

"That's right," said Jefferies, cutting a quick glance to the ranger, then back to the soldier. "We met with *Capitán* Luis Murella, in Esperanza. That is where I was shot *mistakenly* while all of us drank and twirled the whores the *capitán* sent for us." He gave a slight smile, raising his sore shoulder just enough to make notice of it.

Sam sat in silence and listened, observing William Jefferies in a different light. Maybe he wasn't such a big ole kid after all.

"Ah, you two twirled *putas*, compliments of *el capitán*, eh?" The sergeant beamed, raising a finger and twirling it above his head. "I knew *el capitán* went to Esperanza. If only I could have gone with him."

"You would have enjoyed it," said Jefferies. He seemed perfectly at ease, Sam noted. The men behind the sergeant nodded in gleeful unison.

"Perhaps another time," the sergeant said. Changing the subject, he said, "You men provide us with the very best!" As he spoke his hand flipped his holster flap up. He jerked out a big army Colt pistol so fast Sam almost reached for his own Colt before he realized the sergeant was only showing them the gun.

"Look at this. Never have I owned such a magnificent firearm." He handed the pistol up to Sam, butt first, for Sam to admire.

"Very nice," Sam offered, looking the pistol over good. He noticed the U.S. Army ordnance stamp above the trigger guard. Realizing that this gun had either been taken off of a dead American soldier or stolen from an army munitions shipment along the border, he held the revolver by its barrel and handed it back to the sergeant. "Glad we could be of service," he said flatly.

"But look how foolish of me, to show this to you!" said the sergeant. "You have seen far more of these beauties than I." He took the gun, holstered it and gestured a hand to one of the men behind him. "Show him your rifle, Private, quickly!" he said with a show of authority.

The young soldier stepped forward and held a Winchester repeating rifle up at a high port arms position.

"There, you see," said the sergeant. "It is much good you are doing for my government." He gestured a hand around at the horses lined along a hitch rail beside the well. Winchester repeaters hung from saddle rings. A brace of Colt revolvers in saddle holsters lay across one of the saddles, the sergeant's no doubt, in addition to the Colt on his hip.

"We're only glad we can help," said Jefferies, without the slightest glimpse of insincerity. "Will you direct me who to go to to get this wound checked and cleaned?"

"*Sí.* There is a French doctor in Sol de Oro. His name is Lafluer," said the sergeant. "Tell him Sergeant Torio sent you to him. Tell him he better take good care of you, or he will answer to me." He pounded a fist on his chest.

"Thank you, Sergeant," said Jefferies. "Is there anything else?"

"No, you go, get yourself taken care of," said the sergeant. "Give *el capitán* my best regards."

Jefferies and Sam turned their horses back to the street

and heeled them into a walk. "That was pretty smooth of you, Jefferies," Sam said quietly. "I don't think you're going to have any trouble making your way home on your own. You seem to know the right words to say."

Jefferies smiled thinly. "Prew told us to use his name if we got stopped and questioned by *federales*. I threw in the part about twirling the whores just to make it sound real. We were supposed to each get a letter to carry on us. But it never happened." He gave Sam a look and asked, "Did I do something wrong, speaking up like that?"

Sam, already having given it thought, said, "No, you did good. It just surprised me, is all."

"I'm young, Ranger," Jefferies said, without taking offense, "but I'm not stupid."

"I never thought you were," said the ranger. They rode quietly along the stone-paved street.

When they walked into Dr. Lafluer's hacienda, just off the main street of Sol de Oro, Sam waited and watched as the elderly Frenchman unwrapped Jefferies' wounded shoulder and washed it with clean water. Once the doctor gave Sam a nod, telling him that the wound appeared to be healing, Sam stepped forward with his sombrero in hand and said, "Well, Jefferies, it looks like this is where we part company. Stick to the main trail. I expect you'll find your way home from here."

"Yes, I know the trail from here," said Jefferies. "Much obliged, Ranger, for all your help. Maybe someday our trails will cross again."

"Maybe," Sam said. "Until then, *adios*. And stay out of trouble," he added.

"You can count on it," Jefferies said. He watched as the ranger turned and left, closing the large oak door behind himself.

Moments later, as soon as Dr. Lafluer had completed redressing the wound, Jefferies stood and walked purposefully to a window that faced onto the wide stone street. Looking out, he saw the ranger come out of a supply store carrying a shovel under his arm. He watched curiously until he saw him step into the Appaloosa's saddle, lay the shovel across his lap and ride away.

"How much do I owe you, Doctor?" Jefferies asked. Stooping, he ran his hand down into his boot well, brought out a folded leather wallet and flipped it open. As he took out crisp new American dollar bills, he asked, "Where can I buy rifle ammunition and a good pair of binoculars?"

The doctor looked at the money in Jefferies' hand and said dubiously, "You will need binoculars on your way home?"

"I was born with a curious nature, Doc," Jefferies replied. "I like to see everything that's going on around me."

Outside, Sam rode back past the town well and along the stone street until it turned into dirt. He rode straight to the cedar thicket where he'd left Fadden's body. Unhitching Fadden's horse, he led it out of the thicket onto a flat stretch of brushy soil.

Fifty yards out, Sam dug a shallow grave, rolled Dallas Fadden's body into it and shoveled the dirt over him. He gathered stones, covered the grave, then stepped back and wiped his forehead with his bandanna. "It's better than you deserve," he murmured down to the fresh mound of earth. Holding his breath against the terrible stench, he turned and dropped the saddle and bridle from Fadden's horse and slapped its rump.

He watched the horse kick up a low rise of dust as it raced away. Then he stuck the shovel into the ground at the head of the grave, mounted the Appaloosa and rode on. But instead of taking the trail toward the border, he rode back to the hill trail and followed it upward in the direction of Esperanza.

Behind him in Sol de Oro, Jefferies led the tired horse to the town livery stables with his left arm resting in a sling. A few minutes later, he rode out of the livery on a big scrappy black-and-white paint horse he'd traded for. He wore a ragged duster that had been hanging in the stables. He carried a bandolier of rifle ammunition slung over his shoulder and a battered army field lens hung around his neck on a strip of leather.

Instead of heading toward the border, he carefully swung wide around the army encampment and rode the same hill trail the ranger had taken back up toward Esperanza. *Clearly, that's where he's headed,* Jefferies told himself, and that worked right into his plan. But unlike the ranger, he veered off the trail they'd ridden in on and took another trail at the base of the hills. With luck he would get up on a path above the ranger and be able to observe him from within the cover of the hillside.

Part II

CHAPTER 9

Sabio climbed above the secluded pool that lay beneath the waterfalls and looked down on Caridad, who swam naked in the clear water below. "Holy Mother," he gasped under his breath, watching her roll lithely onto her back. Even at such a distance the thin line of dark hair on her lower belly stood out like a glistening black jewel. The sight of her breasts, small but firm and maturing like spring peaches, caused him to close his eyes and whisper aloud.

"My God, why must you tempt us poor mortals in such a manner? Are you as wicked in your torture of us as we are in our cravings for the fruits of your creation?" He looked back down past his weathered folded hands at the naked young woman, and felt a passing need to weep. "Must life be a test of either my will or yours?"

He fell silent, but told himself that there could be no God. What kind of divine presence would have nothing better to do than to test men in this way? Why would any God care if he satisfied himself in the warmth of Caridad's young body? *Well, no sane, caring and merciful God would*, he told himself, nodding, justifying his image of himself and this naked young woman locked together in a lovers' embrace.

Yet, as soon as he denounced God as an insane, noncaring, merciless creature for forbidding man's pleasure, an instinctive fear stirred inside him. He prayed quickly and silently to be forgiven for such blasphemy in his thoughts. Then, letting out a breath and looking back down at the naked swimmer, he shook his head, needing to pray again immediately, for both the thoughts and the urges surging inside

He whispered almost bitterly to himself, or to God, or to all the forces around him, "Perhaps I should save up my prayers until I have come to some resting point in my long carnal journey." His eyes sliced upward as if to admonish heaven for its cruelty, rather than argue it out with God.

Caridad, unaware of Sabio's eyes on her, stood up from swimming and walked back to the water's edge. Standing in shallow water, she raised one leg at a time and rinsed herself, using only her cupped hands. In the same manner she washed her breasts, her stomach, her inner thighs. As she finished, she pulled back her long black hair, squeezed water from it and laid it down her back, its ends loose on her rounded hips.

"Jesus, Sonny, she stepped out. Come take a look at this," said Robert Koch, staring down at the naked woman from a higher edge of rock nearly a half mile away.

"I'm not looking anymore," said Sonny with determination. "Get your horse. We're going down there."

Koch scooted back from the edge and scrambled to his feet. "I hope you wasn't expecting some kind of argument out of me," he said, slapping dirt from his shirt and trousers front. "Part of me is already down there."

"Then hurry up. Let's go," said Sonny, already swinging up onto his horse.

Peering down for another quick look from the cover of a scrub pinon, Koch said, "There's that ghostly-looking little sonsabitch. He's climbing back down toward her."

"Come on, damn it," said Sonny, losing patience, "before he scoops her up and runs off with her."

Jumping up into his saddle, Koch asked as they turned their horses to the narrow trail, "Is this going to be all right with Prew, us dipping ourselves some honey from this sweet little *rannúculo?*"

"The hell is a *ranun—ranuncu*—whatever?" Sonny asked, appearing agitated.

"A buttercup," Koch said with a tight grin.

"How about talking English, damn it?" Sonny asked in a sore tone. "It's bad enough every damn Mexican down here has to speak Spanish, let alone you."

"Sorry, Sonny." Koch gave him a confused, bewildered look as they rode at a fast walk down the trail. "So what do you think? Will it be all right with Prew? I mean, if we both *do* her."

"It's all right with him if it's all right with us." Sonny grinned. "I wasn't aiming to go back and say, 'Prew, guess what we did.' Was you?"

"Well, no, I wasn't," said Koch, looking a little embarrassed. They hurried their horses, side by side on the trail.

"He asked us to find the new kid and kill him—the ranger too, if we see him. He never said we couldn't have ourselves some fun in the doing of it."

"I just thought I ought to ask," said Koch.

"And so you did," said Sonny. "Now don't worry about it. Prew wouldn't care if we both do her and the little monk too."

"Now that sounds ugly," said Koch, with a disgusted face.

"Sabio, you fool! You imbecile!" the former monk cursed himself as he hurried down the jagged rocks toward the pool of water. He had caught a glimpse of the two horsemen just as they'd turned and put their horses on the trail. He knew beyond any doubt that they had seen the naked girl and were now on their way down for her, like hungry wolves. "You were to be looking out for her!" he chastised himself, hurrying, sliding, and struggling to regain his footing.

"But no, you despicable fool! You were too busy deflowering her with your eyes—you and your lustful desires! It is no wonder God loathes you!"

Beneath the roar of the waterfalls, Caridad did not hear the two horses coming down the trail. She'd taken her time washing and pulling back her hair. Now, rather than dress wet, she stretched out on a flat rock to allow the warm sun to dry her.

From a foliage-covered ledge, Sabio saw the two horsemen step down from their horses and lead the animals into a stand of trees. He watched as they slipped quietly on foot toward the unsuspecting woman. "Oh God, no! My poor, sweet Caridad!" he whispered to himself, cupping his palm over his mouth. He scrambled sidelong on the thin ledge, hugging tightly against the jagged rock wall to keep from plunging to his death.

"Koch, circle around in case she sees us and tries to bolt away!" Sonny said as the two of them crouched, moving closer.

"You've got it, Sonny," Koch whispered with a grin, easing away from him. "This is more fun than cornering a young deer."

But as he crept away, he tripped, fell forward and landed with a grunt. His gun slipped from his holster and clanged across the sloping rock.

Startled, and seeing the gun slide past her into the water, Caridad sprang to her feet and grabbed the dress that lay beside her. She raced away a few feet before stopping and turning to see the two men, Sonny still crouched and ready to spring toward her, Koch back to his feet and rubbing his sore chin. "Damn it to hell!" Koch cursed, seeing his gun go into the water.

"Easy, now, little lady!" Sonny said, keeping his voice level, hoping to calm her. "We're not going to hurt you. No sir-ree! Not at all. We just come down to make friends, is all. Sort of get to know one another. Do you understand me? *Hablo englo*— Ah, hell," he cursed. "Koch, help me out here. Talk Spanish to her."

"Uh—*señorita*." Koch stalled. He'd started to circle wide of her again, but Caridad sidestepped along the water's edge, ready to plunge in and swim if she had to. "We, that is him and me here—*nosotros dos*," he said, pointing back and forth between Sonny and himself. "Us two—would like to sit down with you and visit for a spell—" He chuckled darkly, then said, "Hell, you don't even have to dress on our account."

But Caridad saw their intentions and she sidestepped farther away. "*Por favor!* I do not do that. I have never done that! Please do not make me do that!" She stopped moving sideways as if to make a stand for herself.

"She's not going to run. Are you, buttercup?" Koch's tight grin widened. He saw no more need for pretense. "Now that's real good!" He glanced at Sonny, then said to her, "Well, now, if it's true you've never *done that*, I'll give you some mixed thoughts—both good and bad—about a young woman waiting too long before she opens that all-important door into full womanhood!" As he spoke he hurriedly snatched off his shirt.

"Me first, Koch!" Sonny called out.

But Koch didn't reply. He'd raised a foot in order to take his boot off when an explosion ripped above the sound of falling water. Sonny ducked, his hand going for his Colt. Koch let out a cry and clutched the side of his face. Caridad screamed as the upper half of Koch's left ear fell at her bare feet from fifteen feet away.

"Drop your guns, both of you!" Sabio shouted, standing above them at a spot near their horses. The rifle shot had come as a surprise to him and it caused his hands to tremble. But he was certain the two men could not tell he was frightened. His knobby knees quivered inside his tattered robe. Yet he stood with a look of complete confidence on his face. "Do not test me! Drop them now!"

Koch stood groaning, blood running down from his cupped hand. "My damn ear!"

"Hey now, take it easy, *Padre*." Sonny's hand was on his gun butt, but he was not sure if he should make a move or not after seeing what the monk had done to Koch. "We wasn't going to hurt her. You saw yourself she wasn't going to run. She might have been waiting for some warm-blooded man to—"

"Lift the pistol slowly and let it fall!" Sabio demanded, cutting him off. "Do not make me say it again."

"But you're a clergy, a priest or whatnot," said Sonny, his hand still poised. "You can't kill a man! Who are you trying to buffalo?" He grinned and winked as if he'd caught on to Sabio's bluff.

Sabio wasn't sure what to do next, but he raised the rifle to his shoulder and said calmly, "It is true I will not kill you. But I am a crack shot, as you have seen. I will leave enough pieces of you on the ground that you will wish I did kill you."

"We'll take our chances," said Sonny. Keeping his hand on his gun butt he said to Koch, "Can you get to your gun as soon as I start shooting?"

"Not without both of his feet, he can't," Sabio said coolly. He turned the Winchester toward Koch.

"Hey, Sonny, wait!" said Koch, his hand still clamped to his ear. "That's my new Winchester he's holding. That thing damn near aims and shoots itself."

"So?" said Sonny, crouched, poised and ready to draw and throw down.

"So! You saw him shoot! I've already lost a damn ear! I can't lose another one, or a foot, or any important part for that matter!"

Sonny thought about it for a moment. Finally he eased his hand up away from his gun butt and said, "Old man, you've got a good day going for you today. I expect you're saving her for yourself." Then he raised his Colt and dropped it onto the stones beneath his feet.

Sabio reddened, his nostrils flared and his knuckles whitened. He felt himself start to pull the trigger. Yet, having no idea where his shot would go, he swallowed his boiling anger. "Walk away from it," he demanded, telling himself to stay calm, that he had everything going his way. "You," he said to Koch, "raise your other hand and move over beside him. Get away from her."

Koch raised his free hand and stepped over beside Sonny. "You've shot my damned ear off. My gun's in the water. What do you want from me?"

"Both of you stand very still," Sabio warned them. To Caridad he motioned a hand and said, "Come quickly, dear child. Don't be afraid of these men." He saw her start to hurry toward him with her dress hugged tightly against her breasts. "Please, put on your dress," he told her. Swinging the Winchester back and forth between the two men, who still stared hungrily in spite of the rifle pointed at them, he growled menacingly, "Look away from her, you swine!"

When Caridad had wiggled into her dress and run to him, Sabio kept the rifle aimed at the two men and directed her toward the two horses. "If you try to pick up your gun, I will see you do it, and I will shoot off your fingers."

"You can't take our horse, *Padre!*" said Sonny. "A man could die out here afoot!"

"It is twenty miles to Esperanza. I believe you know your way there. You will find water like this along the way if you stay on the hill trails. Avoid any bands of blanket Apache, and you will be all right."

"Prew only sent us to find the kid, *Padre*," Sonny called aloud as Sabio and Caridad disappeared out of sight toward the horses. "Stop this now, and we'll let you both live. Take our horses and we're bound to come kill you! Do you hear me?"

But Sabio didn't answer. Inside the trees, Caridad looked at him in amazement and said, "I never knew you were a crack shot!"

Sabio, stunned by having shot a man's ear off, could think of no other explanation than to look at the rifle and say, "As with all things, it is God working through my hands."

Near the water, the two gunmen waited for a second, and when no answer came, Sonny took a cautious step toward his gun lying on the ground. But before he got to it, a rifle shot exploded and Sabio called out from within the trees, "Uh-uh-uh. Stay where you are! I will not warn you again!"

"All right, damn it!" said Sonny, having jerked to a halt at the sound of the rifle, which Sabio had only fired straight up into the air.

"Hurry, Caridad!" Sabio said, giving a boost on her warm bottom to shove her up into the saddle. Even with their lives in peril the feel of her sent a hot rush of desire throughout him. He closed his eyes tight for a second as if attempting to drive away the image of her.

"I'm ready!" said Caridad, in the saddle, her peasant dress hiked above her knees. Sabio tore his eyes away from the smooth brown flesh and climbed atop the other horse, holding tightly to the rifle.

The two horses came charging out of the trees at a run and in no more than three seconds had disappeared again. "Damn it!" shouted Sonny Nix. He'd made a fast dive for his gun, but when he grabbed it and turned toward the two it was too late. He stood crouched, listening to the receding sound of pounding hooves.

"What the hell do we do now?" Koch asked, wincing in pain, his hand still clamped to the bloody side of his head. "They've got our horses! My rifle!"

"Like he said, we walk," Sonny replied.

"Walk? Look at me—I'm bleeding!"

But Sonny only stared at the rise of dust the horses had left above the trail and said bitterly, "Damned if I'm going back and telling Prew we got outgunned and buffaloed by some ragged-assed priest and his naked girlfriend. Nobody's going to know what happened out here, you understand?"

"Yes! But I can't *walk* to Esperanza!" Koch insisted.

"We're not going to Esperanza," said Sonny. "We're going

back to the old mission we tracked them to the other day."

"Why? They're not there!" Koch snapped.

"Go wash your face and attend to yourself," said Sonny. From his tone of voice, all room for discussion was gone. "They'll be gone for a while, just to shake us off their tails. But I've got a feeling that little skin-headed sonsabitch lives in the old mission. They'll be coming back. When they do we'll be waiting. We'll kill them both."

Koch turned and walked to the edge of the water, untying a bandanna from around his neck. "In that case, I still want some of that girl—even more now that she cost me an ear."

Sonny looked at him in disgust and shook his head.

Twenty minutes later, when Koch walked up from the water, he'd tucked his hat down on one side to keep the wet bandanna pressed against his clipped ear. A large bloodstain ran from his shoulder to his waist. Water dripped from the holster housing his gun, which he'd fished from the stream. "I expect I'm as ready as I'll ever be," he said.

"Jesus," Sonny said, looking him up and down. But before he could comment any further, a voice called out, "Hello the water."

The two turned quickly and saw a tall figure seated atop a large silver-gray, leading a strong dun behind him, loaded with supplies. "Well, I'll be damned, pard," Sonny said quietly to Koch. "Looks like our string ain't nearly run out yet." He took a step forward and added under his breath, "Let's kill him."

"Wait. That's Dan Carlson," Koch whispered in reply. "He's one of the men who's supposed to join us in Esperanza. We can't foul-play him! He's Cherokee Jake's cousin!"

"He used to be," said Sonny, smiling at the horseman as he walked toward him. "Or would you rather ole Wind River Dan here ride in telling Prew what happened to us?"

In a loud voice, Sonny called out, "Wind River Dan. How the hell are you?"

"I'm afraid you have me at a disadvantage, sir," the big

man in the flat-brimmed plainsman's hat said, his hand resting on the butt of a large Colt on his hip. He squinted as the men walked closer, trying to recognize the two.

"I'm Sonny Nix, and this is Robert Koch," Sonny said casually. "We've been waiting for you up in Esperanza. I hope you're ready to make yourself rich!"

Carlson relaxed and gave a thin smile. "I'm ready to do my part—help out any way I can."

"Good," said Sonny, drawing his Colt as he continued walking. He shot Carlson twice in the chest. "'Cause we could sure use some horses." He grabbed the silver-gray by its bridle as Carlson pitched over into the dirt. "Easy, boy," he said to the big horse. "You didn't lose nothing."

Carlson lay gasping for breath, one foot still in his stirrup. Blood ran down from his trembling lips and his eyes bulged. "I expect it's a sonsabitch, dying all of a sudden like this," Sonny said down to him. "You just got here at the wrong time." He shot him again, watched him slump into death, then kicked his foot out of the stirrup.

"What are we going to tell Cherokee?" Koch asked, trotting forward and taking the reins to the supply horse.

Sonny gave him a sharp stare. "I just solved one problem for us. Are you already thinking us up another one?"

CHAPTER 10

The ranger had spent the night beneath a cliff overhang overlooking his back trail that lay hidden in a stretch of thick green forest. At early light he'd sat watching the treetops expectantly. Three hundred yards out he'd watched a flurry of birds rise up and scatter on the silvery morning mist. Moments later the scene repeated itself a hundred yards closer. He waited and watched. Then it came again, closer yet.

Yep, he told himself, *somebody's back there*. They'd begun trailing him the day before, no sooner than he'd reached the base of the first hill line. That was when he'd first sensed someone behind him. Was it William Jefferies? *Yes, more than likely*, he thought, easing back from the edge. He rubbed out the small fire and lifted his tin cup for the last sip of hot coffee.

Whoever was coming back there should have started an hour earlier, before daybreak, or else an hour later, in full morning light. The birds would have been less skittish then. Sam swung his saddle and blanket up onto the big Appaloosa's back. He picked his rifle up from against a rock and shoved it down into the saddle boot.

"Well, Black Pot," he said quietly to the well-rested stallion, "let's go find ourselves a good spot and wait them out." Before mounting he took another look down, this time catching a broken glimpse of a horse and its rider as they moved through a thinner stretch of trees. Seeing only the top of the rider's hat, he recognized neither man nor animal as they veered off the trail and to the left, toward a steeper path winding up, circling around the hillside.

Could he have been wrong about the rider following him? Maybe, but he didn't think so, not just yet. It could be that whoever was down there wanted to get above him. If that was the case he'd find out at the top of the trail. Was he wrong about it being Jefferies down there? "We'll just have to wait and see," he said to Black Pot.

On the steep path circling the hillside, Jefferies looked down at the trail behind him and chastised himself under his breath. Had the ranger seen the birds he'd spooked from their tree branches? He didn't know. Odds were, the ranger hadn't seen them. But whether he'd seen them or not, it was too late to worry about it now. Once he topped the hill he'd be ahead of the ranger. So no matter if Sam watched his back trail or not, Jefferies told himself, he wouldn't be back there.

He rode carefully until midmorning. Then he left his paint horse among a bed of sunken boulders and climbed down onto the trail the ranger had taken. Seeing no fresh tracks, he breathed in relief, climbed back up and led his horse out of sight, rifle in hand. All right, this was how he would do it all the way to Esperanza, he told himself.

He would stay with the ranger by keeping in front of him from one turnoff along the trail to the next. He smiled to himself. *Come on, Ranger, let's see you figure this one out.* Taking his arm out of the sling, he eased down and stretched out prone behind half of an up-stuck boulder, his rifle lying alongside him. He pulled the field lens open, raised it to his eye and adjusted it to the trail below. Now, the wait.

But he didn't have to wait long. Before twenty minutes had passed, he saw a thin drift of dust rise up from back along the trail. *Here he comes.* He watched even closer until he heard the first quiet drop of hooves and saw Sam's Appaloosa walk into view. *But wait!*

"Oh no!" he said, seeing the empty saddle and instinctively throwing a hand over on his rifle, knowing full well that he'd made his move in vain. He froze as he felt the tip of Sam's

Colt center on the back of his neck. At the same time, out of the corner of his eye, he saw his rifle seem to crawl backward until it disappeared from view.

The Colt cocked slowly, as if the ranger wanted to make sure he heard it. "I'll trouble you to reach your left hand under and pull your gun up real easy."

"My left arm's awfully stiff and sore, Ranger," Jeffries offered even as he followed Sam's order.

"I know," Sam replied. "That's why my boot's not planted on it right now."

"How'd you know I was back there?" Jefferies asked, pulling the gun from his belt slowly and holding it out left-handed, with much effort.

Sam wasn't about to mention the birds. If Jefferies saw it, good for him. If not, he'd have to wonder, or figure it out on his own. "Call it a hunch born from more than just a few bushwhackings. Roll over, sit up."

Jefferies sighed, doing as he was told. "Sounds like you're giving orders to a dog." Sitting with his forearms in his lap, he sighed again and said, "For what it's worth, I wasn't bushwhacking you."

"It's not the first time I've heard that either," Sam said in a no-nonsense tone. He jiggled the rifle in his hand. "You're saying one thing, but this Winchester says something else."

Jefferies looked down and shook his head, then looked up and said, "Ranger, we need to talk."

"Still nothing new," Sam said, this time with a trace of a wry grin.

"Just hear me out, please," said Jefferies, raising a hand as if to stop the ranger from anything else for a moment. "I'm Captain William Jefferies, U.S. Army, operating as an agent for the United States Secret Service." He let out a tense breath.

"I have to admit, that is a story I don't hear every day." Sam's Colt remained cocked and pointed as if what Jefferies said made no difference at all. "What goes along with it?"

"I'm down here working under the utmost discretion—"

"No, I mean a badge? Something that proves to me you are who you say you are?"

"I wouldn't last five minutes if Desmond Prew caught me carrying a badge," Jefferies said. Pausing, he shook his head again. "The fact is, I don't have anything to prove who I am. But you didn't get your reputation shooting unarmed men, Ranger. So you'll have to give me time to do what I'm here to do—then check out my story back across the border."

"That's a good deal for you," Sam said, "but it doesn't work for me at all."

"Then what can I tell you?" said Jefferies. "Your story about just happening by the old mission above Esperanza with a body in tow didn't sound too real to me. For all I know you could be working for Prew."

"Watch your language, young man," Sam said sternly.

"You wouldn't be the first lawman working both sides of the line," said Jefferies. "How do I know you're not using—"

"Let's stop right there before you make me start thinking I'm the one in the wrong here," Sam said. He took a step back. "Who started the Secret Service?"

Jefferies nodded. "All right, a test then. Good idea. The Secret Service Division was started by Chief William P. Wood." He gave Sam a confident stare. "Next question."

Sam nodded, knowing his answer to be true. "What's the Secret Service's job?"

"The Secret Service was formed to chase down counterfeiters, Ranger. But any schoolboy would probably know the answer to that one, don't you think?"

Sam didn't respond. Instead he asked quickly, "That being the case, what's a Secret Service investigator doing down here checking out Prew and his mercenaries?"

Jefferies cocked his head slightly. "I could ask you what an Arizona Ranger is doing here in the first place, let alone riding up to Esperanza when you've already finished what

Sabio's Redemption

you came here to do."

"Yes, you could ask," said Sam, "but you'd do well to keep in mind who's holding the gun here and who's looking into the barrel."

"All right," said Jefferies. "Prew has run wild down here for too long. He's robbed too many army trains. My chief thinks he has inside men within the army ranks and the railroad. We'll never find out who his contacts are. I'm here to bust up his whole operation. Once that's done his informers will be out of business."

"All by yourself, you're going to bust up his operation?" Sam asked. "Fighting Prew and his Mexican *federales* allies, you'd be fighting an army."

"You know the saying 'One town, one ranger'?" He gave Sam a flat stare. "Here's a new one for you: 'One *army*, one *agent*.'"

Sam considered what Jefferies had said. "How do you propose to bust up his operation?" As he spoke he uncocked the Colt, reached down with his free hand and helped Jefferies to his feet.

"I have some supplies in a leather weapons bag in Esperanza," said Jefferies. "I hid it the night Rance Hurley hanged himself."

"Rance Hurley the bank robber? The murderer?" Sam asked.

"Yep, that's the one," said Jefferies. "He was sentenced to hang. But he agreed to pose as my uncle, get me inside with Prew and the Mexican captain. Then he was supposed to disappear and never be seen or heard from again. Things fell apart when he shot too much cocaine, ate too much peyote and washed it down with too much mescal. He ended up hanging anyways."

"The thing that worries me about you, Jefferies," said the ranger, "is that the story about your uncle and you slid off your tongue so easy. I have to wonder if you were lying *then* or if you're lying now."

"I've learned that lying is a form of art in this line of work, Ranger," said Jefferies. "You should know that by now."

"No, I don't know it," Sam replied. "I do my job without deceiving anybody."

"Come on—you've never told a little lie along the way, to save somebody, or to keep the game running level?"

"Maybe I have," said Sam. He didn't want Jefferies to know one way or the other about how he thought, how he did his job, or anything else until he knew for certain if the man was telling the truth.

Seeing something to that effect in the ranger's eyes, Jefferies shrugged and said, "I'm just a horse-soldier captain hired by the Secret Service to handle this assignment. When it's over I might be right back at the head of a column, chasing renegade Indians, for all I know. You don't have to worry about me."

"I'm not," said Sam. He directed Jefferies toward the horses with the barrel of his Colt. On their way up the steep rock ground, Sam kept to the man's side, not right behind him. He gave a sharp short whistle to bring Black Pot up from the trail.

"If you weren't out to bushwhack me, what was your plan when I rode through here?"

"I intended to follow you to Esperanza," said Jefferies. "I knew that whatever you did there was going to draw attention. I figured while everybody stayed busy with you, I'd pick up my hidden leather bag and get out of town. I'm following Prew to wherever they plan to take down the next army train." He looked sidelong at Sam. "What are you going to do in Esperanza?"

"I told Prew I'd be coming for what's mine," Sam said. "After seeing all the fancy firearms the *federales* had, I decided to get on back up there now instead of later. I wanted to look around, see what I might do to stop Prew and his men. With enough guns like that in their hands, I could see lots of innocent blood spilled before long."

"Yes, and too much of it has been spilled already," said Jefferies.

They walked on.

"Where are you taking me, Ranger, if you don't mind me asking?" He gave a slight wry grin.

"To Esperanza, so you can get your weapons bag and show it to me," Sam replied.

"Whoa, Ranger." Jefferies almost stopped. "If you think you're going in with me on this, you're mistaken. I've gotten too used to working alone."

Sam gestured him on to the horses without commenting any further on the matter. "I have to hand it to you," he said. "You played a convincing role, acting like the big dumb rube. I sure believed it."

"I feel bad about that, Ranger," Jefferies said. "I don't like deceiving you, Sabio and Caridad. You all three saved my life."

"Speaking of Caridad," said Sam, "where does she stand in all this? Was that just a made-up story you gave her, about how you would come back to her? She believed you meant every word of it."

"I did," said Jefferies in a softer tone, stopping at his horse. Sam's Appaloosa walked up from the trail and joined them. "Maybe I was wrong, telling her I was coming back. The truth is I might not be coming back. I could be dead when this is finished. But if I'm alive, I'll be back for her. You can count on that."

"Then I suppose we better see to it you stay alive." Sam handed Jefferies the gun he'd taken from him. The young man looked surprised until he opened the chamber and saw the bullets were missing.

"I told you, I work alone."

Sam held six bullets up in his cupped gloved hand. "As soon as I believe you might be telling me the truth about yourself, you'll get these back. Until then, don't let me see your hands near the bullets in your pistol belt."

"Anything you say, Ranger," Jefferies murmured under his breath.

CHAPTER 11

Sabio and Caridad rode as hard as the horses and the hill trail would allow for over an hour. Then they slowed to a walk and let the animals walk gently and pick their way into the entrance of a vine-covered valley away from any trails or paths. When they'd ridden nearly a mile deep into the valley, they stepped down from the tired horses for the first time since fleeing the two gunmen. Sabio slipped the rifle into the saddle boot and looked back on the silent forest as if someone might be following. Satisfied, he sighed and smiled at their remote, peaceful surroundings.

"We are safe here. This hidden forest is my friend and it will allow no one to harm us," he said. "Tonight it will rain and wash away our tracks. By the time they follow us here on foot, we will have vanished." He gestured toward an ancient tree whose trunk opened at the ground like the entrance to a small cavern. "In there you will find a canvas full of blankets and supplies."

"Oh, Sabio," Caridad said, looking all around in sheer wonderment, "how do you know about such places as this? All my life I have lived in these hills and yet—"

"Shhh," said Sabio, barely above a whisper. "You must speak quietly in this place. This is my special forest. We are guests here. If we are not quiet and respectful it will cast us away." He gazed upward into the tops of tall reaching trees draped in the same thick vines that guarded the entrance to the valley.

"I am sorry," Caridad whispered, turning her dark eyes

upward too, for a second, as if apologizing to the forest itself. Then lowering her eyes back to Sabio, she whispered, "You know everything, Sabio. Again you have protected me from harm." Before Sabio could say a word, she'd thrown her arms around him and hugged him tightly. "Thank God for you, *mi ángel del guarda!*"

Her guardian angel . . . Feeling her breasts hot against his chest even through his tattered robe, Sabio tried not to let lustful thoughts and images seep into his mind. Yet he was only human, he reminded himself. He held her loosely and stroked her long hair, her face nuzzled against the side of his neck. "Please, Caridad," Sabio whispered, almost in the anguished moan of a lover.

"It is true," Caridad insisted, unaware of the effect her warm young body had on him and therefore holding none of herself back. "You are my savior, my confessor, my holy man, my brave rifleman!" She squeezed him tighter, her body naturally undulating against his. "Is there anything you cannot do?"

Sante Madre! He lifted his aging eyes to heaven as if praying for strength. "Caridad, Caridad," he said softly, sadly, "what am I to do with you? What is God to do with the two of us?"

Caridad pushed back from him, to arm's length. "What a strange thing to say. What have we done to make God wonder how to deal with us?"

"Dear Caridad," said Sabio. "How I wish you could stay as innocent as you are now for the rest of your life." He turned her loose and stepped back. "Yet when I see the trouble your innocence nearly brought upon you today, I think perhaps it is time for you to come forward and join the rest of us."

"It was my innocence that caused all the trouble at the waterfall?" Caridad asked. At first she tried to make sense of his words; but then she shook her head, knowing there was no sense to be made of them. "Why do you say such a thing? Did my 'innocence' as you call it draw those men to us and make them want to do things to me?"

"I am sorry. That is not what I meant," Sabio said, hoping to let the matter drop.

"Oh, then what did you mean?" she asked.

Sabio looked at her, wondering for a second if he could explain to her that it was not her innocence that had brought on the trouble. Yet he knew from experience that innocence attracted the wicked the way fresh meat attracted wolves. Still, he knew that what he'd said was not even close to what preyed upon his mind. In his mind he'd meant what must he do to keep from spoiling her? Or, given his lifelong lust for women, what must God do to save her from him? No, he could not explain any of this to her, he thought.

"Caridad," he said instead, speaking benevolently, the way he'd learned to speak to his subjects as a young priest who did not want his authority questioned. "It does not matter what I meant when I said it. That moment is gone. What matters is what I am saying *now*."

"And now you are saying?" Caridad asked, relenting to his will even though she needed an answer.

Sabio folded his hands at his waist in a priestly fashion and smiled gently. "I am saying we must rest the horses and ourselves. It is not good to have so much talking when one is weary from the trail. It makes any of us say things in ways we do not mean them."

"Yes, I understand," Caridad said meekly. "Forgive me for being bold. Please do not think less of me."

"No, my dear Caridad," said Sabio. He stepped back close to her and cupped her cheek. "Nothing you will ever say or do will change how I feel for you. I have raised you from a baby. You are the child I was forbidden to father." He smiled, genuinely, warmly. "Have I not told you this throughout your life?"

"Yes, you have told me this many times," Caridad said,

looking into his eyes. She never quite understood everything she saw there, especially these past couple of years.

"Then do not trouble yourself over what I say or what I mean," Sabio said, caressing her cheek. "Now go lie down and rest out of the heat. We have much more traveling to do before we return to the mission."

"Yes, I will go rest now," she said dutifully. She walked away. She knew Sabio carried secrets about himself. Dark secrets? Yes, she was certain of it. She knew that when his eyes took on the look they now had it was time to leave him in peace, to his thoughts, the profound and troubled thoughts of her holy man. . . .

Sabio watched her walk away, her long hair swaying gently. He considered how many times he had longed to make love to such a beautiful young woman as this, here in this lush forest, on the soft fertile belly of the earth. But *not* with his Caridad, he told himself, as if he needed constant reminding lest his lower nature overwhelm him. He blew out a breath and shook his head.

Do not destroy this one's faith in you, the way you have done with everyone else, he heard his stern inner voice call out. In reply to that voice he bit his lip. No, he would not do such a thing. Not to Caridad, not to the only soul left on God's earth who still thought him divine and without fault. He realized how deeply he needed to be seen with such blind adoration and reverence throughout his entire life; yet he realized too how low and unworthy of such treatment he'd become.

Were he to destroy what Caridad saw in him, his miserable life would end, he reminded himself, taking the reins to both horses and leading them to a small pond fed freshly from a trickling stream. "When God washes his hands of a man, why does he not remove himself from that man's heart and spirit?" he asked the horses under his breath.

But even as he asked, he knew that it was not God who washed his hands of him. "Holy Mother Church," he said bitterly, casting a scowl upward through the towering treetops. Whatever goodness remained in him lay in the eyes of Caridad. She did not see that his powers through God had turned into coincidences he'd learned to play upon, or twists of random fate he'd only purported to understand.

He'd managed to turn God's power into cheap sleight-of-hand tricks like those of a traveling street performer. Shame overcame him. He stopped the horses, sat down in the dirt and buried his face in his crossed arms. Yet even in his shame, he yearned deeply for the cradling mothering arms of a woman—of Louisa, he thought. Or of any woman.

Ah, the women of my life, he pondered, hoping only to take his mind off his misery. Yet, in recalling their faces, their soft naked forms lying beneath him, his misery only grew, until finally he looked over to the large tree and saw Caridad spreading a blanket on the ground beneath its shading canopy. She added a gauzelike sleeping cover that floated weightlessly to the ground. *When you finish with a man*, he whispered silently to God, *you leave him with nothing. No wonder a man must take—for nothing is given to him.*

He watched Caridad step out of her peasant dress, fold it and set it aside. Naked, she lowered herself out of his sight. *In her innocence, did she not know?* he mused. *But how could she not know?* he asked himself. *For the love of God! How could she not know?* He sprang to his feet and rubbed his bald head vigorously in his frustration. "I owe you nothing!" he growled at the sky.

He stomped off into the forest and walked in a wide circle to take his mind off of the sleeping Caridad, lying naked beneath the sheer cover. But at the end of his half-hour circle he found himself standing above her, looking down at the rise and fall of her breasts.

After a moment he stopped and raised the gauzy sleeping cover and pulled it aside, his heart nearly stopping in his chest. He stared in awe, not having to take only a quick glance before looking away. He could look at her—she would not know; and if she awakened, he would say he was only checking on her comfort as any good savior would do. *Shame on you, Sabio!*

No! It's all right! he assured himself. He could look at her, and who but he would ever know? And if no one else ever knew, what harm had he done anyone beyond himself? As he looked at her, he could not keep from reaching out with his hand and holding it near her—just near her, he cautioned himself. Yet, as his hand moved back and forth only a hairbreadth above her warm flesh, he heard her moan in her sleep.

"Oh, Sabio," she whispered, and he swooned headily at the soft, steamy liquid sound of it. What harm would come from him slipping in quietly beside her? She wouldn't mind, he convinced himself. She had grown up sleeping in his arms. . . .

When she awakened, she did so with a start, escaping a troubled dream. She had seen Sabio standing over her and had felt his hands caressing her in a manner that had caused her to writhe and moan in ecstasy. It was like nothing she had ever experienced; yet even in her pleasure, she had known it was wrong and had forced herself to awaken. She sat up, grasping the sheer sleepcover to her, relieved that it had been only a dream, however vivid and real it had seemed.

At a small fire he'd built a few yards away, Sabio sat staring blackly into the low dancing flames. He did not look over toward her as she stood and slipped into her dress. Nor did he look up at first when she'd shaken out her hair and combed her fingers through it and walked over and stooped down beside him. She would never mention the dream; she dared not. Yet when he finally turned his eyes to her, she wondered if perhaps she had spoken her dream aloud, or if he had not somehow known about it.

Such is this holy man's power, she thought. She had had two similar dreams in the past, but neither of them was as real as this, and in neither had his hands touched her, or had she felt him against her, as if he absorbed something from her warmth and her nakedness.

Sabio did not ask how she had rested. He only searched her eyes for a moment, then looked away as if having answered something for himself. "You must eat," he said quietly. He handed her a small wooden bowl of hot crumbled corn cake—*torta de maiz*—that he'd made on a flat rock above the flames.

She took a piece of the soft cake and blew on it, then held it for a moment before eating. "Did you rest?" she asked.

Sabio seemed to stiffen at her question, then breathed in a sigh and said without facing her, "*Sí*, I am rested."

She ate another piece of the cake. After a silent pause, Sabio said, "We must talk about something."

Her dream! She made no reply, but waited for him to continue. If somehow he knew about her dream and confronted her with it, she would not deny it. How could she if his power let him know these things? She would not deny it, and she would not deny how it had made her feel.

But instead of mentioning her dream, Sabio said, "Once your life has returned to normal in Esperanza, I must leave here."

"But, Sabio, why?" She scooted closer to him and hooked her arm into his. "These hills are your home. What would Esperanza do without you? What would I do without you?"

Sabio did not try to explain. "I have been here too long. It is time I go somewhere else, perhaps across the border. Or perhaps it is time to find my ancestors in *la tierra de los muertos*."

"The land of the dead?" said Caridad, giving him a nudge. "Do not talk this way."

"No, I did not mean that," said Sabio, shaking his bald head. "But I must go—for many reasons it is time I leave here."

Again her dream crossed her mind. "Have I done something to cause you to want to leave?" she asked, ready any second for him to confront her with what he knew, with what he'd somehow witnessed while she'd slept.

"No, my dear Caridad, you have done nothing," Sabio said, rounding his arm from hers and taking a short scoot sidelong, putting a few inches of distance between them.

"Oh . . ." She looked surprised and hurt by his actions. It came to her that lately he had been cross and irritable the same way he'd been when last she'd had such a dream. He had mentioned leaving then, too, she recalled, wondering more earnestly if he knew what she had dreamed and felt he must leave rather than shame her with what he knew.

"You are a young woman now, Caridad, and I am an old man," he said, choosing his words carefully. "For a time God brought us together, for you to be the daughter he felt I needed, and for me to be both the father and mother you did not have. But now our lives are changed. You do not need a father and I—" He let his words stop, realizing that what he was about to say was neither honest nor kind.

"I will always need you in my life, Sabio," said Caridad. She risked scooting over against him again and hooked her forearm under his. "I want *you* to always want *me*, no matter what."

"Oh, my dear Caridad, you have no idea how badly I want you," he said, giving in to her and squeezing her arm under his. He closed his eyes tightly and whispered under his breath, "*No idea . . .*"

When she had finished eating the crumbled corn cake, she sipped from a water gourd she'd taken from the supplies beneath the tree and filled at the trickling stream. "Now, then," she said, standing, "no more talk of either of us leaving."

Sabio nodded. "All right, but there is a time coming when one of us must leave the other," he said, "for this is the way life works." He also stood, and adjusted his tattered robe. He looked at her and continued, raising a finger for emphasis. "You may someday want to go across the border and find a better life for yourself. Your father was an American and it shows in your face. You can go there—you have a right to go there."

"But this is my home," Caridad said. "I must—"

"Shhh. Be quiet and listen!" Sabio snapped, cutting her off gruffly.

"But I—"

"Silence!" he insisted, his senses focusing on the way they had ridden in through the draping vines. "They come! The two gunmen!"

"But we took their horses," Caridad said, fear showing in her face and her voice.

"They have found horses. It is them!" said Sabio. He rubbed out the small smokeless fire with his sandal. "Quickly, get the horses while I say the words that will turn this forest against those two and protect us from them."

Caridad hurried away to gather the horses, finding nothing strange in what the old holy man had just said. When she returned, Sabio had rolled up the blanket and sleep cover and hidden them beneath the tree. "Will it still rain tonight and wash away our tracks?" Caridad asked, handing him his reins.

"Of course it—" Sabio stopped and looked up at the sky above the towering trees for reassurance. "Yes, of course it will," he repeated. He climbed up into the saddle and turned his horse deeper into the forest.

But in his heart of hearts he doubted if the forest would still protect him the way it once would have. The forest had seen him and his impure thoughts. What little power had remained was now gone. He was certain of it.

CHAPTER 12

At the narrow entrance to the forest where Sabio and Caridad had entered so effortlessly, Sonny and Koch met with difficulty, attempting to push their horses through the long, draping vines. "Shove them aside, damn it," said Sonny.

"I'm trying!" said Koch. "They're stiff and stubborn as a mule!" The vines he shoved away snapped back at him as if on springs. Struggling along, he and Sonny looked down at the hoofprints they had followed all the way from the waterfalls. Halfway through the hanging vines the two stopped long enough to observe that the prints disappeared into the forest, snaking their way through a bedding of knee-high ground cover that now lay beaten down.

"They ought to be easy enough to follow," Sonny said almost in a whisper, lest the old man and the young woman were within hearing range. The men grinned slyly at one another.

"Follow me," said Sonny, gigging the big silver-gray forward. But as he tried to coax the horse the rest of the way through the tangle of vines, the animal whinnied and balked, as if the vines were some sort of tentacles from hell. "Damn it," he said, struggling with the horse, vines swinging back and forth and almost slapping him out of his saddle.

Behind him, things went even worse for Koch. "Double damn it!" he cursed, shoving the thick springy vines to the side only to have a half dozen more fall into his face as if from out of nowhere. "We're going to need machetes to cut through this stuff!"

Still having troubles of his own with the horse and the tangled vines, Sonny slid down from his saddle and jerked the spooked horse forward. Vines broke loose and fell, whipping across the horse and causing Sonny to duck into a ball to keep from getting hit. A rotten tree branch snapped high up and fell to the ground with a heavy thud, only inches from him. "What the hell is this?" Sonny shouted. He stood and jerked the big silver-gray to the side to keep the vines from lashing them both like heavy whips.

"Maybe we best—*ahhhrgh!*" Koch grunted as a huge vine reached out and slapped him full across the mouth, causing his legs to buckle, almost dropping him to the ground.

"Get over here out of them!" Sonny commanded.

Stunned from the blow, Koch forced the dun over beside the silver-gray, away from the vines. "I've never seen nothing like that in my life!" he said, spitting blood from his mashed lips. "Did he set some kind of trap for us?"

"No," Sonny said bluntly. "Those old vines have hung there a hundred years, then we come along and got them all stirred up. That's what all happened."

"Yeah, I know," said Koch, quickly getting a grip on himself. "It just seemed strange, is all."

"Yeah, strange," said Sonny, "but not a trap." Overhead, a grumbling sound of thunder resounded from a low, darkening sky.

"Damn, now we've got a storm licking at our backs," said Koch. "Maybe we ought to get out of here and go straight up to the old mission. This place doesn't seem real friendly."

"Doesn't seem real friendly?" Sonny gave him a harsh disbelieving look. "This is where their tracks led us. This is the way we're going. What the hell is wrong with you anyway? Is something spooking you?"

"Hell no!" said Koch. "Nothing ever spooks me. You ought to know that." Yet he looked around warily as he adjusted the bandanna covering his maimed ear.

"All right then, pard, let's get after them," Sonny ordered. "I've got a feeling they're not far ahead."

Leading the silver-gray, he stepped forward, stooped down and parted the plush deep ground cover, exposing the fresh hoofprints lying a quarter of an inch deep in the soft earth. Looking ahead at the beaten-down foliage he motioned Koch forward. But as he took his next step, his boot sank ankle-deep into a thick sucking mud. "Jesus!" he cried out. He looked around and saw that his horse had also stepped down into the mud. "Mud? The hell is this?" Sonny shouted, almost losing a boot as he struggled to pull his foot up. "Him and the woman rode through here! Look at their prints! There was no mud!"

"Well, there is now," said Koch. He stepped forward leading his horse, both having the same trouble walking in the sticky mire. "This is crazy!" he shouted through bloody lips. Overhead, thunder roared on a hard rising wind, followed by a bolt of lightning. "Let's back out of here!"

"Like hell," said Sonny. "We're too close to back away. Come on."

"Damn," Koch murmured to himself, struggling forward, leading the dun. "We're in for it now."

They pushed on as the storm set in hard and steady. Lightning stabbed the earth; thunder cracked like cannon fire. The wind whipped and pounded both men and horses. But the two persisted, struggling through stretches of mud, dense storm-soaked foliage and swaying trees whose lower branches lashed out at them like the arms of an angry crowd. After an hour, they stopped and stood soaked and battered beside their horses, out of breath.

"I've lost their tracks," Sonny said in disgust and defeat. He stared ahead at the thickening forest through the hard wind-driven rain. "Maybe we will have to turn back and go wait for them at the mission."

Koch looked all around them in stunned disbelief, then

said, "Well, turning back won't be hard to do from here! Look at us!" He spread his arms, taking in their stormy surroundings. "We're right back where we started!"

"How the—?" Sonny stared slack-jawed. "You mean we've gone in a big circle?" he shouted above the rage of the storm.

"Either that or else we haven't moved *at* all," Koch replied. He looked around warily. "Let's get the hell out of here!"

The two walked backward a few steps, as if they feared turning their backs on the storm or the forest, or some terrible unseen entity that might spring forward and attack them at any second. When they did turn around, they scrambled atop their horses and hurried the animals back toward the trail. This time as they passed through the narrow entrance, the vines hung limp and lifeless.

"Nobody ever hears about this, all right?" Sonny demanded when they'd left the covered entrance and looked back on the forest.

"Hell no, not from me they won't," said Koch, gasping for breath. He slapped his wet hat against his leg. Beyond the tangle of vines, the storm had already begun to subside. As they turned their horses back along the trail, where the rain had fallen only enough to give everything a thin beaded sheen, he added, "I'm not so sure going up to the old mission is such a good idea either."

Sonny gave him a harsh stare. "We're going up to the mission, Koch. That's all there is to it."

Upon leaving the forest, Sabio and Caridad took a secluded trail down to a small nameless village nestled in a deep valley. While Sabio was certain his powers had left him, he was just as certain that the storm on its own had washed out any sign of their tracks through the forest. After three days of rest at an abandoned old thatched-roof adobe, the pair mounted their horses with a canvas bag of food and supplies and took a long

Sabio's Redemption

winding trail around the hills and back up to the old mission.

When their trail led them above Sol de Oro, they stopped in the cover of trees and looked down on the town long enough to see the mercenaries checking their horses and preparing for the trail. In the center of the main street a cook fire still licked upward beneath a rising spiral of smoke. Sabio knew that the people of Sol de Oro would come forward and put out the fire as soon as the last of the men rode away. As long as the fire continued to burn, there were still mercenaries in town.

"Still, there will be men there," Sabio said, observing the men as they checked rifles and tightened saddle cinches. With a sigh Sabio turned his horse; Caridad did the same, and the two of them rode on.

In the wide dusty street below, Desmond Prew caught only a glimpse of the two tiny riders who passed in and out of sight along the up-reaching trail. But at the sight of them he turned to Sway Loden and said, "If Sonny and Koch show up, send them on to catch up to us. I sent Cherokee to search for them." He looked all around appraisingly. "You'll still have plenty of men to hold things down here until we return."

"Yeah," said Loden, looking along the high trail with him. "I wonder what's taking Sonny and Koch so long."

"Who knows?" said Prew. "Who cares, so long as they get that kid taken care of—and the ranger."

Loden scratched the beard stubble on his cheek in contemplation. "Something else I wonder is what the hell happened to Wind River Dan. Cherokee said his cousin Dan wanted to be a part of this soon as he heard about it."

"Knowing Wind River Dan," said Prew, "anything could have happened."

"Yeah, I suppose so," said Loden, still studying the high empty trail after the two riders had passed out of sight.

"He might show up yet," said Prew, unhitching his horse and signaling for the others to mount up. "We'll be back inside a week. This is just a dry run, but you and your men

119

be ready in case anybody's following us." As he spoke, Prew backed his horse and turned it to the street. "I don't want any surprises. If all goes well, we're going to hit the big munitions train as soon as we get word from our inside man."

"Don't worry. We've got you covered here," Loden called out. He watched the men gather on horseback in the street and form into a loose column behind Prew. In a moment they had ridden out of sight in a rise of dust on the lower trail leading toward the border.

On the high trail Sabio and Caridad pushed on throughout the day until by midafternoon they reached the old Spanish ruins. "I do not know how much longer we can use this place," Sabio said, riding into the ruins cautiously. "Too many people have found their way here. It is no longer safe." His eyes searched for anything out of the ordinary that might tell him someone was waiting in hiding for them.

Once satisfied that the old mission was safe, he and Caridad stepped down from their horses, and Caridad led the tired animals away to be fed and watered. But no sooner had she walked the animals to a lean-to and dropped the saddles from their backs, than Robert Koch stood up from behind a pile of hay with his Colt pointed at her.

"Well, well," he said, "look here. The little chickie has finally come home to roost."

Caridad gasped and looked around quickly for Sabio. But thirty yards away in the open courtyard, Sabio had trouble of his own. "Your old *brujo* boyfriend can't help you this time, chickie." Koch grinned menacingly, stepping around toward her. "You're all mine, anytime I want to reach out and grab you."

Where Sabio stood, Caridad saw the rifle lying on the ground at his feet. Sonny Nix had slipped out from behind a large flowering bush alongside a crumbling adobe wall. He stood with his gun cocked beneath Sabio's chin.

"Do not hurt her, please," Sabio begged. "She is not the

kind of woman you men want."

"I hope you don't think I come all this way just to get a sniff of your little darling, old man," said Sonny. To Koch he called out, "Bring her on over here, Robert. Let's find out about the kid."

"The kid?" Sabio asked.

"Yeah, the kid you've been hiding out up here," said Sonny. "The one with the bullet hole in him."

"Him? Oh, my," said Sabio. "You have come all this way just to find *him?*"

"That's right," said Sonny, "so don't waste time lying to me. It'll just get you both killed."

"I am afraid whatever I do or say, nothing will keep you from killing us both," Sabio said.

Sonny chuckled. "You're pretty smart, old man. But sometimes it's how you die that's the most important thing. It can take you all day to die if I want to drag it out."

Sabio shrugged. "I can tell you nothing about William Jefferies, except that I treated his gunshot wound and he left the next morning."

"After losing as much blood as I heard he left on the cantina floor, I don't think so," said Sonny.

"It is true," said Sabio. "I had the power to stop the bleeding."

"Oh yeah?" Sonny gave him a searching gaze. "Speaking of power, what did you have to do with that forest running us in circles during that storm? Was that some more witchery?"

"The forest ran you in circles?" Sabio almost smiled in spite of the circumstances. His power was still with him, wasn't it then?

"Forget I said that," Sonny growled, realizing how foolish it had sounded—*the forest running them in circles.* "Tell me about the kid."

"I healed him and he left here with the lawman from your country—the ranger," Sabio said. He wanted to hear more about what had happened in the forest during the storm, but he was afraid to ask.

"Which way did they head?" Sonny asked as Koch and Caridad arrived. Koch pushed Caridad over beside Sabio. The old monk took her in his arms to protect her as he answered.

"The ranger said he was taking an outlaw's body back across the border. I do not know where Jefferies went after they left here." He turned his face away from Sonny and looked down at Caridad, brushing her hair from her eyes.

"Hey, look at me, old man!" Sonny shouted. "I've still got questions for you."

Behind them atop his horse inside the arched entranceway, Cherokee Jake sat with his Colt cocked and pointed at Sonny's back. "But you're not asking the right question," Cherokee said.

Startled, Sonny and Koch turned toward the sound of his voice. "Damn, Cherokee! Why are you here?" Sonny saw the Colt pointed at him. His own Colt was in his hand, but he did not want a shoot-out with this ruthless gunman.

Ignoring Sonny's question, Cherokee stepped his horse inside, leading the deceased Wind River Dan's silver-gray and the supply horse he'd found tied in a thicket of cedar where Sonny and Koch had left them.

"You should have asked what the hell my cousin's horse is doing standing hidden out front."

"That's Wind River Dan's horse?" Sonny asked, appearing surprised. "You're kidding."

"Does this look like my *kidding* face to you?" Cherokee asked with a cold flat stare.

Seeing the killing intent in Cherokee's dark eyes, Sonny cautioned, "Easy, pard. Let's talk this thing out before we go cutting loads on one another."

With no change in his expression, Cherokee demanded quietly, "Who are these people? Where is the kid? And where the hell is my cousin?"

CHAPTER 13

The ranger and Jefferies stopped three miles outside of Esperanza and took cover until night fell like a dark blanket over the land. "I checked the town out as well as I could without looking suspicious," Jefferies said, bending down onto his knees. "Let me show you the layout in case something goes wrong and I don't make it all the way to my supply bag." A long bowie-style knife appeared in his hand as if from out of nowhere.

"Go ahead," Sam replied, calmly stooping down in front of him. He eyed the blade, realizing the young man would have had more than one opportunity to make a play for it if he wasn't what he'd claimed to be.

Jefferies gave a trace of a smile, letting Sam know that he understood what had just crossed his lawman's mind. With the knife's blade he cut a line in the hard dirt. "Here's the main street in Esperanza." He cut a crude square and said, "Here's the cantina."

Sam nodded.

Cutting a few inches farther down the street line, Jefferies said, "Here's an abandoned old French Trade building—look for a faded sign above the door." He gave Sam a glance to make sure he understood.

"Got it," Sam said, nodding again.

Jefferies continued. "Inside there's a desk in a corner covered with some old record journals and a pile of dried pigeon droppings." Sam raised his eyes from the diagram, having committed it to memory. Jeffer-ies scraped the big blade back and forth on the hard earth and destroyed the markings. "Pull the desk out of the way and you'll find my supply bag."

"If things go bad and you don't make it, what's my best way out of there?" Sam asked.

"Beside the building is a high wall. It looks impossible to climb. But I looked close and found that somebody had chiseled out some toeholds between the stones in the left corner. If you have to go that way, you can get over it."

"But let's keep a good thought," Sam replied, watching Jefferies' eyes closely for any sign of deception. "Nothing's going to happen to either one of us."

"That's my feeling too," said Jefferies, "but it never hurts to look at all the possibilities."

"Right," said Sam. Standing, he slipped his Colt from his holster, checked it and slipped it back in. He took his rifle from the saddle boot and did the same.

"Prew likes to run his gang like they're a military regiment," said Jefferies. "He keeps a guard posted in the old church bell tower. At first light they change guards." He grinned. "But unlike the real army, the guard always comes down and awakens his replacement."

"You observed things pretty good while you were there, Jefferies," said the ranger. "What does that give us, a couple of minutes to slip out of town?"

"Two minutes at the most," said Jefferies, "but that's all we need."

"In at dark and out at first light," said Sam. it made sense to him. They needed the cover of darkness to carry out their plan, but it would be good to have first light for them and their horses to see by if something went wrong.

"Does this all sound good to you, Ranger?" Jefferies asked, knowing that no one who understood this kind of work would argue with his logic.

The ranger only nodded. "We'd best attend to our horses and get them rested up. This could turn into a long night."

Each of them took care of his own mount, and when they'd finished, they ate a thin supper of jerky and tepid water from their canteens. The ranger did not sleep soundly, but he did lower the brim of his sombrero over his eyes and lean back against his saddle on the ground.

He dozed off and on until the moon stood high and the land lay cloaked in a shadowy purple darkness. Then the two arose and saddled their horses quietly. In moments they had left the small clearing and headed for Esperanza, like two wolves set out to prowl the night.

In the bell tower of the church in Esperanza, a powerfully built young Russian gunman named Klevo Kerchkow had spent much of his watch nodding over the rifle he cradled in his large muscular arms. When Sway Loden climbed the ladder to relieve him, Klevo jerked his head up in time to keep from being caught sleeping on guard. But even in the purple moonlight, Loden saw the bleary-eyed look Klevo gave him and said, "You better never let Desmond Prew catch you doing that."

"Doing vat?" Klevo growled menacingly in his thick accent. "Vat does you accusing me ov?" He took a bold step toward Loden, lowering his rifle in his right hand. He looked fully capable of swinging it like a club.

Loden didn't want to push the matter, knowing the young Russian came to the band of mercenaries with a reputation of brutality and hired killings that stretched all the way from Moscow to the streets and alleys of San Francisco.

Taking a quick glance behind him at the long drop from the bell tower to the stone floor fifty feet below, Loden raised a hand and said, "Whoa, I'm not accusing you of nothing, my friend. I just hate to see a fellow get off on the wrong foot with Prew is all." He offered the Russian a thin nervous smile. "I'd hope you'd do the same for me if it was the other way around."

But Klevo only looked down at his broad feet and asked in the same gruff tone, "Wrong foot? Vat is wrong wit my foot?"

"Nothing!" Loden's hand managed to slip around the butt of his holstered Colt as the Russian stared down, puzzled. Laying his thumb over the Colt's hammer, he said with more confidence, "I'm relieving you. Why don't you go on down and get yourself some sleep, or a drink, or a whore or whatever."

"A whore, maybe, I think," said Klevo, giving Loden a dark stare even as he stepped around him to the ladder and started down.

"Yeah, a whore. That's good," said Loden, looking down at the top of the Russian's battered black bowler hat as he climbed down the ladder. He half raised the Colt, just thinking how easy it would be and how good it would feel to put a bullet into the top of the bowler hat and see it explode out of the Russian's belly. "Get one for me while you're at it," he called down, letting his hand ease off his gun butt.

Klevo looked up from the bottom rung and said stoically, "How can I do that, you fool?"

"Forget it," said Loden, waving the Russian away. "Go bite the head off of a rat, for all I care," he grumbled under his breath.

On the ground, having heard the voices speaking back and forth from the bell tower, Sam and Jefferies slipped quickly and silently along from cover to cover across the street from the old stone and adobe church. At the edge of a porch out front of a supply store they froze when a small white dog came trotting up to them. Even though the dog wagged its tail vigorously, it looked as if it would start barking at any second.

"Easy, fellow," Sam purred in the softest tone of voice. He put the back of his gloved hand out toward the playful dog and hoped it would come forward quietly.

Jefferies whispered only a fraction of an inch from the

ranger's ear, "Choke it if you have to."

But Sam ignored his request. When the dog did ease forward and sniff his hand, Sam managed to scratch its bony head and rub his hand along its back, settling the animal. Beside Sam, Jefferies breathed easier, his Colt hanging loosely in his hand. He had just started to motion Sam forward toward the cantina and the abandoned French Trade building when the Russian stepped out of the church into the moonlit street.

The two froze again, hearing the Russian call out toward them, "Hey, vat have we here?"

Sam turned the dog and gave it a boost toward the Russian. Following his command the dog looped playfully across the street and circled at the Russian's feet. But Klevo would not be diverted. "Get away vrom me, mangy *cooaka!* You are lucky I am not hungry. I would eat you with gravy made from your brains." As he spoke to the dog, he walked toward the spot where Sam and Jefferies had hunkered down behind a stack of feed sacks filled with corn. "Who is there?" he called.

Sam and Jefferies remained quiet. Jefferies tapped Sam on the shoulder and moved around behind him to a thick post supporting an overhang at the end of the grain sacks. Sam got his silent message and waited until he saw that Jefferies was ready to make his move on the Russian. Then he pressed his boot heel firmly onto the wooden plank porch and scraped it back and forth.

"Ah! I heard you!" said the Russian, crouching, hurrying toward the sound. As he focused his attention toward the spot where Sam hunkered behind the grain sacks, Jefferies sprang from the other end of the sacks and cracked him a hard blow across his forehead. The big Russian staggered in place. The two lawmen hurriedly grabbed him by either arm, swung him back and launched him headfirst into the thick post.

The porch and the ground shuddered as the man fell backward, his large arms outstretched, and landed flat on his back in the street. The playful dog bounded back and forth at the man's head as Sam and Jefferies hurried on toward the French Trade building. Atop the bell tower, Sway Loden heard only the slightest commotion. When he looked down into the moonlit street, he saw only the pale image of the white dog running in half circles.

"Stupid damn mutt," he grumbled. "Do your cat chasing in the daylight."

At the abandoned building, Sam turned inside the door and checked to make sure all was peaceful behind them. When he then joined Jefferies at the edge of the old desk, the two soundlessly lifted the desk with its debris atop it and scooted it to one side. In the moonlight, Jefferies gave him a grin. Sam nodded in reply as they bent down over the large leather supply bag lying in a shallow hole that Jefferies had hurriedly scraped out when he'd hidden it there.

Jefferies whispered, "You're going to like this, Ranger." Opening the straps on the leather bag, he held it open and slanted toward the pale moonlight.

Sam blinked. In the bag he saw three bundles of dynamite and a coil of fuse. "I needed to store it in a cool dry place for the time being," Jefferies whispered. "Surprised, huh?"

"Yes," Sam replied. But what surprised him even more than the dynamite was seeing what he estimated to be at least a dozen round metal hand grenades piled in the bottom of the bag.

"If these are what I think they are," he whispered, "I'm glad I didn't show up here alone. I'm not familiar with this kind of ordnance." Nestled down in the explosives he saw a bundle of cigars with a string tied around them.

"They are what you think they are," said Jefferies. Reaching into a pocket inside the bag, he pulled out a double spool of telegraph wire with brass connectors on either end. "Do you know code, Ranger?"

"Enough to get by," said Sam. He looked closely at the cut-in connectors and asked, "What are those for?"

"With these I can cut in at any point along the telegraph wires and get word to the army border encampment when Prew is about to hit the train." He shoved the wire spools back inside the bag. "The problem is there's no lines along this side of the border for me to cut in. By the time I get word to the army, Prew's men will have already made their hit and be gone."

"There's too much land for the army to cover," Sam said, speaking from experience.

"You're right," said Jefferies. "We'll be on our own stopping them." He saw Sam looking in the bag at the dynamite and said, "Don't worry. I'm going to show you how to handle this stuff." Closing the bag and strapping it shut, he hefted it up over his shoulder. "Now do you believe I am with the U.S. Secret Service?"

"I believe you've got some powerful explosives and some telegraph connections," Sam replied, eyeing him closely in the darkness. "But I don't know where you got them—or how."

"All right, Ranger. You're still suspicious," Jefferies whispered, easing toward the open doorway. "I suppose I would be, too, if it was the other way around." They both stopped and huddled at the door.

"It's already starting to lighten up out there," Sam said, nodding toward the eastern horizon. "By the time we get out of here and back to the horses it'll be light enough to see along the trail."

Jefferies nodded in agreement. "Let's go," he said. He started to slip forward along the front of the building, but he stopped cold at the sight of five riders entering the town from the far end through a silver-purple haze. "Oh no!" he said almost in a gasp, ducking back inside the open doorway.

"What is it?" Sam asked, creeping far enough forward for a look. He saw the five horses walk single file into sight.

"It's Caridad and Sabio!" said Jefferies. "Prew's men must've caught up to them."

"That means they must still be searching for you," Sam said.

"I can't let anything happen to them just because they helped me," said Jefferies. "Once Prew's men get a good look at Caridad, they'll never leave her alone."

"I'm surprised they haven't bothered her before," Sam remarked, watching Sabio step down into the street and hurry to help Caridad down from her saddle.

"I don't know," said Jefferies. "Maybe it was like Sabio said—he had her under his protection. The men never noticed her before. She did her cleanup work and kept to herself." He looked at Sam for some sort of agreement. Sam gave him a dubious look but said nothing.

"Whatever the case, they're all noticing her now," he said, seeing three more of Prew's men walk out of the cantina where they'd spent the night. Sway Loden had climbed down from the bell tower and now he came walking toward Sabio and Caridad. Sam offered no solution, but rather waited and watched to see what Jefferies decided. How the young man handled this situation would tell the ranger a lot about him.

"If something happens to her . . ." Jefferies let his words trail off, staring out at Caridad. Sam watched him slip the leather bag of explosives off his shoulder as he spoke.

"We can take these explosives to our horses and come back. We'll slip in and get them," Sam offered, seeing the young man about to do something rash.

"No," said Jefferies. "I'm not leaving her alone here for a minute. This trouble has all been about me. If I'm here, the trouble stops."

Sam saw what he was about to do and said, "What about the munitions train?"

"Take the explosives and be ready to follow Prew to the border, Ranger," Jefferies said over his shoulder as he took a step out through the open doorway. "Leave my horse waiting for me."

"Wait a minute, Jefferies!" Sam whispered harshly, seeing him walk without hesitation to the middle of the street. But it was too late. Thirty yards away, eyes had already turned toward him. Sam could only shake his head and watch as he hefted the leather bag up onto his shoulder.

In the street, Loden called out to the lone figure walking toward the men gathered together. "Who goes there?"

"It's me, Jefferies—the Kid. Remember?" Jefferies called out in reply. "Where is everybody?"

The ranger noted that both Jefferies' voice and his demeanor had changed in front of these gunmen. He sounded younger, less seasoned, less confident. *The Kid,* he'd called himself. *Well, Kid,* Sam said to himself, *I sure hope you know what you're doing.*

CHAPTER 14

The ranger lingered inside the abandoned building long enough to see how things were going to go for Jefferies before leaving him there to face Prew's men alone. But upon hearing Jefferies and Sway Loden talk back and forth, he realized that this young army captain knew how to handle himself. While the men's attention centered on Jefferies and Loden, Sam slipped out in a crouch and moved along the shadowed building, the bag of explosives on his shoulder.

In moments he walked along the path Jefferies had told him about. Using the toeholds on the seemingly impossible-to-climb stone wall, he got to the top, then dropped to the ground on the other side and headed out silently to the horses.

On the street, Loden said to Jefferies as the men drew closer around them, "You've got some serious explaining to do, Kid." He stared coldly into Jefferies' eyes.

Without coming back too strong, Jefferies returned the stare and replied with a shrug, "What is there to explain? I got shot. These people took me in and treated me."

"What about us?" Hubbard White cut in, stepping forward, his hand resting on his gun butt. "Tell him what happened to me and Riley here."

Jefferies gave White and Hallit a curious look. "I don't know what you're talking about," he said. Then he said to Loden, "I don't know what these two have told you. But the fact is they came up to the old mission to finish me off. A lawman showed up and ran them away. As you can see, I'm all right now." As he talked he rounded his wounded shoulder as if to prove its fitness. He nodded toward Sabio and Caridad. "I have them to thank for saving my life."

Loden had listened, looking Jefferies up and down, finding no fault with his story. "Nothing against you, Kid, but they were sent to make sure you didn't get left behind *alive*."

"I understand that," said Jefferies, making sure everybody there heard him. "I'm sort of new here, but I know how this life works. I learned a few things from my uncle." He gestured toward the body still hanging up high in the tree. "I knew when that bullet hit me that I was in trouble if I couldn't ride. That's why I did my best to get out of sight and lay low. I wanted to stay alive." He looked all around and added, "Does anybody fault me for that?"

The men murmured in agreement with him. "I might have done the same," said a voice.

"Me too," said another.

"I expect any of us would," Loden agreed. He looked at Cherokee Jake, sitting atop his horse.

"Keep him here. We'll let Prew decide," said Cherokee. He turned a suspicious stare from Jefferies to Sonny and Koch. "I'm going to catch up with Prew and the others. We're going to have a serious talk about you two having my cousin's horse as soon as I get back." He stepped his horse over and gathered the reins to the two animals Sabio and Caridad had been riding.

Sonny and Koch only returned Cherokee's stare as he backed his horse a step, turned it in the street and rode away, leading the two spare mounts behind him.

"The hell was he talking about?" Loden asked Sonny and Koch.

The two shrugged. Sonny said, "We found Wind River Dan's horse out there is all. Cherokee's wanting to make a big deal of it."

"Oh . . ." Loden gave them a speculative look.

"You heard Cherokee," Jefferies cut in. "Now that I'm

all mended, fit to ride, shoot, do anything it takes to earn my share"—he gazed coolly at Sway Loden—"when do I go to work?"

Loden scratched his jaw, liking the way the kid had managed to look out for himself long enough to heal up and walk back bold as brass—*When do I go to work?*

"You've got grit in your belly, Kid," Loden said with a trace of a chuckle. He looked at the gun on Jefferies' hip. "Where's your horse, Kid?" he asked.

"Just outside of town," said Jefferies. "I'll go get it after a while. I wasn't about to ride in here unannounced, especially not with you in that bell tower. I've seen how good you are with a rifle."

Loden grinned, clearly liking the comment. "That was wise thinking," he said. Glancing around at the men, he added jokingly, "Hell, I might have shot you thinking I'd just seen a ghost."

The men chuckled; so did Jefferies, realizing he was back in with them for now. He still had to get things smoothed out with Prew, but it shouldn't be a problem, he told himself.

As he'd spoken to the men, he'd noted the looks on Caridad's and Sabio's faces. He knew that neither of them liked seeing him back here or hearing him talk this way. Yet he was doing it for them, he reminded himself. Soon they would understand.

"Kid, if you like whiskey for breakfast, I want to buy you a drink!" said Riley Hallit, laughing at his own humor. He stepped close enough for Jefferies to smell the alcohol already on his breath.

"Sounds good to me," said Jefferies. Hallit threw an arm around his shoulder and directed him toward the cantina.

"One thing," said Jefferies, stopping and turning toward Sabio and Caridad. "I want everybody to hear me plainly. You've all got the whores *el capitán* sent here." He gestured a hand toward Caridad. "I have taken quite a shine to this woman all the while she was taking care of me. I'm letting everybody know, she's *mine*." He looked all around. "And as long as she's with me, I'm not sharing her. Does that set well with everybody?" He glared at the men with a half-menacing look in his eyes.

"Aw hell, Kid," said Hallit, "that's just the little cleaning gal who swamps the cantina. You can have her. Right, men?"

A couple of faces looked disappointed. "He said, *'Right, men?'*" Loden called out in a louder tone, giving them a stern look.

The men grumbled but nodded in agreement.

"There you have it," said Loden. "Unless Prew says otherwise when he gets back, she's all yours, Kid."

Jefferies nodded gratefully. "All right, then, now that I have a woman of my own anytime I want her, let's go get that drink." He had pulled it off, he told himself. He'd made his move in time to keep these men away from Caridad. Things were going good. But as he turned away and headed for the cantina, he saw the smoldering anger in Sabio's fiery eyes, and the look of hurt and disappointment in Caridad's.

Farther up the street, in the gray morning light, Klevo Kerchkow had dragged himself to his feet and now came staggering forward, bareheaded, a Colt dangling in his broad hand. Jefferies froze at the sight of him and did some quick thinking.

"Everybody hold it right where you are!" the Russian called out in a thick and pained-sounding voice. "I want the man who did this to me!"

Loden gave him a curious look. "Did what to you, Klevo?"

"Look at my head!" The Russian, bowed his head, showing a large welt with a bloody split down its middle. "Whoever did this is going to pay with his life!" he shouted.

"Damn, what a lick," Loden said, stifling a chuckle under his breath. "But if you don't know who did it, how's he going to pay with his life?" Loden looked at the others for support.

"It looks to me like you got sleepy again and walked smack into a post somewhere."

"You want to make a joke? I'll show you a joke!" the Russian fumed, gripping his gun handle tightly.

"Easy, Klevo," White cautioned. "Around here we don't blame folks unless we've got some proof. Like Loden said, it looks like you walked into a post and drew yourself a goose egg."

"I did not walk into a post. I was grabbed and thrown into it!" the Russian insisted, eyeing each of the men in turn.

"Oh, I see," said Loden. "So you admit there was a post involved?" He grinned, hearing the rest of the men make little effort to stifle their laughter.

Jefferies relaxed and let the men have their fun at the Russian's expense. *So far so good*, he told himself.

After he'd finished a couple of shots of whiskey with the rest of the men, Jefferies left the cantina and walked out of town along a footpath to where his big paint horse stood alone, still hitched in the same spot where he and the ranger had left their animals earlier. He looked all around, unhitched the horse and started to step up into the saddle. But the sound of Sam's voice stopped him.

"I wish you wouldn't pop up unexpected like that, Ranger," he said, watching Sam step forward from the brush, leading his Appaloosa behind him. His Colt was in his hand.

"And I wish you'd let a person know when you decide to change a plan the way you did back there," Sam said, nodding toward Esperanza. "You might have gotten us both killed." As he spoke he lowered his Colt into his holster.

"Sorry, Ranger," said Jefferies, "but what else could I do under these circumstances? I wasn't about to leave her to that bunch of wolves."

"Strange, how they never bothered her before," Sam said, curious. "I believe that ole holy man has some sort of power.

It always protected her before. He wouldn't have let anything happen to her. I don't know how, but I believe it."

"I couldn't risk it. Could you?" Jefferies said bluntly, staring questioningly at Sam.

Sam paused, then said, relenting, "No, I suppose I couldn't. If you hadn't done something, I likely would have. As long as you were still missing, they might have killed Sabio. You showing up made everything all right again."

"Then you're not as angry over it as you look?" Jefferies asked.

The ranger offered a thin smile. "I'm never as angry as I look most times," he said. "You made a good move, as it turned out. I was thrown off at first, not knowing how to set up those explosives. That's one reason I stayed around here, hoping you'd come back alone for your horse."

"Don't worry. You'll do just fine, Ranger," said Jefferies. "Cut as much fuse line as you think you need for the grenades, shove one end down into it, light it with your cigar and throw it where you want it." He grinned. "Easy enough?"

"That's not what I mean," Sam said. "I can figure out how to light a grenade and throw it. I meant what is it you had in mind? You've got enough dynamite to make some big changes in the countryside. You must've had something in mind."

"You're right. I do have a target in mind," said Jefferies. "I'm here to do two things. It's important to bust up Prew and his men, kill them if I can. My other objective is to keep any more military ordnance out of *Capitán* Luis Murella's possession."

"By blowing it up," Sam said flatly.

"Yes, by blowing it up," Jefferies replied. "A raid this size, Prew is going to need wagons to haul away his plunder. Once I knew when he was going to make the raid on the army train, my plan was to get to his wagons along the high trail and blow them up, his men along with them if I could."

"There's no need to change your plan now, is there?" Sam asked.

"No," said Jefferies, "the plan is still the same. Only now I've got to get Caridad and Sabio away from Prew and his men before I carry it out."

Sam studied the concerned look on Jefferies' face. "You really do care for that young woman, don't you?"

"I told you I do," said Jefferies. "I have since I first laid eyes on her." He looked a little embarrassed. "I didn't mean for something like this to happen. But it has. When I leave here, she's going with me."

"And Sabio?" Sam asked. "He doesn't appear to be real fond of you."

"I know he's like family to her," said Jefferies. "He can go with us or stay behind, as far as I'm concerned." He paused, then said, "I hope she's not going to hate me for acting the way I was a while ago. I've got some tough explaining to do once I find a chance to get her alone."

"Sabio already knows why you were acting that way," said Sam.

"That's what I figured. But I doubt if he'll be putting in a good word for me," Jefferies said.

"That's your personal matter," Sam said with a trace of a wry grin. He paused for a moment in contemplation, then said, "Maybe it's for the best, you being back in with the gang for a while. You can get more information inside there than out here."

"That's what I think too," said Jefferies, "now that the cards have fallen this way. I've already heard that Prew and most of the men are out on a dry run right now, checking out the train along the border. As soon as they get back, they'll all be ready to go do the real thing."

"A dry run?" said Sam. "That doesn't sound like Desmond Prew to me. What's making him so cautious?"

"I don't know," said Jefferies, "but that's the story I heard from Loden. Cherokee Jake rode out to catch up to him."

"Maybe I better get on his trail, see what he's up to," said

Sam. "He's known to turn as tricky as a fox when it suits him."

"He's got over a full day's head start on you," Jefferies cautioned. "Cherokee took three spare horses with him. I suppose he'll ride them all three into the ground getting there."

"Riding horses into the ground isn't my style," said Sam. "I know a few trails over these hills." He eyed the paint horse. "Having two horses would help, though. Didn't your dear departed uncle leave you his horse, in Esperanza?"

"Yes, he did," said Jefferies. Without another word on the matter, he handed Sam the paint horse's reins.

"Obliged," Sam said, looking the horse up and down.

"Before you leave, store the dynamite in a cool dry place," Jefferies said. "When Prew gets back then I'll know you're back too. If you need to find me, there's a widow who lives in the third adobe on the right when you leave the rear of the cantina."

"I'll stay out of sight, and keep the dynamite cool and stable," said Sam. "As soon as you know the raid is ready to take place, manage to be in the bell tower the night before. At midnight, use two matches to light a cigar. I see the two lights flash at midnight, I'll get the explosives and be ready to go the next morning."

"All right, then," said Jefferies. "We're back in business. I just need to straighten things out between me and Caridad."

"Good luck with that," said Sam. He nodded toward Esperanza. "You better get back there before Prew's men start getting suspicious." He turned with the paint horse's reins in hand, but before he walked back into the cover of the brush where his stallion stood waiting he said, "Be careful, Jefferies."

"Yeah, you too, Ranger," Jefferies replied. "Don't let Cherokee and Prew catch you trailing them."

"I don't plan to," Sam said over his shoulder.

CHAPTER 15

The next morning, as Prew and his dozen handpicked riders were about to break camp and mount up, they turned toward the lone figure riding in from the north. Prew stood waiting expectantly until Cherokee Jake sidled his tired horse up close and stepped down from his saddle. "Tell me something good," said Prew as Cherokee stood stretching his back after the long ride.

"I brought Sonny and Koch back," he said. "I also brought in the old monk and the girl who cleans the cantina."

"What about the kid?" asked Prew. "Is he dead?"

"No," said Cherokee. "He showed up on his own. Claims he's fit and ready to ride. I told Loden you'd deal with him when we get back."

"Well, hell," said Prew, "if he's back in the saddle, I expect the rest doesn't matter."

"Sonny and Koch had my cousin's horse when I caught up to them," said Cherokee, giving him a look. "I expect to get to the bottom of it when we get back to Esperanza."

"Yeah," said Prew, "you bet we will." He nodded toward the coffeepot still sitting beside the campfire. "Pour yourself a cup and carry it with you. We're moving out."

"Moving out?" Cherokee gave him a look. "I just killed two horses and been stuck in the saddle nearly twenty hours getting here."

"Then pour yourself two cups and carry them along," said Prew with no sympathy. "We're still moving out."

A moment later, with a steaming cup of coffee in his

gloved hand, Cherokee rode alongside Prew at the head of the column of riders. They rode until noon, still following the same trail they'd taken outside of Esperanza. The trail led east, in the direction of the American border. But upon reaching a fork in the trail, Prew turned his horse southwest and rode on. Beside him Cherokee said with a puzzled expression, "Hold on, boss! We're going the wrong way."

Prew gave him a smug grin. "Maybe you are, Cherokee, but I know exactly where I'm going."

Cherokee looked back, seeing the confused expressions on the faces of the men behind them. Turning back to Prew he said, "Want to let me in on what you're up to? Or is this a secret?"

"Not a secret now." Prew gazed straight ahead as he spoke. "We're not going on any dry run across the border, Cherokee."

"Oh? Then where are we going?" Cherokee had to work at keeping his voice from sounding a little sharp and testy. He didn't like having to squeeze information out of Prew this way.

Prew's smug grin widened. Without looking around at Cherokee, he said in a flat tone, "We're headed for Plaza Fuerte."

"Plaza Fuerte? It's a two-day ride out of our way if we're going to make a dry run across the border," said Cherokee.

"Forget the dry run," said Prew. "We never was going to do that. We've always been headed for Plaza Fuerte."

"But there's nothing for us there but *federales*. It's their main encampment west of Mexico City! It has been for the past year or two." Cherokee looked stunned. He almost stopped his horse. But thinking better of it he nudged the animal forward and asked, "What the hell are we going there for?"

"How does gold sound to you?" Prew asked in a calm quiet voice.

"Gold, you say?" Cherokee's eyes lit up. Looking back,

he saw a couple of the men start to ride forward to find out what was going on. But he waved them back into ranks with a gloved hand, then said to Prew, "Gold has always held a warm and special place in my heart." He seemed to consider it, then asked, "I take it you *are* talking about *stealing* gold? Not digging it up out of the ground or anything as foolish as that?"

"Please," Prew said with a disdainful sidelong glance. "Do you see picks or shovels in my gear?"

Cherokee looked closer at Prew as if to see if he was serious. "But Plaza Fuerte is always crawling with soldiers. We'll have the fight of our lives. How is *el capitán* going to feel about us doing this?"

"I've got a hunch the soldiers won't be there when we arrive," said Prew. "As far as Captain Murella . . ." He shrugged, unconcerned, and let his words trail off. He gazed ahead as if he had nothing more to say on the matter.

After a moment of studying Prew's profile, a knowing look came to Cherokee's face, followed by a sly grin. "Ah, I get it. This is all something you and *el capitán* cooked up between yas."

"We decided why keep robbing army trains, having to lug all those heavy crates around," Prew said. "What we all need is a good strong dose of Mexican gold in our saddlebags."

"Yeah, I always found that it makes a horse run straighter," said Cherokee, suddenly jubilant. He added in a tone filled with awe, "The Federal Bank and Gold Exchange of Mexico."

"Yep, *El Federal Bank y el Intercambio de Oro de México*," Prew replied. "It is a big one."

"Big?" said Cherokee. "It's bigger than any job I ever dreamed of in my life."

"*El capitán* said the government moved the bulk of their gold from Mexico City to Plaza Fuerte last year. Said they thought it would be safer with so many troops always there."

"Well, I for one applaud their decision," Cherokee said

in a mocking tone. "Man! You and *el capitán* have come up with a good one." He shook his head at the idea of running his fingers through ringing gold coins. "He gets the troops out of town, we clean out that big ole bank, and split it up with Murella when he comes to hunt down the thieves who did it!"

"Something like that," said Prew. "I figured you'd be interested." He pointed at a clearing along the trail ahead. "As soon as we get up there, we'll stop and let everybody else in on it."

Cherokee looked back at the others. "Why so many of us? This being a setup, we could have done it with half this many."

"But then it might begin to look like a setup." Prew gave Cherokee a close look and said, "Don't start getting greedy on me, Jake. I need you to be my right-hand man, now that White has let me down. Are you up to it?"

"Hell, you know I'm up to it, boss," said Cherokee. "I was just thinking out loud is all." Considering what Prew had said, he added, "You're right. Too few men would make it look like a setup."

"Leave it all up to me and *el capitán*," said Prew. "Believe me, we've thought of everything."

"I'm with you all the way, boss," said Cherokee. "You do the pointing, I'll do the shooting."

"That's the kind of talk I like to hear," Prew said, turning to face the trail ahead.

When they reached the clearing along the trail, Cherokee motioned for everyone to gather up beneath the overhanging branches of a tall white oak tree. As they settled, Prew looked from face to face, silently saying their names to himself. Sitting closest to him were four gunmen from Texas, Clifford Elvey, Ethan Crenshaw, Bud Stakes and Bud's half brother, Dan Farr.

Cherokee Jake called out, "All right, everybody listen up. We've made a change in plans. But it's one I think you're all going to like."

As Cherokee spoke, Prew continued looking from man to man. Off to the right sat Hemp Knot Russell, Cur Dog Kerr, Matt Harkens and Stu Wakeland. To the left sat Indian Frank Becker and Niger Elmsly, an English outlaw who'd fled the London countryside ahead of the law.

"Men," Prew called out, "Cherokee is talking about a job that Captain Murella and I came up with that is going to make all of us rich."

Cherokee sat back comfortably in his saddle and listened to Prew explain to the men what he himself had heard only moments ago. Yet he took on a wise and confident look, one that purported to say to the men that he'd known about the big bank job all along.

The ranger hid the bag of explosives inside a shaded stand of piñon beneath a low rocky overhang. Looking around closely to make sure no eyes had been on him, he walked back to the horses and stepped up into his saddle. *Now to make some time*, he told himself. He knew the backcountry from the many times he'd tracked men in this area. A day and a half head start didn't discourage him. He'd trailed desperate outlaws who'd known he was coming for them. Prew and his men wouldn't be in that kind of hurry. *If Cherokee Jake can catch up to the gang, so can I,* Sam told himself.

With one of the horses always at rest on a lead rope behind him, the ranger rode diagonally over the hill country, nonstop. He took trails that had been abandoned so long they'd become little more than deer and elk paths. At night when it grew dark and dangerous on the high trails, he did not stop. He only slowed the animals' pace, and rode on.

The next morning, with the sun already making its ascent, he found the day-old hoofprints of several riders. Curious, he stopped the big Appaloosa at the fork in the main trail and watched the prints veer off to the right. Following the tracks led him to the same tree where Prew and his men had gathered up before heading to Plaza Fuerte.

"So, you're not even headed for the border, are you, Desmond Prew?" he murmured. "I knew a dry run didn't sound like your style."

He sat silently for a moment, gazing out along the trail Prew and his men had taken, in his mind drawing images of what towns he knew lay in that direction. "Nothing that way but more *federales*," he said as if discussing it with Prew. "But then, lately, some of your best friends are *federales*, aren't they?"

He nudged the Appaloosa away from the tree. Instead of turning back to the main trail, he took a thin path into the woods and followed it for over an hour until he reached a point where a wide swift running body of water lay stretched before him. "Rio Perdido," he whispered to himself.

Here was where he would gain ground on the mercenaries. Stepping down from the saddle, he prepared the horses, his weapons and his meager supplies for the trip across. He was certain that Prew and his men weren't about to swim Lost River. *Not unless they're running and desperate*, he reminded himself.

When he'd finished with the animals and his guns, he took off most of his clothes and rolled his boots up in his trousers. He put the trousers and boots inside his shirt, buttoned it and tied the sleeves around it. Along with his guns he put the bundle inside his canvas duster, wrapped it and tied it with the rope he carried hanging from his saddle horn. He hefted the bundle up onto his shoulder.

Wearing only his summer johns, he climbed back into the saddle, lead rope in hand, and said to the Appaloosa, "I know you don't like swimming any more than I do, Black Pot. But here goes."

He nudged the Appaloosa down the short cutbank into the water. He did not tie the lead rope around his saddle horn and take a chance on losing both horses if something went wrong.

Instead he wrapped the lead rope one turn around his hand, so he could let go if he had to. He led the spare horse behind him, feeling it resist only slightly before stepping forward into the rushing river.

Letting the Appaloosa have its way, he turned sidelong on the saddle and kept his canvas bundle high and dry. When he'd gotten far enough out into the water to know the paint horse would not turn back, he let the lead rope slip from his hand. The animal drifted apart from the Appaloosa but still swam in the same direction.

The two animals floated and bobbed and swam forward even as the current swept them along sideways. The ranger let himself slip back from the saddle to give the Appaloosa less weight on the center of its back. Keeping his clothes and guns raised high in his right hand, he hooked his left hand into the strap of his saddlebags and let himself bob along, most of his weight off of the stallion's rump.

When he felt the stallion's hooves find the first purchase on the solid bottom, he pulled himself into the saddle and lowered his dry bundle onto his lap as the animal rose higher out of the water with each step.

"Good work, Black Pot," he said, patting the stallion's wet neck as it plodded up onto rocky dry land. Looking downstream he saw the paint horse step out of the water, shaking itself off. Turning the stallion, he rode down to where the paint had already found itself a clump of wild grass and begun nipping at it. Reaching down and taking the wet lead rope, he led the horse out of the sun to a place where he stepped down and sorted out his clothes, guns and supplies.

The canvas duster had taken no more water than it would have from a light summer rain shower. Yet he inspected his rifle and Colt before slipping the pistol into his dry holster. The rifle he would leave out and carry in his hand until the sun dried his saddle boot.

He loosened the wet saddle, swung it and the dripping

saddle blanket off the Appaloosa's back and laid them out in the sun to dry. Stripping out of his wet johns, he wrung them between his hands and laid them on top of clumps of tall wild grass next to the saddle.

He stooped down against the rough trunk of a large chokecherry tree and rested both himself and the animals until the saddle blanket and his johns were only damp. Then he gathered the damp saddle and blanket and swapped them over to the paint horse. He pulled on his damp johns and the rest of his clothes, his dry boots, and stepped into the saddle. In moments he was back on the trail.

Stopping only long enough to rest, feed and water the horses and himself, by late evening in the waning light of day he picked up the group of many hoof-prints again on a wide dusty trail. Beneath him the paint, although trail-wary, stepped back and forth restlessly. On the lead rope beside him, Black Pot did the same.

"Easy now," the ranger said, patting the paint's sweaty withers. "You've done good." As he spoke under his breath, Black Pot crowded in close beside him, appearing jealous of the dun. "You've *both* done good," Sam said, patting the Appaloosa's damp muzzle. He corrected himself as if the animals understood his words.

Looking out along the flat meandering trail before him, he saw the large rise of trail dust hanging in the hot evening air. "Well, Desmond Prew, we'll soon be close enough to shake hands." He nudged the paint forward. "But I doubt if we will."

Instead of making a camp for the night, he swigged tepid water from a canteen, poured the rest into his hat and gave each animal a drink. Then he rode on.

Taking advantage of the silvery light of a full moon, he kept an eye on the trail dust until it settled and the glow of a campfire rose up in its place. Keeping the firelight to his left, he traveled steadily throughout the night until by the first glow of dawn the campfire had fallen back over his left shoulder.

"We're ahead of them," he whispered thankfully to the animals. In the near distance he saw the shadowy purple hill line overlooking Plaza Fuerte. "Let's get on up there where we can watch them ride past," he said, stopping and stepping down from his saddle. He quickly reached down, loosened the cinch on the paint's belly, and swung the saddle over onto the Appaloosa. When he'd changed bridles and slipped the lead rope over the paint's sweaty muzzle, he mounted Black Pot and rode on.

Part III

CHAPTER 16

By midmorning, the ranger stood on a cliff overlooking the town of Plaza Fuerte on his right and the long stretch of dusty flatlands off to his left. He'd arrived there and spent the past hour lying on the ground in the shade of overhanging juniper and wild laurel. At a thin trickle of water beneath a rock ledge the horses drank and grazed hungrily on clumps of wild grass.

Rested, Sam pulled his telescope open and raised it to his eye. "Good morning, Mr. Prew," he murmured, centering on Prew and Cherokee Jake Slattery in the lens before taking a good look at the rest of the riders. He watched Prew's lips move in the wavering field lens, then saw the column come to a halt as Cherokee Jake rode back and spoke to the men.

"Time to get ready, fellows," Sam said under his breath, watching most of the men check to make sure they had bandannas hanging around their necks. A few reached into their dusters or saddlebags, pulled out their bandannas and tied them on, leaving them draped down their chests for the time being.

The ranger was about to watch a crime take place, and for the first time in his life, he realized there was nothing he could do to prevent it. He knew he was out of his jurisdiction, but jurisdiction had nothing to do with it. If he'd thought it would help, he would have already ridden into Plaza Fuerte and warned the *federales*. But knowing the relationship between Prew and Captain Luis Murella, he was certain the only thanks he would get would be a bullet in his back as he rode away.

"This one is all yours, Mexico," he said to himself as if

talking to the wide endless land. He scanned the lens over the men until he saw Thomas Russell and Braden Kerr talking to Cherokee Jake. "But Hemp Knot and Cur Dog are *all mine*."

On the flatlands, Prew waited until Cherokee returned to the front of the column. Having heard Cherokee and the two gunmen raise their voices to one another, Prew asked, "What are those two bellyaching about now?"

"Same as always since they heard what the ranger said about giving you your horse and you turning them over to him," said Cherokee. "They're both too spooked to know what they're doing. If you ask me, I'd say give them both the boot before we ride in here and get all that gold. Why share it with a couple of yellow—"

"Shhh. Hush now," Prew said, cutting him off. "I *didn't* ask you." He looked back along the men and saw Russell and Kerr gazing expectantly at him. In a lowered voice, he said, "Even a couple of saddle tramps like Russell and Kerr have some value."

Cherokee smoldered at being hushed like an unruly child. But he held it in check and said, "If there's value there I guess I missed seeing it."

Prew grinned. "That's the difference between being the *segundo*, like you, and being *numero uno*, like me," he said, tapping a thumb on his chest.

Cherokee saw it as Prew flexing his muscle, reminding him that he was only second in charge. All right, Cherokee told himself, he knew his place here. He didn't need reminding.

"I understand, boss," Cherokee said in a stiff but humble tone.

Prew saw he'd struck a sour note with his right-hand man. "Here's the thing you need to know about me, Cherokee," he said, the two nudging their horses on. The men followed in a loose column behind them. "I don't do nothing without a damn good reason." He gave a tight short grin. "If I do something that doesn't make sense right then, pay attention. It'll all make sense later."

"I got you, boss," said Cherokee, wanting to dismiss the subject. "I shouldn't have said anything. If you think those two turds are worth something, I guess I'm not obliged to argue it with you."

"Good," said Prew. "Now just sit tight, be patient, and help me carry all this gold."

"I can do that right enough," said Cherokee. He wondered how quick and easy it might be to set up Prew and gut him the way he had gutted Sibbs.

"That's what I thought." Prew smiled knowingly and gazed ahead toward Plaza Fuerte.

A half hour later, reaching the outskirts of Plaza Fuerte, Prew and the others looked over to their right at the empty army encampment, where row after row of canvas tents billowed gently in the hot wind. Empty corrals stood with their gates swung open. "This is perfect," Prew said with satisfaction.

Off to their right, a group of townsmen had gathered noisily around a makeshift arena constructed of weathered wooden fruit crates, fence rails and baling wire. As Prew led his column of men along the trail past the gathering, they looked at the townsmen and saw two roosters rise up with a flurry of wings, locked in battle.

"Cockfight," Thomas Russell said quietly to Braden Kerr, who rode beside him. "Nothing I enjoy more."

"Yeah, me too ordinarily," Kerr replied almost in a whisper, keeping an eye on Prew at the head of the slow-moving column. "But I keep getting a bad feeling about things. Prew's going to hand us over to that lawdog. I just know it."

"Not if we play it smart," said Russell.

"Play it smart how?" Kerr asked.

"Just watch me and go along with what I do," Russell said, glancing around to make sure no one was listening.

Prew's men had stared at the cockfight for only a moment. Russell and Kerr watched them turn their eyes dutifully forward toward the busy stone street ahead of them. "I'm with you," Kerr said to Russell under his breath.

"Collars up, hats down," Prew said sidelong to Cherokee as they drew closer to a large stone and adobe building standing at the center of a circling stone-paved street.

Half turning in his saddle, Cherokee passed the word back quietly among the men. Then, seeing only two young uniformed soldiers standing slumped at ease on either side of a large arched open doorway, he whispered gleefully to Prew, "Looks like *el capitán* didn't leave much for us to deal with."

"Just the way he said he would," Prew whispered in reply.

Fifty yards from the bank, Indian Frank Becker and Niger Elmsly drifted away from the column and took up positions on either side of the busy street. A few yards closer to the bank, Matt Harkens and Stu Wakeland did the same. Harkens wandered a few feet away from Wakeland, leading his horse to a watering trough and letting the animal drink while he kept watch on Prew and the others. Beneath the edge of his long riding duster, an inch of rifle barrel protruded with each step.

Seeing the rifle barrel, a young boy ran into a store where his father, a local farmer, had just hefted a bag of grain onto his shoulder. "Papa! Papa!" The boy tugged excitedly at his father's trouser leg.

"Not now, Jesus," the farmer replied in their native tongue. But the boy followed him outside, all the while tugging and pleading in earnest until the man shouldered the bag over onto a mule cart.

"Now, what is so important, child, that you couldn't wait until I loaded our supplies?" he asked.

Gesturing his father down to him with urgency, the boy whispered into his ear as he nodded toward the men stepping down from their horses in front of the bank. When the boy had finished, his father straightened up with a grim look on his face. Seeing the men raise their bandannas over their noses as they walked toward the open doors with saddlebags over their shoulders, he said, "Quickly, Jesus, quickly!"

He gave his son a push. "Go inside and do not come out! Tell the proprietor everything you told me!" Even before the boy ran across the plank walkway, the farmer reached into the mule cart and slid a battered French army rifle from beneath a folded canvas cover.

On their way into the bank, Cherokee Jake and Clifford Elvey grabbed the unsuspecting guards right and left, snatched their rifles from their hands and shoved them into the building. The two frightened young soldiers fell to the floor with stunned expressions. Before they could retaliate in any manner, rifle butts swiped across their heads, knocking them senseless. "Not exactly crack troops, are they?" Cherokee chuckled to Elvey, speaking behind his bandanna mask.

Seeing the looks of panic and fear on the faces of the bank customers and tellers, Prew stepped forward with two big saddle Colts held out at arm's length and shouted in Spanish, "This is a robbery! Nobody move!"

A woman shrieked and fainted. Two men reached and grabbed her before she hit the hard stone floor. Prew grinned and said sidelong to Cherokee, "This is a dream come true." Then louder, "Everybody fill their bags. Let's go! Hurry it up!"

Filling the bags quickly with gold coins and bundles of pesos, the men returned to where Prew, Cherokee and Elvey stood holding their guns on the frightened customers and tellers. "Somebody take these," said Ethan Crenshaw, wobbling with the weight of an extra pair of saddlebags he'd carried in.

Without turning to face him, Prew said angrily, "Can't you see we've got these people covered? Hand them to somebody outside!"

Turning with the others and hurrying out the door, Crenshaw hefted the saddlebags to Russell, who stood beside Kerr, the two of them holding everybody's horses.

"Sure thing!" said Russell. Taking the heavy saddlebags and throwing them onto his shoulder, he gave Kerr a knowing look. "Take these reins," he said quickly.

Kerr grabbed the reins as Russell shoved them at him. He watched Russell step quickly around to the side of his horse, swing the bags up behind his saddle and tie them down tightly.

"Hey, damn it! Give me my horse!" shouted Dan Farr, poking Kerr with his gun barrel. Kerr turned, shoved his reins toward him and hurriedly passed out the rest of the reins to the other riders as they ran from the bank with their gold-filled saddlebags.

Then, standing with only his own reins in hand, Kerr looked up at Russell, who'd mounted his horse and sat looking down at him. "Well! Are you coming with us?" Russell shouted. He deliberately stalled as Prew and the others swung their horses around.

"Yes indeed!" Kerr said, seeing what Russell had in mind. He swung up into his saddle and gigged his horse around beside Russell's. The two of them raced away from the rest of the fleeing riders. Cutting across the stone street, the two ducked into an alley and disappeared.

As the riders thundered along the street, sending pedestrians, wagons and buggy traffic scurrying out of their way, the armed farmer raised up from behind a stack of wooden crates and fired on the robbers. A few feet away, two more armed townsmen rose up and fired, one with a big Spanish revolver, the other with a shotgun.

At the rear of the column of riders, Matt Harkens felt shotgun pellets nip at his thigh. His horse whinnied in pain and tried to veer to the side, but Harkens managed to keep the animal running straight as a rifle shot whistled past his head. In front of him, Crenshaw and Bud Stakes turned in their saddles and sent a hail of pistol shots toward the farmer and the townsmen, giving Harkens cover until he caught up with them.

"Where's the other two?" Stakes called out, slowing his horse enough to let Harkens catch up to him. He saw the blood on Harkens' thigh, and the red pellet wound on the horse's side.

"I don't know," said Harkens, riding hard, bent low in the saddle. "Dead, I guess!"

At the cockfight, the townsmen had turned from their bloody sport toward the harsh sound of gunfire resounding off the stone streets of Plaza Fuerte. As the riders thundered along the trail toward them, the men drew pistols and ran toward the trail. But before they arrived, the oncoming riders slowed and circled in the dirt trail.

"Nail a couple of them!" Prew shouted, still wondering about the gunfire behind them. "We've got to get out of here." Almost before the words had left his mouth, pistols swung up from holsters and fired in one long volley.

"Whoo-*eeee!*" shouted Cherokee Jake as two men crumpled to the ground. The others turned and ran for cover. In the fighting ring, two bedraggled roosters circled, locked in a death waltz, oblivious to the world of man surrounding them.

Turning his horse restlessly, Prew saw the three straggling men come riding up. Harkens had a hand pressed to his bloody thigh. "What happened?" Prew shouted at Stakes and Crenshaw.

"Some damn townsfolk ambushed us!" said Crenshaw. "They buckshot Harkens here. We held them off him while he got away."

"Where's Russell and Kerr?" Prew asked, staring back along the trail.

"My guess is the townsfolk got them," said Harkens. "They were right behind me when we mounted."

"Are you going to be able to ride?" Prew asked him bluntly.

"Hell, yes, I can ride!" said Harkens, knowing the consequences of *not* being able to ride. "Ain't that what I'm doing?" He slapped his wounded leg. "This is just a couple or three buckshot pellets, is all." He gestured at the horse's side. "Ole Henry here took a couple himself. But we're both fine as can be."

"Then you best keep up," said Prew. Dismissing the matter, he looked at Crenshaw's single pair of saddlebags and said, "Ethan, who'd you hand the other saddlebags to?"

"I handed them to Russell," said the lanky gunman. As soon as he'd said it, he realized his mistake and looked back toward town. "Damn. They're laying there in the street beside him," he said.

"In a pig's eye," Prew said. He stared from one side of the street to the other, looking for a rise of dust. Seeing none right then, he looked over at where the townsmen had taken cover. "Let's get the hell out of here before these cockfighters decide to turn into heroes." He batted his heels to his horse's sides and rode away, firing shots toward the hiding townsmen.

High above, on the same ridge where he'd waited since Prew and his men had ridden past him into Plaza Fuerte, the ranger watched through his field lens. Hearing the gunshots had piqued his interest. Now, seeing Prew and his mercenaries riding back along the trail below, he counted silently. "You're coming out two riders short," he said under his breath.

Raising his lens to the trail on the other side of town, then to the trails on either side, he searched for the missing riders. Just as he'd begun to think that the missing two might be dead or captured, he homed in on Russell and Kerr. "There you are," he whispered. The two looked back on the town as they raced along a flat trail headed east, toward the same line of hills he stood upon.

Lowering and collapsing the lens, the ranger shook his head slowly and walked to the horses. "It looks like we've got company coming," he said to Black Pot and the paint. He picked up their reins and walked them up a steep path to the rocky trail. "Why don't we just ride over and meet them?"

CHAPTER 17

Ten miles from Plaza Fuerte, Prew brought the riders to a halt on a tree-studded hillside fifty yards off the trail. As the column followed him and Cherokee Jake up the hillside, Ethan Crenshaw leaned in his saddle and said quietly to Bud Stakes, "It looks like I'm in big trouble now."

"Yeah," said Stakes, "and I hope I'm not in trouble along with you, for stopping to help Harkens." As he spoke, he watched Prew's back. "A man hardly knows what move to make around here. Anybody else I ever rode with would applaud helping a fellow who's shot—but not so with this bunch. Prew looked like he was about half sour on the idea."

"And look at me," said Crenshaw. "All I did was hand a man some saddlebags to carry. Now I'll be lucky if I don't get shot and dumped along the trail."

"Not trying to side against you, Crenshaw," said Stakes, "but I learned long ago in Texas you never give the horseman any bags of money to carry."

"I realize that," said Crenshaw, "but mistakes can happen."

Stakes continued as if he'd not heard him. "First of all, you know the horseman is going to be the last man leaving town. That means if he gets shot, there goes the money."

"Yes, but—"

Stakes cut him off. "No buts to it. The other reason is you can't watch behind you every second. The last man out can cut and run with the money without you knowing it till it's too late. Which in this case he did, or they did—Russell and Kerr, that is."

"You don't believe that circumstances matter?" Crenshaw asked.

"Sure, I believe circumstances account for a lot," said Stakes, the two riding up into the trees, at the center of the column.

"Well, I should say so," Crenshaw added, seeming somehow relieved.

"But what I believe doesn't matter," said Stakes. "I ain't the one who'll blow your head off over it."

Behind them, Harkens chuckled, having overheard their quiet conversation. Looking back at him, Crenshaw growled, "What's so damn funny, Harkens? I don't recall you doing any laughing when we lagged back to save your ass from them wild-eyed Mexican townsmen."

"Sorry, Crenshaw," said Harkens. "I shouldn't have laughed. But the fact is nobody is going to get shot over this. Hell, Prew needs good men to get things done down here. I wouldn't worry about it if I was you."

"You really think so?" Crenshaw asked.

"If I didn't think so, I wouldn't have said it," Harkens replied.

Crenshaw looked at Stakes for confirmation. Stakes shrugged and said, "There you have it."

Crenshaw felt a little relieved. But his relief was short-lived. Upon entering the wooded hillside, Prew led the riders into a circle and came to a halt straight across from Crenshaw. "Boy, that was some winging there for a while," Crenshaw said, trying his best to force a smile through the worried look on his face. He raised his bulging saddlebags from his lap, having to use both hands, and heaved them to the ground.

Prew and Cherokee sat staring at him blankly. The rest of the men followed suit, not wanting to respond in any way that would offend Prew. Crenshaw said nervously, "I was just thinking, since I made what you might call a little mistake back there, why I don't just take less of a cut than the rest of—"

One of Prew's big Colt saddle pistols bucked in his hand as the shot picked Crenshaw up and flung him backward from his saddle. He hit the ground doing back flips like some limp and mindless circus clown; then he lay facedown as still as stone. His horse bolted and raced away along the sloping hillside.

Prew said to Dan Farr, "Go get his horse and bring it back."

"Right away, boss." Farr turned his horse quickly and sped after the runaway animal.

The men sat silent, watching, waiting, not knowing what to expect next. Prew said to Stakes, "Bud, take your rifle, put a few shots in his back, roll him over and do it again."

Stakes looked puzzled. "Why, Prew, he's already dead."

The big Colt bucked again. Stakes flew from his saddle, rolled and stopped flat on his bloody chest. "Oh Lord," he groaned, trying to push himself up from the ground with both hands. "I'm a . . . mess here." Before his horse could bolt away, Indian Frank Becker jumped his horse forward, caught the animal by its reins and held it in place.

"Harkens?" Prew said quietly, the Colt smoking in his hand. He jerked his head toward Stakes.

"Yes, sir, right away, boss!" Harkens replied, his words running together in his haste. He yanked his rifle from its boot as he answered and levered a round into the chamber.

A hundred yards away, Dan Farr had caught up to the fleeing horse. He held its reins firmly as both his horse and the runaway reared at the sound of more gunfire. "My God! Are they killing one another?" he asked aloud, hearing shot after shot resound from the trees. He quickly calmed both animals and raced back to the others.

"That settles everything," Farr heard Prew saying as he hurried in leading Crenshaw's horse behind him. Farr looked across the circle and saw Harkens tying down the heavy saddlebags he'd swung up onto his horse's back. Then he stepped back, rolled both bodies over onto their backs and shot them some more. Rifle smoke loomed around him in a gray cloud.

"Bud?" Farr said, staring at Stakes' bullet-riddled body on the ground. The men sat staring in silence.

"He's some kin of yours if I'm not mistaken," Prew said in a calm even tone. "Your brother, wasn't he?"

"Huh?" said Farr, looking up from the body and over at Prew, who sat holding the big saddle Colt.

"Whoa!" he said in shocked surprise. "*Half* brother! That's all he was," Farr said quickly, raising a hand as if to ward off any hasty response on Prew's part. "We got along, Bud and me, but just barely. There was times I could have killed him myself."

"So, I shouldn't have to worry about you getting all whiskey-bent and wanting to take some revenge for me killing him?"

"Me? Over ole Bud here?" Farr looked amazed at the suggestion. "Naw, hell no!" He felt a sheen of sweat appear across his forehead. "Like I said, there was times when I wished I'd—"

"Yeah, yeah," Prew said, cutting him off. "Let me ask you this. If I give you his share of the gold to take home to his family, say to a wife, a kid? You'd see to it they got it, wouldn't you?"

"Would I? Well, *hell yes* I would," said Farr with great commitment. "Just as sure as a duck pulls a worm, I'd take every cent back to Kansas and . . ."

His words trailed to a halt as he looked around, hearing the sound of stifled laughter from the men. Looking back at Prew and seeing the big pistol slide down into a saddle holster, he let out a tense breath. With a face reddened by embarrassment, he gave a sheepish grin and said, "All right, I get it—you're funnin' with me."

"Yeah, I'm only joking," Prew said with a smug grin. "We

wouldn't ask that much of any man. Tie their horses to a tree where *el capitán* and his soldiers can find them." He looked all around at the men. "It would look bad for him if every one of us got away." He and Cherokee turned their horses and rode back toward the trail. The circle of riders followed behind them.

* * *

The ranger waited behind a tall rugged cedar at the top of the steep trail leading up the far end of the hill line. When he'd arrived, he'd dropped the saddle from Black Pot's back, and for the past half hour he'd let the horses graze on sparse clumps of wild grass in the shade of a small meadow. He'd cleaned and checked his guns and taken a few minutes to rest himself. Then he'd taken cover behind the tree until Russell and Kerr led their tired horses into sight.

"Stop right there," he called out, stepping from behind the cedar into the center of the rocky trail. The two outlaws were clearly caught off guard as they stared back along the trail behind them.

"What the—!" Thomas Russell exclaimed, his hand going instinctively around his holstered gun butt.

Kerr's hand did the same. But seeing the ranger standing no more than thirty feet away, his Colt already out, cocked and pointed, the two froze.

"Thomas Russell and Braden Kerr," the ranger said in an officious tone, holding up his wrinkled list of names in his left hand. "You are both wanted in Arizona Territory for murder, robbery, forgery, land fraud, counterfeiting of American currency, destruction of a—"

"Damn it all to hell! We know what we've all done!" said Kerr, cutting him off. He dropped his horse's reins and took a step farther away from Russell. "Prew already had us sold out!"

"Whatever you're thinking about doing, Cur Dog," said

the ranger, "you best check yourself down and give it more thought."

Seeing Russell take the same kind of short sidestep, Sam said, "You too, Hemp Knot. I'm taking you both in. Lift your hands away from your guns."

"That damn Prew," said Kerr. "He *did* trade us both for his bay horse. I reckon I always thought he would. This has been gnawing at us ever since you sent his horse to him."

"Tell me something, Ranger," Russell asked. "How did you and Prew manage to set us up this way? How'd you know we'd come up this trail?"

"This is no setup," said the ranger.

"The hell," said Kerr. "Everything Prew does is a setup. That bank robbery back there. The military trains. Him and *el capitán* sets everything up."

The ranger wasn't about to tell them how wrong they were about this being a setup. Instead he said, "Raise your hands away from your guns. We'll talk more about it along the way."

"We ain't going back with you, Ranger," Kerr said with resolve. "We're not outlaws no more. We came here and changed our lives. We're respectable mercenaries here."

"Yeah, Mexico is our home now," said Russell. "Your badge ain't worth spit here." As the two spoke they put a few more inches of space between themselves. "So, you and Prew can both go to hell. Your little trading plan didn't work."

"Don't do it," Sam warned, seeing in their eyes and their demeanor that at any second they would make a move on him.

"Now!" shouted Russell. No sooner had Sam warned them than their guns came up fast from their holsters.

The ranger's first shot hit Russell in the heart before he got his gun up to fire. The ranger's second shot hit Kerr in the center of his chest just as Kerr sent a bullet whistling past the ranger's head.

The ranger stood for a moment in a ringing silence,

watching the two men fall backward down the hillside. Russell's body slammed into a tree. Kerr slid down the rocky trail, his fingers clawing into the dirt. The two tired horses stepped back and forth nervously, but then settled and nickered under their breath.

Kerr moaned. His fingertips scratched the ground toward his pistol, only an inch out of reach. Sam stepped down and kicked the gun away. "Damn you, Ranger," Kerr rasped, looking up at him in pain. "I could have . . . lived good on this gold."

"You made the move, Cur Dog," the ranger replied. "I warned you not to."

"Warned us . . . ha," said Kerr, struggling for breath, blood pouring out of his wounded chest. "You never meant to take us in." He gestured a weak hand in the direction Prew, and his men had taken. "We heard the shooting. You and Prew were just thinning the herd."

"I had nothing to do with Prew," said the ranger. "All I did was send him his horse and tell him I'd be coming for you and Russell. Everything else you thought about was all in your heads."

Looking down at Kerr's blank eyes, Sam wasn't sure how much the wounded man had heard before he'd died. But Kerr's last words, "Thinning the herd," had given him pause for a moment. He'd heard the two pistol shots and the repeated rifle fire earlier. Had that been Prew killing some of his own men, leaving a body or two behind for the *federales* just to make things look good?

The ranger thought about it as he turned to the two tired horses standing in the center of the trail. He loosened and dropped the saddlebags full of gold coins to the ground, then stripped the saddles and bridles from the horses and gave them a shove on their rumps. The horses only moved away along the hillside at a walk.

Without taking time to bury the two men, Sam dragged

their bodies off into the brush. He carried both of the saddles in and tossed them over their faces. "That's all you get today," he said. Moments later he rode away back in the direction of the earlier gunfire, the bags of Mexican gold on the paint horse's back.

On his way along the high trail he stopped once to look down and back along the flatlands toward Plaza Fuerte. Seeing the rising dust of many horses, he murmured to himself, "*El capitán*, no doubt." Then he hastened his horses' pace and rode on, in the direction of the earlier gunfire.

Over an hour later he stepped down where the bodies of Crenshaw and Stakes had been laid out side by side. A few feet away the dead men's horses stood hitched to a tree. *Cur Dog was right*, he told himself. Prew had been thinning the herd.

Looking around, Sam led his two horses closer. Using his gloved hands he scooped half of the gold out of the mercenaries' saddlebags and into his own. Then he swung the half-full saddlebags down from the paint horse and dropped them against the tree. He gazed back toward the distant rise of dust. Thinning the herd wasn't a bad idea, he thought as he set about the task of loading the two bodies across their horses' backs.

CHAPTER 18

Captain Luis Murella stopped a few yards back from the tree and stared blankly for a moment. To Sergeant Simon Cordova, who sat his horse beside him, Murella said in their native tongue, "Is this his idea of a joke?"

"If it is, I don't think it's so funny," said Cordova. The two stared for a moment longer at the saddlebags lying against the tree. "But perhaps there has been an error of some sort," he offered warily, knowing how many times he'd seen the captain fly into a rage over a thing of much less importance than gold.

"No, Sergeant, there has been no error," said the captain, shaking his head. "I know how the mind of this criminal works." He tapped his finger to his head as he spoke. "He is leaving me a message here, telling me that he has grown much more powerful than me."

"A message, *mi capitán?*" the sergeant asked in a meek tone of voice.

"He robs the bank and leaves no bodies as he said he would," the captain said, sorting it out. "And instead of waiting to split up the gold after the train robbery as we agreed to do, he leaves this miserable set of saddlebags?"

"Yes, it is most disturbing, *mi capitán*," said the sergeant.

"Most disturbing indeed," the captain growled, giving him a sharp look. He gestured a nod toward the saddlebags. "Get them, bring them here. We will see how much is in them." He paused and looked back down the hillside to where his men sat waiting at ease in their saddles. "But if that is *half* of the gold coins in the Mexico National Exchange Bank, this

167

country of mine is in worse shape than I thought."

The sergeant quickly stepped his horse forward, climbed down and opened the saddlebags. Looking inside, he shook his head, closed them, shouldered them and walked back to the captain, leading his horse behind him. "*El Capitán*, it is as you suspected." He held open the flap so the captain could see inside.

"Close it and get it out of my face," the captain said with bitterness and contempt.

Just feeling the captain's smoldering fury unnerved the wiry little sergeant. He lowered the saddlebags, walked to his horse and slung them easily up behind his saddle. If Desmond Prew thought he could treat *el capitán* this way he was badly mistaken, Cordova told himself. When he'd finished tying down the saddlebags, he stood silently at attention.

The captain looked all around the deserted hillside, then said in a low growl, "He left none of his men for me to take back either." Staring down at the sergeant he added, "Does he think me a fool, Sergeant? Am I the kind of man who will stand still for such a double cross as this?"

The sergeant, uncertain how to answer, simply said, "It is he who is the fool, *mi capitán*, not you." He stiffened more even though he already stood at attention. "You have only to say the word. We will ride to Esperanza and slice off each and every important part of his body."

"No," said the captain, "we will not ride to Esperanza. Desmond Prew knows that we need him right now, to rob the train and bring us the explosives we need. That is why he thinks he can get away with this. But he is wrong. We will wait until we get the explosives. Then we will settle all accounts with him."

"But for now, Capitán," the sergeant asked, "what do we do about taking in someone for robbing the bank?"

"For now we do nothing," said the captain. "But when we meet up with Prew and his men after the train robbery, we will have plenty to choose from. He grinned, his fiery temper cooling a little. "Who knows? Perhaps we will take in Prew himself." He turned his horse and rode back down to join his column of troops. The nervous sergeant scrambled into his saddle and followed him.

From a thin overgrown trail atop the steep hillside, the ranger focused his telescope lens and watched the two ride down and take their positions at the head of the column. A trace of a smile came to his face when he saw the captain's angry expression. Beside the captain the sergeant raised a gloved hand, brought the men forward into a sharp turn and headed them back toward Plaza Fuerte.

"The more stones I can throw in your path, Desmond Prew, the more likely you are to trip over them," the ranger said to himself. He collapsed the telescope and walked to the horses, where the bodies of Crenshaw and Stakes lay across their saddles.

He rode for the next twenty minutes along the high trail until he found the best spot to roll the bodies, saddles, tack and all down into thick brush on the rocky hillside. The two horses he turned loose the same way he had done with the others. Then he rode on, working his way back toward Esperanza to tell Jefferies what Prew and his mercenaries had been up to.

At Louisa's small adobe house in Esperanza, Sabio and Caridad had taken lodging until such time as they could disappear once again into the hills. Sway Loden had warned them not to leave until after Prew and his men had returned. Yet, Sabio wanted to take Caridad and leave quietly, and the two of them would not be missed.

But Sabio knew that staying at Louisa's removed the temptation of anything happening between him and Caridad, the way it had almost happened that day in his secret forest. He would not risk being alone with her under such circumstances again, he told himself, keeping a watchful eye on William

Jefferies, who had come to the house once more to plead for Caridad's forgiveness.

For the past two days, he had sat silently by and watched and listened to Jefferies try to make Caridad understand why he'd rejoined Prew's men. But Caridad would have none of it. "When you left with the ranger, you said you were going across the border," she replied, "and that you would return for me someday. You said you wanted nothing more to do with these kind of men." She looked at him with deep hurt showing in her dark eyes. "You lied to me."

"Yes, and I am sorry," said Jefferies. He did not tell them that he'd come to town with the ranger, or what he and the ranger had planned to do. The less they knew about their plan, the better, he thought. "Caridad, I had to come back here, just for a little while," he continued. "I came back because I was worried about you. Won't you please believe me?" Jefferies knew how weak it sounded, yet he was unable to tell her why he'd been here when she and Sabio rode in with Cherokee Jake Slattery and the other two mercenaries.

"How could you come here for me, when you knew that Sabio and I were going to stay at the old mission?" she asked.

She had him there, Jefferies thought, knowing he could take it no further without endangering her. It wasn't that he didn't trust her. It was that he didn't want her knowing something that would bring her harm if Prew ever found out about it.

When he could offer no explanation, she gave him a disappointed look and said, "That is what I thought." Then she turned and walked out the back door to where Louisa stirred a simmering pot of goat stew over a small stone *chimenea.*

Turning toward Sabio as Caridad stepped into the backyard, Jefferies said, "I think it's time for you and me to have ourselves a talk. I think you understand why I walked out into the street when I saw the two of you ride into town."

"Yes, I understood right away," Sabio admitted. He stood up from his straight-backed chair and picked up a clay pitcher of cool wine. He walked over to the table where Jefferies sat and poured a cupful for the young American.

"Then why won't you talk to her, let her know that I'm not lying?"

"Why have I not done that?" Sabio considered. "I will tell you why I have not." Having come to a decision regarding Caridad, Sabio sighed deeply in his resolve and said, "I have remained silent all this time because I love that one very much."

"You mean . . . ?" Jefferies let his words trail off.

"No," Sabio said. "Not in that way." He sat down across the table from Jefferies, poured himself a cup of wine and said, "But let me tell you a story that will help you understand how things are with me and with my precious Caridad."

Jefferies watched him bow his bald head for a moment as if in prayer. When Sabio looked up, a tiny bud of a tear lay in the corner of his eye. "When I was a young man here in Esperanza, I fell in love with a beautiful girl whose name I still forbid myself to speak aloud. But throughout my life I have been endowed with both a blessing and a curse. My blessing has been this gift of power which you have witnessed." He looked Jefferies in the eye. "You do believe in such a thing as a spiritual gift, do you not?"

"I've had reservations in the past," said Jefferies, "but I won't discount such a thing. I came to you bleeding and you stopped it. I can't say how—I can only say you *did*."

Sabio nodded and continued. "It was because of that power that the priests took me in and made me one of them. They wanted people to witness my power and think it came from the holy mother church. But it did not. It came directly from God, from God's hand to mine, with no one between. Do you understand me?"

"Yes, I believe I do," said Jefferies. "If this power came from God, you didn't want anyone or anything else claiming to be the source of it?"

"Yes, you *do* understand," Sabio said, seeming a bit surprised at the young American's insightfulness.

Jefferies only sipped his wine and listened.

"That was my *gift*," said Sabio. "And even my gift was not an easy thing to bear." He gave a thin sardonic grin and said, "But wait until you hear about my *curse*."

Jefferies nodded and looked deep into Sabio's dark eyes as he continued.

"My *curse* has been an unrelenting carnal desire for women," Sabio said bluntly. "Throughout my life I have never been able to satisfy my hunger for them. It is a terrible affliction, one that has cost me everything over the years. And now it seems, it is taking my gift from me, as I should have known it would."

Jefferies only stared at him silently, not knowing what to say.

"The young woman I loved?" Sabio said. "I refused to allow myself to hurt her as I knew I would someday. So I gave in to the leaders of the church and joined their brotherhood, thinking that God in his mercy would take this craving from me, or at least give me the strength to overcome it. Because how could a man be given such a gift as this and yet be plagued by such a curse?" He asked Jefferies in a way that pleaded for an answer; yet, clearly, he knew no answer was forthcoming. "Why does God do such things as this?" he said, shaking his bald head sadly.

They both drank from their clay cups.

"So," Sabio said at length, "my beautiful young woman married another—and why shouldn't she, knowing that as a priest I was forever forbidden to take a wife and build a home like other men do? He was an American like you, a good man, her husband. Yet I despised him for having what I knew could never be mine."

Jefferies reached out, picked up the clay pitcher and refilled the cups, encouraging him to continue.

"It is harsh and terrible, the punishment God lays upon those to whom he has entrusted his gifts, especially when they repeatedly offend him, as I did with my insatiable appetite for women." Sabio sipped from the fresh cup, needing the wine to soften his pain.

"When my beautiful woman had recovered from birthing her only child, his daughter, my Caridad, she and her husband and the baby set out across the badlands at a time when the Apache ran wild and murderous."

Jefferies began to see where the old monk's story was headed.

Sabio appeared to relive the hurt even after all these years as he said in a trembling voice, "The two were barely breathing when the *federales* arrived in time to chase away the Apache. The baby lay wrapped in a blanket and was not seen by the warriors." He crossed himself. "It was a miracle."

"Yes, indeed," said Jefferies, starting to understand the feelings between Sabio and Caridad.

"They brought my beautiful woman and her husband to me, for me to use my gift to save them, as I did you, and as I had done with countless others at that time."

"But, God forgive me, in a moment of selfishness, I tried to save *her*, yet at the same time let his life slip away." He swallowed a tight knot in his throat. "But God would not stand for my foolishness that day. He knew I held back with my gift and allowed the husband to die. Because of it, he took them both. It was his way of telling me they would be together for eternity while a fool like myself would go on forever alone."

"But he left you the child, Caridad," Jefferies offered quietly. "The child of another man, yet still the flesh and blood of the woman you loved so dearly."

"Yes, and I have raised her as my own daughter, and I have never harmed her." He paused as he studied Jefferies' eyes. "But when I look at her, and I think of how badly I am still cursed . . ."

"But you would never allow yourself to—"

"Do not tell me what I will allow myself to do," Sabio interrupted, "unless you have lived inside me and seen my thoughts and know how weak I am. When it comes to sins of the flesh I have found no end to my depravity." He paused, then took the conversation back to the past.

"After I misused my gift and allowed the deaths of her mother and father, my gift has never been the same," he said. "Sometimes it acts with the certainty of God—other times I seem to have to prod it along and make up excuses for it when things do not go right."

"Things went right for me. You saved my life," said Jefferies.

"Yes, and now, seeing you return at such a time that I have become more concerned about Caridad, am thinking that saving your life was meant to be."

More concerned about Caridad? Jefferies was afraid he understood too well what that meant.

"Now," said Sabio, "because of my terrible thoughts I fear my gift has been taken away from me entirely." His expression darkened as he added, "If Caridad stays with me, I fear what will someday happen."

"Then send her away with me, Sabio," Jefferies said suddenly. "I love her—I fell in love with her the minute I laid eyes upon her. You won't have to worry about her. I'll take good care of her. I'll make her happy, I swear it."

Sabio paused and took a deep drink of wine, as if needing it in order to relive painful memories. "I see her face, and I see the face of the only woman I ever loved. Yet, now that she is a woman, I find myself fighting with my lower nature to keep from someday defiling her, the way I have defiled all things I ever loved."

Jefferies saw the tears stream down from the old holy man's eyes. He wanted to reach across the table and place his hand down over Sabio's, but he couldn't bring himself to do so. "Then it's settled," said Jefferies, his voice taking on a decisive edge.

"Speak to her on my behalf while she still idolizes you, Sabio. Send her away with me before it's too late."

"I will speak with her," said Sabio. "I suppose I knew from the moment I saw you that you would be the one to take her from me." He arose slowly from the table. "It is better that I lose her to you than to any of those," he said, nodding in the direction of the cantina. "Or to myself," he added in a grim tone of voice.

Before Sabio walked away from the table, Sway Loden appeared in the open doorway and said to Jefferies, "So there you are, Kid. We've been looking all over town for you."

"Why? What do you want?" Jefferies asked, standing and walking toward the open door.

"Nothing," said Loden. "We're just gathering everybody up for some serious drinking before Prew and the others get back. Are you interested?"

Jefferies gave Sabio a look, then said to Loden, "Oh, yeah, very interested." He snatched his hat from a peg on the wall and put it on as he stepped out the door.

CHAPTER 19

On the last stretch of their ride back to Esperanza, Prew and his men had gathered beneath a cliff overhang and divided up their half of the gold coins. With the loot separated out and each man carrying only his share in his saddlebags, Prew and Cherokee kept *el capitán's* share in three bulging sets of saddlebags they had slung over Cherokee's horse's rump.

"Let me make sure everybody understands," said Prew. "This bank raid is our own little secret. If any of yas start flapping your tongue about it, just expect to catch yourself a bullet in your head." He stared from one face to the other as if to make certain each man heard his threat.

"All right then," he said, "all of yas ride away now while Cherokee and I stash Captain Murella's share somewhere for safekeeping. Wait for us at the fork in the trail. Anybody caught snooping around here, sniffing for the captain's share, won't live long enough to find it."

The men understood. They formed up in their loose column and rode away. When they were out of sight, Cherokee said, "There goes some happy men. Let's hope they've the good sense to keep their mouths shut about the bank job."

Prew nodded, not seeming too concerned about it. "It's only for a few days. Once we ride to the border and take down the train, everybody's going to split up anyways. If they want to shoot their mouths off about it then, that'll be their business."

"Right," said Cherokee Jake. He straightened up in his saddle and looked all around the hillside. "Now then, what about *el capitán's* share? What do you think we ought to do with—"

"Get off your horse," said Prew, cutting him off.

"What?" Cherokee looked stunned. He glanced at Prew's hand to make sure he wasn't holding a gun on him. Relieved to see that he wasn't, Cherokee said, "Don't you want me to find a spot for—"

"I said get off your horse!" Prew demanded impatiently. "Are you deaf?" This time his hand did go to his gun butt, instinctively.

"All right, boss, easy now," said Cherokee. He stepped down, giving Prew a worried look.

Prew's hand came away from his gun butt and took the reins to Cherokee's horse. "Start walking," he said. "Stop and wait for me down by the trail. I'll be there after I hide the captain's share of the gold."

"Oh, yeah, sure thing." Cherokee, looked relieved, recalling how quickly Prew had killed Crenshaw and Stakes the day before. "I figured you'd want my help is all." As he spoke, he stepped down and handed Prew his horse's reins.

"Not with the captain's share," said Prew. "I'll take care of it from here."

He watched Cherokee walk away in the same direction as the others. Before he'd even gotten out of sight, Prew turned his horse, leading Cherokee's behind him and rode farther up the steep hillside and to a narrow rock crevice. Stepping down, he looked back and listened closely for the slightest sound of anyone following him.

Satisfied that he was alone, Prew carried the saddlebags of gold into the narrow crevice. Where the crevice narrowed beyond shoulder width, he pulled back a thick wall of draping vines and laid the bags behind it. Leaning for a moment, he looked down at the skeletal remains of a man stretched out along the ground. "Hello, Charlie Lowe. I see you're still here, watching over things as usual," he said in mockery.

A thin lizard perched in an empty eye socket, looking up at him curiously, its tongue flicking. A bone hand protruded from the end of a rotted shirtsleeve. At the end of the outstretched calcium fingers lay a rusted, dirt-covered Colt, its hammer still cocked and ready. A rotting hat lay only inches from the skull.

"You wasn't hard to replace, Charlie," Prew said. "It only took one trip to the nearest saloon." Taking a step back, he grinned and said in parting, "You take care now, don't go 'way." Then he let the vines fall back into place as he turned and walked out. At the horses, he looked back into the crevice and said, "The *captain's share?* Ha, in a pig's eye. This is my last train job, Charlie. All or nothing!" He stepped into the saddle, took the reins to Cherokee's horse and rode away.

Moments later, riding down the trail, he pulled the horses over and stopped where Cherokee Jake sat atop a half-sunken boulder. Cherokee stood up, dusted the seat of his trousers and stepped down off the rock. Without another word about the gold, he stepped up into his saddle and said, "I can't wait till we get the go-ahead on that military train."

"Me too, Charlie," said Prew with a thin speculative grin. "I'm thinking it won't be much longer."

"*Charlie?* Who's Charlie?" Cherokee asked. "My name is Jake, remember?"

"Sorry, Cherokee," said Prew, gazing ahead. "I was thinking about something else."

At the fork in the trail, the two rejoined the rest of the men and started the uphill ride toward Esperanza. When they'd reached a point where they could stop and look down on the trail meandering beneath them, Prew glimpsed a lone rider pushing his horse hard, his black duster tails flapping out on either side like the wings of a low-flying bat.

"Well, well," said Prew, "look who's coming here. It's Dick Spivey." Turning to Cherokee, he said, "Take a man with you, ride down and bring him to me."

"Dead or alive?" Cherokee asked, ready to turn his horse and ride away.

"Alive! By all means, *alive*," said Prew. "This man is important to me."

"Sure enough, alive it is," said Cherokee. He looked at the gathered men and said, "Indian Frank, you're coming with me."

Indian Frank Beeker turned his horse alongside Cherokee's without a word. The two rode away at a gallop while the others stepped down from their saddles and led their horses out of the sun.

On the trail below, Dick Spivey didn't see the small spill of rocks tumble down off of a rock facing. But his horse saw the rock spill and spooked. Veering hard, the animal sent its rider flying from his saddle into a bristly tangle of stiff juniper. Before the horse could regain its balance, its hooves slid in the loose dirt and it toppled over into a roll, its legs splaying wildly.

"Jesus!" Spivey growled, thrashing about, pulling himself from the low stubby juniper bushes. "Crazy son of a bitch!" he shouted at the horse. He scrambled back onto the trail and saw the animal roll up onto its hooves and shake itself off. His hand snapped shut around his gun butt. "For two cents I'd—" But his threat stopped short, as he saw the horse favor its left front leg.

"Damned if this ain't all I need, a horse gone lame on me," he said, spitting bits of dirt and juniper from his lips.

From one of the higher trails the ranger had taken, he'd heard the shrill whinny of the horse resound across the hilltops and valleys from a long way off. Searching with his telescope he found the rider and watched him dust himself off and amble over to the limping horse. *One of Prew's men?* Sam asked himself. If so it wasn't any he'd seen before. He watched the man inspect the horse's injured leg, then pick up the reins and lead the animal on up the hill trail.

Headed for Esperanza . . . ? Of course. Where else? he asked himself. Then it dawned on him. Jefferies had said Prew and his men were awaiting word from their inside informant at either the army or the railroad shipping office. *Was this him?* Sam watched the man walk along for a few yards, then saw him duck to the side of the trail as two of Prew's men came riding down toward him. "Uh-oh," Sam murmured, seeing the two riders spot him before he could get himself and the limping horse out of sight.

But then Sam smiled to himself. "That's more like it," he said as he saw the man on foot recognize the two riders and walk toward them, their lips moving silently in the round circle of the telescope. "I see who you're with," he whispered. "Now what part do you play?"

He watched for a moment longer, then collapsed the telescope, put it away and climbed back into his saddle. He'd have to push hard to catch up and stay atop them on the high trails. But he had a feeling this was the man they'd all been waiting for. Things were going to start happening fast, he decided, nudging the stallion and leading the paint horse behind him. He needed to let Jefferies know.

Riding double with Cherokee, Dick Spivey stepped down where Prew and his men waited along the trail. Taking the reins to his injured horse from Indian Frank, Spivey stretched and dusted the front of his shirt. Cherokee stepped his horse forward toward Prew. "There he is, boss, alive, just like you wanted him," Cherokee said between the two of them.

Prew noted the scratches on Spivey's face and the torn places on his shirt. "What the hell did you do to him?"

"Oh, that wasn't our doing," Cherokee pointed out quickly. "His horse took a tumble before we got there. He was already leading it up the trail. Lucky for him we come along when we did."

"I'll say," said Prew, riding on over to where Spivey stood

looking his horse up and down. "Having a hard time keeping a saddle under you these days, Dick?" he said to Spivey.

Spivey turned to face him. "I pushed him too hard on these Mexican trails." He looked around to make sure no one was close enough to hear him, then said in a lowered tone, "Everything is set for four days from now."

"Good," said Prew. "That's the news I've been waiting to hear." He stepped down from his saddles and looked Spivey's horse over as he asked, "Is the signal still the same as before?"

"Yep," said Spivey, in an even lower tone. "Look for three signal lanterns hanging on the caboose."

Prew smiled. "Simple enough. It looks like everything's going as planned."

"Except for one thing," said Spivey, stepping in closer and looking all around again. "Sherard says tell you there's a lawman snooping around. According to Sherard's information he might be trying to weasel his way in on the operation and break it up."

Prew stiffened. But then, thinking about the ranger, he looked relieved and said, "We've already had a brush with him. It's that Arizona Ranger, Sam Burrack."

"Burrack?" said Spivey. "Damn, he's trouble, that one."

"Ordinarily, yes, he is," Prew said. "But not to me. He sent my horse back to me after some fool let him take it from him. He said he gave me back my horse so I'd turn two of my men he's looking for over to him." Prew grinned. "I suppose you could call that trying to weasel in."

"Yeah, I suppose," said Spivey. "He's nobody to fool around with."

"Obliged for the warning," said Prew. "Now that we've settled on who the lawman is, what else?"

"That's all," said Spivey. "Sherard said warn you about him, so I did."

"Yes, you did," said Prew. He rubbed Spivey's horse on its dirt-streaked muzzle. "Now, if you want to swap horses with one of the men, you can get back under way. Tell Ike Sherard I got his message."

"If it's all the same with you," said Spivey, "I'd sooner spend a day or two in Esperanza. I hate swapping out a good horse when all he needs is a couple days' rest and mending time. Sherard won't be expecting me back this soon anyway. Besides, I get the willies thinking that ranger is prowling around out here."

"Don't worry about that ranger," said Prew. "He tried to weasel in, but I cut him off before he got started."

"Still, if it's all the same with you," said Spivey, "I could use the rest myself."

"Suit yourself," said Prew. "Find somebody to double with. We're heading out."

As Prew stepped back into his saddle and motioned his men to form up on the trail, high above them the ranger, gaining ground, slowed only long enough for another look at them. Then he closed the telescope and pushed on.

CHAPTER 20

In Esperanza, Jefferies drank in the cantina with the rest of the men, yet he kept himself in check, managing to drink only one shot of whiskey to everyone else's third and fourth glasses. When the others began to get drunk and more talkative he managed to get in a couple of questions about who provided them information on the army munitions shipments. But he soon began to realize that these men had no idea. Prew kept his contacts close to his vest, he decided, and he ceased asking rather than draw suspicion to himself.

"Now that you're up and feeling fit," said Loden in a loose whiskey-slurred voice, "why don't you shinny up that tree, cut your dear departed uncle down and give him a fit burial?"

Jefferies made an effort to appear as drunk as the others. "I'd do about anything for kin. But I don't climb trees. I leave that for monkeys." He tipped his shot glass as if in a toast and only sipped it.

The Russian, Klevo, with his forehead swollen and purple, said in a drunken surly tone, "If you were any kind of rifleman, you wouldn't have to climb like the monkey. You would stand on the ground and cut it with a bullet."

"Hey, that ain't a bad idea, come to think of it," said Loden. "You want your uncle down—here's a good way to do it and at the same time show the rest of us you can handle a gun."

Jefferies tried to wave it off. "Naw, I'm too drunk today," he said, knowing he would allow them to talk him into it.

"Oh, too drunk? Maybe you are not so good with the rifle,

eh, Kid?" Klevo said in his thick accent.

"Or maybe you don't care as much for your uncle as you let on?" Loden said.

Hallit joined in. "If it was my uncle I wouldn't leave him hanging up there."

"Neither would I," said White, still dejected and angry over Prew dropping him as his second in command. "As much trouble as you've caused me and Hallit and some of the others, I think we've got a right to see what you've got when it comes to shooting."

Hesitating a moment longer as if contemplating the matter, Jefferies finally said, "I'll tell you what. I'll cut him down with one shot or the drinking is all on me the rest of the night."

"Hell yes!" said Hallit with a grin. "Now that's being a sport."

"Let's get to it right now," said White.

"But"—Jefferies drew everybody's attention, his finger raised for emphasis—"if I cut him down with one shot, you fellows have to dig the grave for me to bury him in."

"Like hell," White growled.

"What's wrong, White?" Jefferies asked. "Are you afraid of a little bet?" Now it was him doing the needling. "You've never seen me shoot. How do you know I'm not bluffing? If you turn down the bet you'll never know for sure, will you?"

Slamming his hand down on the bar top, White said, "Damn it! I'll take that bet! Get your rifle and let's go see what you've got, Kid."

Sonny Nix cut in. "Let's all make sure we understand the bet. If the Kid loses, he pays for all the drinking. If he wins, Hubbard White digs a grave for the Kid's uncle." He looked all around and asked, "Right, everybody?"

Heads nodded and murmured in agreement. "Wait a minute," said White in protest. "I don't dig it by myself. Everybody helps."

"That's not how I heard it," said Sonny, shaking his head.

"Yeah, Sonny's right," Hallit said to White. "You agreed to dig it, not us."

"All right, then, damn it, I'll dig it by myself!" White fumed. "What's the difference, he ain't going to hit it anyway, first try."

"Are you, Kid?" Loden asked, sizing the Kid up.

"That's the bet," Jefferies said. He tossed back the rest of his drink and walked out front, the men on his heels. At the hitch rail stood Rance Hurley's horse where Jefferies had hitched it when he'd brought it from the stables. A Winchester stood in its saddle boot. Jefferies pulled the rifle out, checked it, and levered a round up into its chamber. "From the middle of the street suit you?"

"Middle of the street." White chuckled darkly. "Well hell yes." He eyed the distance up to the limb above the hanging body, judging it to be over fifty yards. "Take a couple steps closer if it makes you feel better."

"Middle of the street will do," said Jefferies. He took five steps to the middle of the street while White turned and said to the men with a laugh, "Hope everybody here's as thirsty as I am. Kid here will have his part of this deal spent before we ever even cross the border and—"

The single blast from Jefferies' rifle shut White up. The man flinched and turned quickly, in time to see the body drop from the tree and hit the ground like a bag of dirt. "Jesus!" White shouted, taken aback by the suddenness of it.

"Good shot, Kid!" said Loden.

"*Damn* good shot," said Sonny Nix.

"Wait!" said White. "I didn't even see it!"

"You should've been watching," said Nix, "instead of running your mouth."

"That ain't fair!" White protested. "I didn't see him shoot, how do I know he did it?"

"Oh, really?" said Loden. "What do you think, he has

somebody hidden up there? They cut the rope, or what?"

"I didn't see it, how do I know?" said White. He looked around for some support, but found none.

The Kid levered another round into the chamber and said flatly, "Are you saying I cheated?"

Before White could reply, Loden cut in. "Hey, Kid, we all heard him. He's going to crawfish out of this. He bet and he lost." He turned to White. "Now get yourself a shovel and start digging, else we'll tell Prew when he gets back and let him be the one to decide."

White cursed under his breath, then said, "All's I'm saying is I didn't see it, that's all!"

"That's because you looked slower than he shot!" said Loden, not backing off. "Now shut up about it, or take the next step you need, to get the taste of it out of your mouth!" He clamped his hand around his gun butt.

White raised his hands chest high to show he wanted no fight with Loden. Jefferies, Loden and the others watched him stamp off toward the stables. "Come on, Kid, we're buying *you* a drink. I have to admit I was hoping you'd miss so we could all drink this cantina to the ground on your dollars." He gestured a thumb toward White. "But nobody likes a poor sport." He and the others escorted Jefferies to the cantina.

Late in the afternoon, Robert Koch, from the bell tower, spotted Prew leading the column of men up the last hundred yards of winding trail toward Esperanza.

"Here comes Prew! Pass along the word!" Koch shouted down to Sonny Nix, who sat out front of the cantina with a half-naked whore on his lap.

"You heard him, sweetheart," said Sonny. He stood up from the straight-backed chair and the whore fell to the ground. With a shriek, she regained her footing and ran away cursing, covering her naked breasts with a forearm.

Stepping over and sticking his head inside the cantina,

Sonny called out to Loden, "Koch says the boss and the others are riding in. Grab a bottle for the boss. Everybody get out here and welcome them back."

Standing next to Jefferies at the bar, Loden grinned and said, "It's about damn time!" Waving to the bartender for a fresh bottle of whiskey, he said to Jefferies, "Come on, Kid, stick with me. I'll be talking to Prew on your behalf." He took the bottle from the harried bartender and turned toward the door.

"Obliged," said Jefferies. He finished the shot from the glass in his hand and followed Loden out to the street.

When Prew and Cherokee led the men onto the street from the dusty winding trail, Jefferies stood back and observed as Loden and the others crowded around Prew's horse. From where he leaned against a cedar post he watched Prew take a long swig from the bottle Loden handed him, then pass it on to Cherokee Jake.

The bottle of whiskey made its way from Cherokee to Dick Spivey and Indian Frank, who'd ridden double the last few miles. They passed it along, the bottle going from hand to hand until it hit the ground empty. Jefferies watched coolly as Prew stood listening to Loden, the two with their heads together in secrecy. Finally, Prew looked toward Jefferies as he raised a hand to settle his men.

"Kid," he called out, causing all eyes to turn toward Jefferies, "I see you're up and around."

Straightening from against the post, Jefferies stepped forward and said in his young, inexperienced-sounding voice, "Howdy, Mr. Prew. Yes, sir, I'm up and around and ready to do whatever my job calls for." He added humbly, "If that's all the same with you, that is."

"Oh, it's fine with me, Kid," said Prew. "I've checked everything out. We're ready to *ride*." As he spoke he looked around with a grin, seeing the excitement his words caused among the men.

"Whooo-ee!" bellowed White, throwing back his head like a varmint howling at the sky.

"All right!" shouted Sonny, waving his battered hat in the air.

Raising his hand again to settle the men, Prew said to Jefferies, the two stopping with ten feet between them, "So I'm needing all the good men I can get, Kid. How's the shoulder?"

"Never better, Mr. Prew." Jefferies rounded his shoulder to show its fitness. "I'm game for whatever the job takes. Just count me in."

"I'll say he's game and able," Loden cut in. "We all just saw him stand there where you're standing and cut his uncle down with one shot!" He pointed toward the body of Rance Hurley lying on a pushcart a few yards away at the edge of a small cemetery.

Prew looked over at the tree where Rance Hurley had hanged himself. "You cut the rope from here?"

"Yes, sir," said Jefferies, "I did."

"First shot?" Prew asked. He was trying not to look impressed, Jefferies thought.

"First shot, *only* shot!" Loden called out drunkenly, spinning a finger in the air.

"I want *you* to shut up," Prew snapped, with a harsh stare at him. He looked back at Jefferies. "Well, Kid?"

"That's right," said Jefferies. "One shot."

Prew nodded. "Not bad." He stepped in closer to Jefferies. "Look, Kid, about me sending those two looking for you. I want you to know it was nothing against you. I run a tough business. It requires that some things be handled a certain way."

"I understand, sir," said Jefferies, being the polite kid now, showing his youthful manners. "If I'd had any ill feelings, I wouldn't have come back. Me and my uncle came to do a job." He nodded toward the body in the pushcart. "My uncle didn't make it. But I'm sticking until the job's finished."

"That's what I like to hear, Kid," said Prew. "You stick through this job, we've got plenty more coming." Looking around at the men, he said, "As you can see, four men didn't come back with us. They decided they didn't have the stomach for making big money. So we left them behind." He grinned and added, "But I don't expect any of yas here have any objection to getting rich!"

Around them the men hooted and cheered. "See what I mean, Kid?" said Prew. "These men will tell you, living by the gun is the only way to live."

Having slid down from behind Indian Frank's saddle, Dick Spivey stood holding the reins to his injured horse in one hand and a bottle someone had passed to him in his other. Raising the bottle to his lips as he listened to Prew and Jefferies talk, he glanced at the body in the pushcart, then at one of the horses standing in line at the hitch rail. His expression turned curious as he looked back at the body, then at the horse and shook his head as realization set in.

"What's your uncle's name, Kid?" he called out, loud enough to bring attention to himself. The men fell silent.

Jefferies looked at him and said expectantly, "Ward Tidrow, sir. And who are you?"

Also taking on a curious look, Prew said, "This is Dick Spivey, a friend of mine from across the border. His business is information. He rode down here to tell us it's time to go."

Spivey passed the bottle on to one of the men and wiped a hand over his mouth. "Yeah, and I've got some more information," he said, looking with suspicion at Jefferies as he spoke. "The body laying there belongs to Rance Hurley, the most awful jackpotting sonsabitch I ever knew."

"My uncle was no angel, mister," Jefferies countered quickly. "He might have gone under lots of other names, for all I know. But he never jackpotted nobody in his life."

"Rance Hurley never went under any other names. Last I heard he was selling everybody out to the government. I think there is something slippery afoot here."

"You're calling me a liar?" Jefferies asked, taking a step toward Spivey.

"I expect so," Spivey said. He pulled back his riding duster and revealed his holstered Colt. "Unless you can prove otherwise."

"Whoa! Everybody cool down!" said Prew, raising a hand toward the two. He looked at Spivey. "I've heard of Rance Hurley. He betrayed everybody he ever rode with. But how can you say this is him, from this far away? Look at this wretch, his eyes pecked out, half his face eaten by buzzards."

"Because *that's* his barb horse," said Spivey, pointing at the horse at the hitch rail.

Jefferies stiffened, his hand ready to make a grab for his Colt. "Easy now, Kid," Prew cautioned. To Spivey he said, "Horses are apt to wind up anywhere. What else have you got before you offer this man your apology?"

"I've got no apologies," Spivey said confidently. He pointed toward the pushcart. "Somebody bring the cart over here, roll that sonsabitch over and you'll find a stab wound and a scar running half across his back. I know 'cause I put them there, four years ago in Brownsville." He stared hard at Jefferies as he spoke.

Hallit and White had already turned and trotted over to the cart. When they returned, together they tipped the cart instead of handling the half-eaten, odorous remains. "Damn if Spivey ain't right," White said after reaching down with his rifle barrel and raising the tattered remnants of a shirt from the dead man's back. "There's the stab, and the scar, what ain't been et of it."

Jefferies saw the men began to spread out, half circling him. Sonny Nix had disappeared from his sight. "Hold it, everybody, this is crazy," Jefferies said. "I'm here to make myself some money." But as he spoke his hand streaked up with his Colt cocked and ready. Fanning it back and forth he said, "This man doesn't know what he's talking about."

The half circle of men advanced a step in spite of his cocked gun. Prew took a step to the side and said in a low growl, "Take him, Sonny."

Jefferies started to turn, but he was too late. Sonny Nix's rifle butt came forward with a hard solid punch to the back of Jefferies' head. The young lawman crumpled to the ground like a house of cards, his Colt falling from his hand.

Across the street, hidden from sight, Sabio had to grab Caridad to keep her from running out to Jefferies. As three of Prew's men picked him up and carried him inside the cantina, Sabio lowered his hand from Caridad's mouth and loosened his arm around her waist. "Do not try to go to him. It will only make matters worse. If he could he would tell you to stay put and keep away from these men," Sabio whispered.

"But we must help him!" Caridad said.

"Yes, and we will," said Sabio. "But first we must ask ourselves how."

"With your power!" said Caridad frantically. "Use your power to keep them from killing him! You must." Tears welled in her dark eyes.

"Caridad," said Sabio, trying to calm her. "My power is gone, child. Can you not see that I have lost it?" He gestured toward the men in the street as they filed into the cantina. "Even if I still had it, the power to do good has never worked for me against evil such as this."

Caridad pulled free of him. "I have come to realize that your power, your gift, works only when you need it to work for yourself!"

"No, Caridad, that is not so," said Sabio, crestfallen to hear her talk this way. "I have done too many bad things and it has caused me to lose my power."

"I know of these bad things," Caridad said. "Louisa has admitted them to me. But these things are things people do because they are weak, or frightened or lonely. God does not punish for being weak or lonely or imperfect. That is the punishment we deliver to ourselves."

"Louisa has told you—" Sabio hid his face in his hands for a moment. But then he raised his face, stared in her eyes and said, "All right, I will do what I can to save your young man. But if I save him, you must promise me to leave here with him and never return."

Caridad took Sabio's hand between hers and held it to her bosom. "I will do as you ask, only save him, Sabio. Please save him, *mi hombre santo*."

"Your holy man . . ." said Sabio, repeating her words. Reaching his hand up from between hers and cupping her cheek, he said gently, "Always I have been *your* blessed holy man, and yet to myself, I have always been the tortured fool." He looked at the dark open doorway of the cantina.

"Don't worry, my darling Caridad. I will save him, somehow." He spoke silently to himself as he gazed off across the endless hills east of Esperanza. *Ranger Burrack, where are you?* But he quickly stopped him-self from even hoping that the ranger might show up at a time like this. By now the ranger would be far away, in his own territory.

You have misused your power and now it has forsaken you, Sabio told himself. *No such miracle will ever come your way again. . . .*

Yet, as if in defiance of his inner voice, he said to himself, *Ranger, if you can hear me, you must come back. You must. . . .*

CHAPTER 21

Inside the cantina, after a long swig of whiskey, Spivey corked the bottle and slipped it into his duster pocket. "That's it for me," he said to Prew. "I'm lighting out of here while there's still enough daylight to get me down the hillside. He looked at Jefferies, who sat tied to a chair in the middle of the dirt floor, his battered face bowed over his bloody chest.

Beneath the sound of the men drinking and laughing, and the snappy whine of accordion music, Prew asked, "What's your hurry? I thought you needed a couple of days for your horse's leg to heal."

"I did," said Spivey. "But that was before I realized you've got lawmen sniffing at you." He nodded toward Jefferies just as Loden stepped forward, took a handful of the battered man's hair and raised his face. "I'm glad I could help, but now it's time to say *adios*." Spivey grinned. "When there's a lawman around I break out in hives and itch and twitch something awful."

"What about that good horse of yours?" Prew asked, as a loud backhanded slap from Loden sent Jefferies' head bobbing sideways from its impact.

"Indian Frank had an extra horse," said Spivey. "We managed to dicker up a trade."

Prew nodded. "Then you have a good ride back. Tell Sherard I said, 'Obliged' and that he'll be hearing from us real soon."

"I'll tell him," said Spivey. He turned and sauntered to the chair where Jefferies sat struggling to remain conscious.

Bending down, he grinned smugly into the bloody swollen face. "You try to have yourself a good evening in spite of its many pitfalls and obstacles, you hear?"

"I'll . . . try," Jefferies moaned.

Spivey chuckled and said to Prew, "He's got a sense of humor, this one." He thumped Jefferies on top of his head, like testing a ripe melon.

"He won't have any *humor* left when I'm through with him," said Loden, rubbing the back of his sore hand as Spivey left the cantina.

At the bar Sonny refilled Cherokee Jake's shot glass and said to him, "I'm glad you and me got things straightened out between us. It was him who killed your uncle Wind River Dan." He jerked his head toward Jefferies at about the time Loden slapped the hapless lawman again. "Not that I saw it. But hell, he's the one who had Dan's horse when we took it from him. It had to be him who killed him. Who else?" He shrugged at the end of his lie.

Cherokee only eyed him closely for a moment before saying, "We're going to let it ride that way for now, Sonny. If I get any other notions about it, I'll be sure and let you know."

Sonny returned his stare, picked up his glass and his bottle of whiskey and moved away. Robert Koch saw what had happened and sidled up to Sonny as he found himself a new spot at the bar. "All this lawman did was buy us some time," he said. "If we're smart we'll kill Cherokee before he guts us both, the way he did Sibbs. He's fast and he's sneakin' and we ain't clear of him yet."

Looking toward the table where he knew Cherokee had killed Sibbs, Sonny said, "I know you're right, Robert. Let's watch one another's backside until we can get it done."

In the middle of the floor, Sway Loden backhanded Jefferies across his face again, then stepped back rubbing his blood-splattered hand. "I knew something wasn't right about this sonsabitch. I would've seen it soon enough."

At the bar Niger Elmsly called out, "Yeah? When? About the time he led all of us up onto a gallows and slipped a noose around our necks?"

The cantina roared with laughter. Loden fumed at Jefferies, "Let's see how you like the taste of gun metal!" Slipping his Colt from his holster, he drew it back to swing.

"All right, Loden," said Prew, "that's enough for now. If you kill him, he's of no use to us."

"What use is he anyway?" Loden asked, checking himself down. He slid the pistol back into his holster with his sore and swelling gun hand.

"I'll be sure and consider your question before I make a decision," Prew said coldly. "Meanwhile, keep breaking your hand on his face if you want to, but he lives till I say otherwise."

"Sorry, boss," Loden said sheepishly, backing away and working his stiff swollen fingers.

While Prew had turned toward Loden, Dan Farr stepped over beside Cherokee at the bar and said quietly, "Prew said if anybody asks about the four men who didn't come back with us, we're supposed to say they changed their minds and cut out. But what if that ain't good enough?"

Giving him a hard look, Cherokee said, "If that ain't good enough, you tell them to come see me." He thumped himself on the chest. "I'll make sure it's good enough for them." Out of nowhere Cherokee's big knife flashed in the dim light and plunged into the bar top. "You understand?"

"Whoa! Yes! Yes, I do!" Farr backed away quickly, shot glass in hand, and didn't stop until he stood at the far end of the bar, able to keep an eye on Cherokee without being noticed.

Out front of the cantina Spivey had gigged his newly acquired horse up into a trot just to get a feel for the animal before heading down the winding trail. Satisfied with his trade after putting it through its paces for a half mile, he slowed the horse to a walk, patted its neck and took the bottle of whiskey from his duster pocket.

"You'll do," he said to the animal. Pulling the cork from the bottle, he half turned in his saddle toward Esperanza and raised it in a toast. "Here's to hope!" he called out, referring to the English translation of *Esperanza*. He took a long swig, then let out a deep hiss and said in a whiskey-dulled voice, "*Hope* you all go to hell and rot there!"

He cackled with laughter, started to stick the cork into the bottle, but upon staring at the swirling amber liquid for a second he said, "Don't mind if I do." He raised the bottle in another toast, this one toward the darkening evening sky. "Here's to you up there who wish me well—if you don't you can go to—"

His word stopped short. The ranger had him. Behind him in the saddle, Sam tightened his arm around his throat and jammed the tip of his gun barrel into his ear. "Rein him down, mister," Sam said sternly.

"Jesus!" Spivey shrieked. "Don't shoot! I've got no money! You can have the horse, the saddle, my rifle! Hell, my boots! They're almost new!"

"Slide down," said Sam, already pulling him down from the saddle with him. "Who are you, mister?" he demanded. Sam pulled Spivey's pistol from his holster and tossed it over beside the high trail. Spivey eyed the gun lying in the dirt.

"Who am I?" He sounded surprised. "Is that why you waylaid me? You wanted to know my name?"

"Not if I have to ask you twice." Sam made sure Spivey heard the Colt cock in his ear.

"All right, take it easy. My name is Henry Akerman. I'm up here scouting for cattle."

"Spell it," Sam said.

"What? 'Cattle'?" said Spivey. "C-A-T-T—"

"Your name, mister. Quit wasting time," Sam demanded, jamming the gun barrel more firmly.

"It's not Akerman." Spivey let out a sigh in defeat. "You're that ranger, ain't you?"

"Yes, I am," said Sam. "Now who are you? This time pick a name you can spell."

"I'm Dick Spivey. So what? I'm not on that list I've heard so much about."

"Not yet you're not, but I can fix that. What are you doing up here?" Sam asked.

"I told you. I'm—"

"Don't start," Sam snapped. He pushed Spivey an arm's length away. Spivey turned facing him with his hands raised chest high. "I know you came here to tell Prew it's time to raid the munitions train," Sam said, playing a hunch. "If you tell me who else is on Prew's payroll and when the train comes through, you'll ride away from here. If you want to be tight-lipped I'll put a bullet in you and go on. That's your only choices today."

Spivey took a step back toward the edge of the trail, hoping to get closer to his gun before making a leap for it. "All right, Ranger." He shrugged. "I don't owe Prew nothing. The train is running across the badlands in four days. Prew knows he's got to hit it near Choking Wells at the water stop."

"I already know the name of the other inside men working for Prew," Sam said, bluffing. "But you tell me anyway. Don't let me catch you lying."

"Art Smith—want me to spell it?" Spivey said smugly.

"Wrong name. So long, mister," said Sam, pokerfaced, knowing this one would try to lie first. He leveled the Colt at Spivey's chest.

"Wait!" said Spivey, seeing the ranger's gun hand tighten. "It's *Sherard*. His name is Ike Sherard!"

Sam shook his head. "You're lying when the truth could've saved your life, mister."

"Wait, please, Ranger, for God sakes!" said Spivey, seeing the look on Sam's face. "It *is* Ike Sherard. I swear it is! He used to be sheriff in Texas. Now he's the rail station manager who handles all the military shipments running along the border! If that's not the name you have, somebody has given you the wrong information!"

"Ike Sherard," the ranger muttered to himself. It made sense. He'd heard of Sherard, seen him a couple of times; and lately he'd heard the man had gone over to the other side of the law. "Who's the other?" he asked, not stopping until he had everything he wanted to know.

"I don't know," said Spivey. "Some army sergeant. I've never been able to find out his name. Sherard won't let it out who he is."

It stood to reason Sherard didn't want anybody to know his contact, Sam thought. The name would come up when the time was right. That was Jefferies' job. He let his gun hand relax a little, having bluffed the truth out of the belligerent outlaw. "Four days, you say?"

"Four days," said Spivey. "And that's the truth too." He inched backward as he spoke. It didn't matter that he told the ranger the truth, he thought. The ranger wasn't leaving here alive. "But I don't think it's going to do you any good knowing it. You can't stop it by yourself, and your partner is in no shape to help you."

"What partner?" Sam asked sharply. "What are you talking about?"

"Prew's got him, Ranger," said Spivey. "No point in denying it." Spivey grinned slyly. "They've already beat the hell out of him. Your plan is out of the bag. Anything you didn't want him to tell, he's told by now." He inched backward another short step as he spoke, seeing the news had hit the ranger hard.

Sam saw him turn and make a dive for the gun at the edge of the trail. He didn't want to fire the Colt this close to town, but now he had no choice. He leveled the gun quickly. But he held up on firing as he saw Spivey's dive send him sliding in the loose dirt, picking up the gun on his way, then failing to stop at the edge. Sam stood frozen for a second, hear-ing a long scream trail downward, then stop abruptly.

He walked to the edge and looked down. Spivey lay dead on a rock ledge eighty feet below, his black riding duster spread out around him, a startled look on his face. Sam shook his head and holstered his Colt. There was not a moment to spare. He had to get into Esperanza and get Jefferies out of there if he wasn't already dead. Walking to Spivey's horse, he took off its saddle and bridle and tossed them into the brush.

"Get!" he said, slapping the horse on its rump. He realized how many horses he'd sent galloping off in the Mexican hills lately.

Riding in closer to Esperanza in the fading evening light, he observed the empty bell tower through his telescope from the cover of brush and low-standing juniper. With Prew and his riders back in town, he speculated that a night of drinking lay ahead. Yet, even with the tower unmanned and Jefferies' life in question, he stayed put until after dark before slipping into town.

He left the two horses near the spot where he'd last met with Jefferies and walked quietly through the trees and foliage until he'd made his way to the dark empty street. In the bell tower he saw the glow of a cigar and realized someone had once again taken up the guard position. But that was all right. He intended to stick to the shadows behind the cantina, find Sabio and see what he had to do to get Jefferies out of Prew's hands.

Following Jefferies' directions to the third small adobe on the right in the alleyway behind the cantina, Sam eased up to an open window and looked inside. This was the place. Inside, Caridad and a stout older Mexican woman huddled in a circling glow of firelight at a small hearth. He saw the woman's arms encircling Caridad, comforting her.

At a wooden table in the center of the dirt floor, Sabio

sat bowed over the flame of a small candle, his fingertips to his temples as if in deep contemplation, or prayer. Looking all around the shadows in the dimly flickering firelight and seeing no sign of Jefferies, Sam whispered softly through the window, "Sabio. Sabio. It's me, the ranger."

Sabio bolted upright in his chair, his face turned to the ceiling. His hands lifted into the air as if paying homage to heaven. "Oh, Ranger, yes! Yes, I hear you! Thank God I hear you!"

"Over here, Sabio," Sam said a little louder. "At the window."

Sabio turned quickly, facing him in the moonlight at the open window. Making the sign of the cross toward heaven, he collected himself, slipped from his chair and hurried to the window. He clasped the ranger's gloved hand and squeezed it tightly, saying with tearful eyes, "I knew you would hear me. I knew you would come. I still have my faith!" His gaze steadied on Sam. "You did hear me, did you not?" he asked.

Sam only stared, having no idea what Sabio was talking about. The old priest waved it away. "It does not matter if you heard me or not. God heard me. Sometimes he goes about his will in strange mysterious ways."

Across the room Louisa and Caridad had heard the two men's voices and moved closer to the window, watching and listening with the same awestricken looks on their faces.

"I don't know what's gone on here, but I came to get Jefferies."

"See?" said Sabio, half turning toward the women, an arm gesturing toward the ranger as proof once again that his mystical power had worked.

Sam began to understand that the old priest had been praying for his return, but he had no time to dwell on the matter. "I need your help," he said to Sabio.

"Yes, of course, anything!" said Sabio, offering Sam a hand as he climbed in through the open window.

"Can you create a diversion for me?" Sam asked.

Sabio shrugged in shame. "Some would say my entire life has been a diversion of sorts."

Sam let his self-debasing remark pass. "Will these men allow you among them?" he asked, looking toward a straw sombrero hanging on a wall peg.

"I—I think so," Sabio said hesitantly. "Why? What would you have me do?"

Looking toward the open hearth, Sam said, "It's night and there's a chill moving in. Let's see what good we can make of that."

CHAPTER 22

Inside the cantina the drinking continued. Half-naked whores twirled to the lively sound of the accordion. Prew's men clapped, stamped their feet and tossed money at the girls. Dark bare breasts jiggled and flashed in the glow of lanterns and candlelight. Knocked out in his chair, Jefferies sat propped against a table.

One of the men had taken a black-and-white checked harlequin mask from the wall behind the bar and pulled it down over his swollen eyes. Blood trickled from beneath the mask like dark tears. "Let me go on and cut his damn throat," Cherokee said to Prew at the far end of the bar. "Loden was right. He's no use to us."

"Are you cocksure of that?" Prew asked above the rim of his whiskey glass.

"I'm damn cocksure of it," Cherokee said in a surge of drunken confidence.

"You might be right," said Prew. "But wouldn't you hate to kill a man tonight while you're *cocksure,* and find out in the morning that you were dead wrong?"

"Is that one of them questions that's meant to snarl a man up and make him look like a fool?" Cherokee asked. "Because if it is—"

Prew cut him off. "No, it's not a trick question," he said. "I like to keep a man alive long enough to decide whether or not he's of any value to me. In this case you and Loden are right. He's not." Prew shrugged, feeling his whiskey. "Cut his throat if it fills any inner need you might have."

"What does that mean?" asked Cherokee.

"It means go *ahead*, damn it," said Prew. "Kill him and get it out of your system."

"That's more like it." Cherokee straightened up at the bar, loosening his big knife from where it stood gleaming, stuck in the bar top. "I like things said to me in plain English."

But before he could turn and leave the end of the bar, Prew's hand on his forearm stopped him. "Look who's coming here," Prew said in a low tone, nodding toward the stooped figure entering with a tall load of firewood in his arms, the straw sombrero barely visible above it. "I suppose he's going to try and set Jefferies free while we're not looking."

"Good luck," said Cherokee, looking over where Jefferies sat unconscious in the propped-back chair. "He's too knocked out to walk anyway, let alone what I'm fixing to do to him." He started to go over to Jefferies' chair, but again Prew stopped him.

"What's your hurry?" Prew asked. "Let's watch the old *brujo* make his move." He gave Cherokee a strange patronizing grin and said, "That way you get to kill two men with your big sharp knife."

Cherokee just stared at him, not knowing how he should take his remark. But he settled at the bar and let the big knife slump in his hand. The two watched the crafty interloper move back and forth, bowed at the hearth, stacking some of the wood to one side of the blackened open fire pit and jamming two logs into the glowing embers.

"You called him a *brujo*," Cherokee said quietly between them, watching the hearth closely. "Do you think he really is a witch?"

"I don't know," said Prew, "but lots of these ignorant townsfolk think he is. That's all that mattered to him, I suppose. The accordion player told one of the whores that he used to be a priest, but he couldn't keep his pecker under his robe. Stuck it in anything that moved."

"Amen to that." Cherokee chuckled, laying his knife down on the bar top. He watched the hearth as he listened to Prew.

"The accordion player told her that the church hated to lose him because he has some kind of hocus-pocus power or some such nonsense. Instead of getting rid of him outright, they made him a monk and sent him up to live with some other monks in the old Spanish mission. But he spent more time in the women's bedrooms of Esperanza than he did at doing whatever monks do. They finally tossed him out of the church altogether."

"So now he tends fire in the cantina?" Cherokee asked curiously.

"I think he just started tending to the hearth tonight," Prew said, giving a knowing grin.

Cherokee looked across the back of the cantina as if searching for Caridad. "Wonder where that skinny gal is who's usually with him."

"You mean his daughter?" Prew said.

"His *daughter?*" Cherokee looked surprised. "Damn, he sure did keep that thing of his busy."

"That's what the whore said," Prew continued. "She said he was bedding with a young woman he'd known before he became a priest. He got her fixed up with child, then killed her husband so he could have her and the baby. But then she died too."

"A priest killed a man?" said Cherokee, staring at the glow of firelight growing stronger in the hearth, bits of fiery ember racing up the stone chimney.

"I wouldn't put much faith in what a whore says, though, especially one all the way from Mexico City," Prew concluded. "What would she know about things here in Esperanza?"

Cherokee tossed back a drink of whiskey and set his shot glass down. "*Brujo*, priest, monk, magician—they're all the same to me. There's nothing to all that foolery anyway. A man gets what he can take from this world, by gun, knife, or whatever means he has to. If I was God I wouldn't care what happened to anybody, long as I got what was coming to me." Staring coldly toward the figure stooped down in front of the hearth sweeping up bits of charred cinder, he added, "Why don't I ease over there right now and put his fire out for good."

Prew threw back a shot of whiskey and said, "Hell, go on, enjoy yourself."

Yet once again, before Cherokee could walk away from the bar, Klevo called out from his guard position in the bell tower, "Fire in town!"

"So what?" Prew said to Cherokee. "Let it burn." But no sooner than he'd said it, Clifford Elvey stuck his head in the front door and cried out loudly, "Fire at the stables!"

"Damn it, let's go!" Prew shouted, racing for the front door. He stopped at the open doorway and shoved Dan Farr and Matt Harkens back toward the bar. "You two, stay here. Watch him!" He nodded toward Jefferies. Then he turned and ran ahead of the others toward the fiery orange glow above the stables.

As soon as the other men had left the cantina, the barkeeper looked toward the hearth and said in a frightened voice, "Sabio, you fool, what are you doing?"

At the open doorway of the cantina, the two men stood craning their necks toward the flames. Upon hearing the barkeeper they turned quickly, in time to see the Colt aimed at them from ten feet away. "Cut him loose," the ranger demanded, pushing the straw sombrero up off of his forehead. He gave one short nod toward Jefferies sitting slumped in the chair.

Harkens and Farr had raised their hands only an inch after seeing the Colt covering them. They stepped slowly inside the cantina and spread apart a few feet instead of doing what the ranger told them to do. "Can you really kill a man, *Padre?*" said Farr. "I mean, pull a trigger and watch the life go out of his eyes. What will God think of you doing—"

"Damn it, Dan! Don't you *get it?*" said Harkens, staring at Farr in stunned disbelief. "He's no priest! He's a lawman!"

Farr looked confused for a moment, then recovered and said quickly, "Whoever he is, he's not fool enough to risk shooting that Colt and bringing all the men back here, are you, *Padre?*" He gave a dark grin, his hand lowering to just above his gun butt.

Padre . . . ? The ranger stared at him, his first shot hitting him squarely in the forehead. The bullet sent Farr's hat and a spray of blood and bone matter spewing above the open doorway. But even as the first shot exploded, the second shot nailed Harkens in the chest as his hand lifted his gun from its holster. He slammed back against the wall beside the doorway and slid down, saying to Farr, "You stupid . . . son of . . . a bitch!"

"What the hell is this?" Prew said when he arrived at the stables and saw no sign of any fire, but only an orange glow moving away quickly on the other side of the long lean-to stables.

"That's a wagon!" said Cherokee. He stared at the moving orange glow, seeing it get smaller, as if somebody was struggling to extinguish it. "Want us to chase it down?" he asked.

Before Prew could answer, the two shots echoed from the cantina and he turned, cursing loudly in revelation. "That damn monk!" Pistol still in hand, he waved everybody back toward the cantina. "Come on, hurry it up!"

"What about the fire wagon?" Cherokee shouted, already running along behind him, but staring back over his shoulder.

"Forget it!" Prew shouted angrily. "We've been tricked! Two of yas stay here, guard the horses. We can't lose the horses, not this close to the train job!" Behind him Indian Frank Beeker and Niger Elmsly slowed, stopped and turned in the darkness, looking all around the dark shadows surrounding the stables.

In the cantina, behind the bar, the barkeeper helped the ranger cut the rope from around Jefferies and load him up over the ranger's shoulder. "I am sorry I called out to you and gave you away," the barkeeper said. "I truly thought you were Sabio, and that you had lost your mind—his mind, that is."

"Don't apologize," Sam said, moving toward the rear door. He knew that Prew and his men had heard the shots and were by now on their way. "And don't take a beating over this. If Prew asks, tell him it was me, and that I took the Kid with me. You don't know where. Tell him I said Spivey told me everything. He can come on out and face me tonight, in the darkness if him and his men feel up to the job."

The barkeeper's eyes widened as he pulled the rear door open. "You really want me to tell him this?"

"I'm obliged if you will," said Sam, knowing that Prew had to weigh his choices tonight. Should he come after him and the wounded Kid, or get ready for the big job that he knew awaited him and his men across the border. "*Gracias*," said Sam. He stepped out through the rear door and disappeared into the darkness.

A moment later, as the barkeeper stood behind the bar wiping it with a wet rag, Prew rushed in, his men right behind him. Taking only an unsurprised glance at the empty chair where Jefferies had sat, he said expectantly, "All right, what did he say?"

"First of all, *Señor* Prew," said the barkeeper, "I do not like to get involved in troubles between two men who are—"

"Hey, Hosea! Will you tell him quicker if I lop off a couple of your fingers?" Cherokee asked, stepping toward the bar with the big knife gripped firmly.

"*Por favor, Señor* Prew! He said tell you that *Señor* Spivey told him everything. He say come face him in the dark if you and your men feel up to the job!" the barkeeper said, speaking rapidly in broken English.

"The ranger . . ." Prew said in an exasperated sigh.

But on the floor next to the open doorway, Matt Harkens, his hands clasped to his chest, said in a rasping halting voice, "Yeah, it was . . . that damned . . . ranger."

Prew looked down at Harkens in contempt. He noted the smear of blood running down the wall above him. "Well, thank you, Harkens. Now why is it you're dying and he's still alive?" In a fit of anger, he drew his gun and shot the dying man four times in his bloody chest.

The men stood staring in silence. After a tense pause Cherokee asked cautiously, "Want us to get after him?"

Prew stood mulling it over. Tomorrow at dawn he'd have to have himself and his men on the trail, headed for the border. He looked at the two dead men on the floor, knowing he'd been left two men short. Looking at the barkeeper, he asked, "Is that the way he said it? He said to tell me to come face him *tonight* in the dark?"

"*Sí*, that is how he said it, *señor*."

"Then that settles it." Prew uncocked the gun in his hand.

Looking uncertain, Cherokee asked, "You mean we're all going after him, right?"

"*No*," Prew said firmly. "That's what he wants us to do. Spivey has jackpotted us."

"Yeah, well, let's go kill the dirty lawdog and be done with it," Cherokee said, seeming puzzled, not understanding Prew's reasoning.

"And he'll whittle us down by another man or two," Prew growled. "And every man we lose fighting him in the dark, that's one less man we'll have when we need every gun we can get!" He scowled at Cherokee, his revolver still hanging in his hand. "Use your head, Jake! We've got a big job coming up! He knows about it!"

Cherokee looked surprised. "So, we're not going to do anything? We let him walk in here, kill two of us, and take the kid from under our noses. We're doing nothing?"

Prew fought back the urge to put one of his last two bullets in Cherokee's belly. But he took a deep breath and let it out slowly and with it some of his killing rage. "Yes, we're going to do something, all right," he said. "We're going to get our horses, saddle up and get the hell out of here tonight, instead of waiting till in the morning."

CHAPTER 23

Not wanting to risk Prew's men finding them at Louisa's home, Sam carried Jefferies to where he'd left the horses hitched in the cover of trees and brush. On the way there he'd heard Jefferies moan and felt him try to raise his head. "Don't worry, Jefferies. It's me, the ranger," Sam said. "I'm getting you out of here."

"What about . . . Prew?" Jefferies asked.

"I don't think he'll be coming after us," said Sam. He eased him gently down against a tree near the horses, stepped over and took a canteen from his saddle horn. "I told him to come face me in the dark," Sam continued as he jerked the bandanna from around his neck and wet it with canteen water. "He's got a lot at stake. He can't afford to lose any more men."

"That was . . . good thinking," Jefferies managed to say. "Now, if I . . . just knew where—"

"Near Choking Wells at the water tank," Sam said, interrupting him. He stared at the harlequin mask on Jefferies' face, eased it off over his bruised forehead and laid it aside. "It all happens four days from now." He pressed the wet bandanna carefully against Jefferies' swollen eyes.

"That much I overheard." Jefferies groaned. "Good work, Ranger." He strained to open his purple eyelids and look at Sam. "Too bad we couldn't . . . find out who is working with him inside."

"Ever hear of a former lawman named Ike Sherard?" Sam asked, wiping the young captain's swollen face gently.

With a moan Jefferies said, "No . . . but I'm betting you

210

have."

The ranger managed a thin smile. "That's right. I have. Spivey, the man I caught coming out of town, told me everything I wanted to know about Prew."

"Spivey is the one . . . who ruined it for me," Jefferies said. "Is he . . . ?" He let his words trail off.

"Yep," said Sam.

"Good work, again."

"I didn't kill him," said Sam. "I was on the verge of having to, but he slid off of the hillside, landed on a stone ledge."

"Well, that's . . . one more out of the way," Jefferies replied through split and swollen lips. "I suppose you got the name . . . of the other inside man too?"

"No," said Sam. "The other is an army sergeant. Spivey said Sherard won't let his name out to anybody."

"It figures," said Jefferies. "If Sherard let these outlaws know his connection . . . they wouldn't need him anymore."

"Feeling better?" Sam asked, noting how Jefferies' voice had already sounded stronger.

"Yes, I do, just knowing we're about to get these rats rounded into the same trap." He looked closely at Sam through swollen eyes. "You stored the dynamite in a good place, didn't you?"

"Yes," said Sam. "I took care of everything. Are you going to be able to ride come morning?"

"Nothing feels broken," Jefferies said, laying a hand to his ribs as if checking himself. "I just took a hard beating. Lucky for me you showed up when you did. I've got a feeling things were going to get a lot worse."

"Lucky for both of us, Sabio set up a diversion on the other side of the stables, gave me the time I needed to get you out of there."

"That's twice he has saved my hide," Jefferies said in a soft tone.

From the edge of the trees, Sam heard a rustle of brush

and swung around toward it, his Colt out and cocked in one motion. "It is us, Ranger," said Sabio, stepping from the trees into the open moonlight.

"Speaking of Sabio . . ." the ranger said. He slipped his Colt back into its holster.

Caridad walked at Sabio's side. A horse walked behind him, its reins dangling from Sabio's hand. "If not for this noisy horse, you would never have heard us coming," he said.

"I know that, Sabio," said Sam. "Much obliged for your help. I hope all went well for you?"

"Yes. I built the fire in three whiskey barrels in the bed of a buckboard wagon the way you asked me to. Caridad drove the wagon. By the time I rode away the barrels themselves had caught fire." He stopped and stood with the ranger's shirt and trousers sagging down around him. His free hand held the loose trousers at the waist. "Now, I must have my clothes back," he said. "I have gone so long in a robe and sandals I can wear nothing else."

Beside him, Caridad stepped forward. Upon seeing Jefferies' battered face in the moonlight, she gasped and ran to him. Sam stepped back out of her way as she took the wet bandanna and held it gently to Jefferies' cheek. "What have they done to you, *mi querido?*" she whispered tearfully.

Stepping away from the two, Sam stood beside Sabio, who said under his breath, "Look. She calls this one her darling." He sighed. "If my Caridad cares so much for him, he must be a good man."

"I believe him to be," said Sam. The two stepped into the trees and exchanged clothing.

"I must tell you, Ranger, on the way here I saw Prew and his men riding out of Esperanza," said Sabio, pulling his robe down over him and straightening it.

"So he decided to leave tonight," Sam said. "Then Jefferies and I need to get mounted and move out ourselves. I don't want to lose Prew and his men." He walked from the trees to where Jefferies lay with his head cradled in Caridad's arms.

Catching up to him, Sabio said, "But he cannot ride tonight. Look at the shape he is in."

Jefferies raised his head from Caridad's lap and said, staring through swollen eyes, "Oh, yes, I can ride." He sat the rest of the way up and took the wet bandanna from Caridad's hand. Struggling to his feet, he said to Caridad, "The fact is I'm a lawman, Caridad. I'll explain it all to you later. But right now, the ranger and I have to get after these men. They are about to commit a terrible crime against the American government."

Caridad stood up too. "If you go, I am going with you," she said firmly.

"I'm afraid that's out of the question, Caridad," said Jefferies. "Things are going to get dangerous—"

"If you do not take me along, I will follow," she said, cutting him off. "Sabio will not let me go alone. So he will come too." She looked back and forth between Jefferies and the ranger, then asked, "Why are we wasting time here? If you must go, let's go."

"Sam?" said Jefferies, looking to the ranger for guidance.

"Just as far as the border trail," said Sam, looking at Sabio, then at Caridad. "But you both have to stop there, without any argument about it."

"*Sí*, we will stop and await your return at the border trail," said Sabio.

Helping Jefferies into his saddle, the four rode quietly into Esperanza, where even in the middle of the night, the townsfolk had ventured out warily and looked all around, making sure Prew and his mercenaries had left. When the townsfolk saw the whores from Mexico City walk toward them on the dusty street, many picked up sticks and rocks and stared menacingly at the bedraggled women.

"What do you *putas* want?" one of the townswomen called out to the dark shadowy figures.

"We have no way home," one of the whores replied, holding a blanket wrapped around her naked breasts. "*El capitán* told us we would have transportation."

Dark laughter rose and fell. "As you can see, *el capitán* is not here," the same woman called out.

A farmer in his wide straw sombrero stepped up beside the woman, holding a large rock in his hand. "Now it is time you pay for disgracing us with your nakedness, your drinking and your fornication on our streets!" he called out to the whores.

But as he raised the rock threateningly, Sabio, Caridad and the two lawmen rode in out of the darkness and Sabio shouted in authoritative tone, "Jorge! People! What are you doing to these women?"

Seeing Sabio, the man dropped his stone and stood looking ashamed of himself. The other townsfolk did the same. "The mercenaries are gone, *Padre*," Jorge said, looking down at the ground and only facing Sabio with quick glances.

"Jorge, Jorge." Sabio shook his head patiently. "Why must I keep telling you, I am no longer a priest?"

Shrugging, Jorge said, "You are still my *padre*." He swept an arm toward the others. "You are always our *padre*."

"What can I do?" Sabio said to the ranger before swinging down from his saddle and walking over to the farmer. "If I am your *padre*, tell me what is going on here."

"They have left these *putas* stranded with us," Jorge said, gesturing toward the women who stood in the dark with their heads lowered.

"Oh?" Sabio looked at the whores, then back to Jorge and the other townsfolk. "Then, I say make them welcome here until I return and can help them find a way home." He turned and smiled at the whores.

"But we have never allowed these sort of women to live and practice their profession in Esperanza," Jorge said quietly. "I don't think we can do what you ask."

Sabio bent down and picked up the stone he'd dropped

and said grimly, "Then who will cast the first stone? Certainly I cannot!" He looked all around at the gathering, seeing Louisa look down to avoid his eyes. "Can you, Jorge? Are you an innocent, without sin?" He held the rock out for him, but Jorge folded his hands, refusing to take it.

"No, I am not without sin, as you know, *Padre*," Jorge said. "We thought this was what we should do. Forgive us, por favor."

"I forgive you, of course, even though I am no longer a *padre*," said Sabio. Making a quick sign of the cross toward the man, he added, "And I pray God will forgive you." He looked around at the townspeople. "I forgive each and every one of you." Turning toward the whores he said, "And I will forgive each of you, *personally*. As soon as I return from my journey with these two American lawmen, I will hear your sins, and we will spend some time together—"

"Sabio," Caridad said from atop the horse she shared with Jefferies, "we must go. There is much we have to do to prepare for the trail."

The four traveled throughout the night and the following day, stopping only long enough to rest and water the horses and themselves. They carefully stayed back far enough to avoid being seen by Prew and his men, at the same time keeping their trail dust in sight. Before leaving Esperanza Jefferies purchased a horse and a tough little donkey from Jorge. Caridad rode the horse. Sam secured the leather supply bag of dynamite and grenades to the donkey's back with lengths of rope.

When they arrived at the border trail, the four riders made camp for the night. The next morning the two lawmen headed out before dawn, leaving Sabio and Caridad to await their return. The following morning as they broke camp and prepared for the trail, Jefferies felt both of his battered cheeks and said, "You might think it sounds foolish, but I believe just being around Sabio has caused me to heal quicker."

Sam looked at him. "Is this Sabio the priest or Sabio the *brujo* we're talking about?"

"I know he's a hard one to figure out," said Jefferies. "But it's a fact that he stopped me from bleeding to death and took out the bullet with his bare hands. I saw it with my own eyes."

"Not to cast aspersions," said Sam, "but there are Hindus on the other side of the world who have been doing that sort of thing for hundreds of years."

"Holy men?" Jefferies said.

"Some say they are."

"Then that only proves my point," said Jefferies. "If they are holy men, then why isn't Sabio too?"

"I never said he's not," Sam replied. "I believe there are powers greater than what we understand. But since you saw and felt that power firsthand as you did, I suppose it's only natural that you believe it stronger than I might."

"I see what you mean," said Jefferies. "It's easier to believe something is real once you've held it in your hand."

"Yep," said Sam. "But all that aside, I expect there is something holy about saving a life, regardless if a man does it with his bare hands or with a tray full of surgical instruments."

"What do you make of Sabio?" Jefferies asked, keeping watch on the distant rise of dust as they neared the border.

"He's a man born with extraordinary gifts," Sam replied, gazing ahead. "Neither he nor the rest of the world understood them or knew what to do with them. The church leaders saw his power and tried to use it to prove their own beliefs. But they expected Sabio to be perfect, and the man is far from it. He thought he had to be perfect too."

"None of us are perfect," said Jefferies.

"But because Sabio thought he had to be, every time he fell he thought God was punishing him, taking away his gift." Sam shook his head. "Now he goes from thinking one day that he has his gift back, stronger than ever, to thinking the next day that he's lost it for good."

"What exactly is his gift?" Jefferies asked. "I know he can stop bleeding. But what else is it? What is this power?"

"I expect he'd have to be the one to tell you what it is," Sam replied. "It's all about faith somehow. I expect if he really knew what it is, he wouldn't be so tortured by it."

Jefferies shook his head. "So, the believers, the faithful in Esperanza whose lives he's touched, still call him *padre*."

"And the ones who don't believe, or who have no faith in anything or anybody, call him a *brujo*—a witch."

"What do you call him, Ranger?" Jefferies asked.

"I call him what he called himself the day I met him," the ranger said. "He's Sabio Tonto, the wise fool."

At midmorning the next day, they crossed the border and rode toward the badlands station and water stop at Choking Wells. Five miles from the water stop they watched the dust settle and knew Prew and his men had stopped. "They've ridden down onto the flatlands to Choking Wells," Sam said. Motioning toward a mesa rising up ahead of them, he added, "There's where we want to be for now. If we ride about halfway up we can look down on every move they make."

The two of them stopped. "I'll take the cut-in connectors, go find a place along the lines and wire the army camp," Jefferies said. "They've got to be warned." As he spoke, he sidled up to the donkey, rummaged through the leather supply bag and came out with the telegraph cut-ins.

Looking at the connectors and the coil of wire in Jefferies' hand, Sam said, "I've got a feeling you're going to find the wire has been cut between Choking Wells and the army camp."

"I've got to try." Jefferies reached back and shoved the connectors into his saddlebags.

"I know," said Sam. "When you're finished, follow my trail up. I'll be waiting at the end of it." With no further discussion, they turned their horses in opposite directions and rode away.

CHAPTER 24

From a rocky perch high up on the side of the mesa wall, Sam watched the Choking Wells water station through his telescope. He saw nothing out of the ordinary. A thousand yards east of the station, three of Prew's men sat on the ground in a dry creek bed, their horses' reins in their hands. But looking back and forth in all directions, Sam could see no more of the mercenaries.

Yet, as his lens made another sweep back to a stretch of trees and brush, he spotted three freight wagons lying in wait. "There they are," he murmured to himself. A thousand yards north along the barren rails, he caught a glimpse of Jefferies on his paint horse, riding back into the cover of trees from a telegraph pole. "Now we wait."

It was late afternoon when Jefferies rode up, stepped down from his saddle and hitched the paint beside Sam's stallion. "You were right, Ranger," he said, crouching as he walked out closer to the edge. "The lines are cut somewhere. It could take days to find out where."

"Maybe it's just as well." Sam nodded, raising the lens back to his eye. "From the look of things, this is going to go smooth and quiet. Prew has his men spread a long ways along the rails. He's wanting to keep this quiet and bloodless is my guess."

"Let's hope so," said Jefferies. "If we stop him and his men right here, we won't get Captain Murella."

"Then we need to sit tight and let Prew play this out before we hit them," said Sam. He lowered the lens long enough to point toward a set of rails running off of the main track and stopping three hundred yards south. "He's got to get the munitions car over onto those tracks, out of the way. He needs time to get it unloaded onto his wagons."

"You've located his wagons?" Jefferies asked, easing down beside the ranger.

"Yes. There are three of them." Sam handed Jefferies the telescope and directed him toward the hidden wagons. "Go a thousand yards to your right. You'll see three of his men."

Raising the lens carefully to his swollen eye Jefferies looked out first at the hidden wagons, then scanned to the right until he found the three men. "There's Loden," he said quietly, "the one who did most of this to me."

Testing him, Sam said, "I suppose you'll want to settle with him once we get started!'

"Only if it works out that way, Ranger," Jefferies said, staring at Loden in the round circle of vision. "I'm here to do my job. Loden is only one small part of it. I want them all."

Sam nodded to himself, liking the answer.

They spent the night listening, watching for any lantern lights or campfires below. There were none, save for a dim light spilling from a window onto the wooden platform. Two hours before daylight, Sam stood up from a blanket he'd spread on the ground. Checking his rifle he said to Jefferies, "Time to go to work."

Jefferies arose quietly. He poured fresh water onto his bandanna, wrung it out and pressed it to his swollen eyes. Ten minutes later they were on their way down the side of the mesa, riding silently, keeping their horses at a quiet walk. But before they'd ridden halfway down, Sam halted his stallion and said, "Listen—hear that?"

After a second's pause, listening to a low roar approaching from out on the distant flatlands, Jefferies said, "It's the train! It's not supposed to arrive here for another two hours!"

"It's early," said Sam. "Let's get down there. I expect if

he's got a station manager in his pocket, Prew can have him set things up however he wants them done."

They hurried downward as fast as they dared risk their horses in the darkness. But before they reached the bottom of the mesa they heard the roar of the train move across the land in front of them and realized they wouldn't make it to Choking Wells in time. "We haven't heard any gunfire. Things are still all right," Sam offered as they hastened their horses' pace across the flatlands. "They can't shake us off their trail, not with three loaded wagons."

By the time they reached the edge of the clearing surrounding the station, the train had finished taking on water and chugged on into the silvery darkness. In the east, the first sliver of red sunlight wreathed the rolling horizon. "Nothing happened," Jefferies said in a whisper, stopping his paint horse and looking back and across Choking Wells.

"I wouldn't say that," the ranger whispered in reply. The two listened to the creaking sound of one car rolling freely along the set of rails south of the deserted station. "We hoped this would go smooth and bloodless," he added, "it sounds like we got what we wanted."

Jefferies smiled, listening to the railcar slowing as it rolled along the siding rails. "They cut the munitions car loose as the train pulled out and switched it onto the siding rail." He paused, then said, "But what about the caboose?"

No sooner had he said it than the ranger's gun streaked up from his holster and pointed at the two startled faces that had just stepped out of the silvery darkness. They froze at the sight of the Colt. "Oh, Lord, mister! Don't shoot!" said one frightened railroader, both of them throwing their hands in the air. They wore bib overalls and floppy railroad hats.

"No, please don't," said the other one. "We never saw nothing, honest we never!"

"I'm an Arizona Ranger," Sam said, lowering his gun an inch. "What's gone on here?"

"A ranger!" Their attitudes improved instantly. "Man, are we glad to see you. We just got an army car and our caboose stolen out from under us." The railroader pointed toward the creaking sound of the railcar. "Soon as we seen they'd switched us, we hopped off and let it go. What else could we do?"

Noting their voices getting louder, Sam said, "You did right hopping off. Now keep quiet and get out of here before any shooting starts. Find the nearest place to get a wire off and let the army know they've had a munitions shipment stolen."

"We'll do that," one of them replied, and both hurried away.

Sam and Jefferies watched the two scurry along the rails. Then, listening to the sound of the single car rolling away, Jefferies said, "So far, so good. We'll find the caboose sitting somewhere along there. They cut it loose, braked it down and left it blocking the tracks for them."

"Prew knows his business," Sam said. He nudged his stallion forward, leading the donkey beside him.

"So do we," said Jefferies. "We'll catch up to them while they load the wagons, then we'll stay back and keep a close tail on them back across the border. So far Prew has everything going like clockwork. Let's hope he keeps it up."

"It would help if we had some light to work by," Elmsly said under his breath to Stu Wakeland and Sway Loden. The three of them hurriedly carried crate after crate of ammunition, blasting powder, and dynamite out of the munitions car and handed it down to Indian Frank, who stood stacking it in one of the freight wagons.

"Keep complaining and see if you don't get a bullet in your head instead of a cut of the money," Loden replied in a harsh whisper.

"He didn't mean nothing by it," said Wakeland, realizing Elmsly had made a mistake.

"You don't have to mean anything to get yourself cut out of the pay is what I've heard," said Loden. "Alls you need do is keep running your mouth."

"Yeah," Wakeland said to Elmsly as the two hefted either end of a larger crate. "Once these wagons are loaded, the need for men lessens by half, the way I figure."

"You figure right," said Loden. "Something went on when Prew and some of yas made that dry run. I ain't figured it all out yet, but I will." He looked along the side of the car in the grainy predawn light at the three wagons being loaded feverishly out of the long two-door railcar. Prew stood at the other door, his rifle in the crook of his arm. Cherokee stood across from him, his Colt hanging in his hand.

Wakeland and Elmsly gave one another a blank stare in the darkened railcar, then moved out and hefted a crate over into Indian Frank's big powerful arms.

"Now we've got somebody else joining us," Loden whispered as the two walked back into the railcar.

At the other freight door Prew lifted his rifle and waved it back and forth at a rider who appeared out of the silver darkness. Seeing the men loading the wagons tense and lay their hands on their guns, Prew said, "Everybody keep at it. This is our man, Ike Sherard."

When the rider sidled up to the railcar and stepped up into it from his saddle, he said, "Morning, Prew. How'd it go?"

"Sweeter than a birthday cake." Prew grinned. As he spoke he reached inside his coat and took out a thick brown envelope bulging with cash. As he handed the envelope to Sherard, he hesitated turning it loose. "You might ought to leave this with me a while longer. I've had an Arizona Ranger pestering me the past two weeks. He's still hanging around somewhere, no doubt."

"It's probably the lawman I told Spivey to warn you about," said Sherard, seeming unconcerned. "Didn't know it was a ranger though." He gave a tug, freeing the envelope. "If it's all the same, I'll take it up front, the way we always do. My army friend likes it this way." He opened the envelope, smiled, fanned across the bills, then closed it and put it inside his long yellow riding duster. Looking back at Prew he asked, "Who is this ranger? Anybody to worry about?"

"Sam Burrack," Prew said flatly, watching for what effect the name had on Sherard. "Does that name ring a bell?"

Sherard's smile went away. "Ring a bell? Hell, it fires a cannon." He half turned and said, "My army friend ain't going to like this and neither do I, you showing up with a ranger 'pestering' you, as you call it. Most people Burrack *pesters* end up being shit out of a buzzard's ass, all across these badlands."

"Hey, take it easy, Sherard," said Prew. "I told you so you'd be warned, not so you'd soil yourself."

"Soil myself?" said Sherard. "I'll act like I didn't hear that, Prew, 'cause I ain't taking the time to be offended this morning. You and Burrack have yourselves a real good time out here. Maybe I'll see you flying over or splattering down the side of a cactus." He stepped down onto his horse and gave it his heels, riding away quickly.

"For two cents I'd have staked him to the ground and burned the name of his army friend out of him with a cigar," Prew said to Cherokee as they watched Sherard ride away, his yellow duster tails flapping behind him.

"Say the word, boss," said Cherokee. "I've got a cigar. I can ride him down and get to it."

"Naw," said Prew. "We'd be taking a chance on losing what we've got set up with him. Maybe he'd lie to us. Maybe there is no army friend. Maybe whoever it is will only deal with Sherard instead of us." He gazed off toward Sherard's galloping horse. "We'll stick with what we've got."

Along the trail leading back to the main set of rail tracks, the ranger and Jefferies heard Sherard's hooves slow down to a walk as he moved cautiously toward the rail station. They pulled their horses into a stand of trees until Sherard drew closer. Even in the grainy silver light the ranger recognized Sherard as the man stopped his horse, raised his hat, wiped a hand across his forehead and looked behind him with a worried expression.

"It's Ike Sherard," Sam whispered. "Let's take him."

With a troubled look, Jefferies said, "No, let's let him pass. We'll get to him later—"

His words cut short as the ranger's big Colt jammed into his side. "I say we take him now, William Jefferies, and see what he's got to tell us." Before Jefferies could make a move, the ranger's free hand slipped his gun from his belt. "Walk forward," he said quietly.

"Who's in there?" Sherard called out, his hand clamping around his gun butt as he saw the two horses stepping out toward him.

"It's me. Don't shoot," Jefferies said flatly as his horse walked into sight, the ranger's stallion close beside him.

"Oh, it's you, Captain," said Sherard. His hand came away from his gun butt. "At first I thought it might be that ranger . . ." His words trailed off as he recognized Sam. His hand clamped back around his revolver and raised it halfway from his holster, then stopped, seeing the ranger's Colt already drawn, cocked and ready to fire.

"Drop it or fall with it, Ike Sherard," Sam demanded.

"Hey, what's going on here?" Sherard asked. Instead of dropping the Remington he slipped it back into his holster, as if the ranger wouldn't notice such a move.

Sam let the move go and said, "I'm glad to see I don't have to introduce you two."

"Damn it," Sherard said to Jefferies, "I never trusted you, you sonsabitch. This setup went to hell when Sergeant Keough died. Like as not, it was you killed him."

"Like as not it was," Jefferies replied. Then to Sam he said, "Listen, Ranger, you're making a big mistake here."

"He's right, Ranger," said Sherard. "I've got twenty thousand dollars in my duster. What say give it to you two to split however you like, and I just ease away from here, no harm done?"

"Not today, Sherard," said the ranger. "We're going to ride into the trees and have a good honest talk about who's who and what's what—"

Before Sam's words had left his mouth, Jefferies shouted, "Look out, Ranger!"

Sherard had made his play—the play Sam knew was coming when he saw the former lawman hadn't dropped his gun the way he'd been told to. But his play wasn't fast enough. Sam's bullet lifted him from his saddle and dropped him to the ground as his horse bolted in fear and raced off along the rails.

"A man can sure stay busy riding with you, whoever you are," Sam said, reaching over and snapping a cuff around Jefferies' wrist. His smoking Colt had swung back to Jefferies almost before Sherard hit the ground. "Now the other one," Sam said firmly.

Jefferies let out a breath and held his other wrist over. "Ranger, you've got to listen to me. You're making a big mistake."

"Oh?" said Sam, gesturing for him to step down from his saddle. "Bigger than the one I made trusting you to begin with?"

Jefferies dismounted and led Sam to the body on the ground. "I am Captain William Jefferies, Ranger. Everything I told you is the truth, except that I am the inside contact man who set this up."

"I see," said Sam. He stooped down and took the envelope full of money from Sherard's duster. "The part about you being the main one who set this up slipped your mind?" Keeping his gun on Jefferies, he dragged Sherard's body into the trees. Jefferies tagged along, his wrists cuffed in front of him.

"No, I didn't tell you I set this up because I knew how you

would take it," said Jefferies.

"Save it, Jefferies," said Sam, knowing that any minute some of Prew's men would be riding from the siding rails to investigate the gunshot. "Whatever you want to tell me, you can tell the tree."

"The tree?" Through swollen eyes Jefferies gave the ranger a questioning look.

"Yes, the *tree*," said Sam, waving him back to the horses with his Colt barrel. "Let's go. I still plan on putting your operation out of business."

CHAPTER 25

Standing with his face only inches from the trunk of a wild cherry tree, his arms cuffed around it, Jefferies said, as if speaking directly to the tree, "It's true I'm the one who killed Sergeant Keough. I found out he was the one informing Sherard when there were arms and ammunition headed this way. Instead of agreeing to cooperate with me, help me bust up this thieves ring, he tried to kill me. I killed him first." He paused for a moment, then said, "Ranger, are you listening to me?"

"Hmm? Oh, yes, of course I am," said the ranger, sitting on the ground a few feet away as he cleaned his Colt and his Winchester. "You just keep telling me your story over and over. I'll let the tree decide when we've heard enough."

Jefferies let out a breath and stared at the tree, shaking his head. "You're going to need my help with the dynamite, Ranger," he said. "When we get there, at least let me wire everything up. You can hold your gun on me while I do it. But please don't let these men get away from us. Do you have any idea how much they have stolen from the army?"

"You *can* relax, Captain," said Sam. "Nobody is getting away, including you." He continued cleaning his rifle. "As for what they've stolen, I don't see how they would steal anything else if you hadn't set it up for them after killing this Sergeant Keough."

"Prew and Murella would have replaced Keough soon enough," said Jefferies. "I had to set this up in order to stop them, once and for all. You can check with the army. I am who I say I am, blast it!"

Sam smiled thinly to himself. "Yes, I could do that, but like you said, the lines are down. I can't reach anybody."

"It's true they are down," said Jefferies. "But later, after this is over, you can check and see that what I've told you is the truth."

Sam stood up and walked to the tree. "Rest your tongue a while, Captain." He drew the keys to the cuffs from his pocket. "We've got to get behind Prew." He reached out to unlock the cuffs, then stopped and said in a grim tone, "Make no mistake. If you try to interfere with what I'm doing I *will* kill you."

"I understand," Jefferies said, rubbing his wrists as Sam released him from around the tree. "But you've got to tell me what I have to do to make you believe me."

Sam gave him a nudge toward the horses. "Just keep talking to the tree every chance you get."

Once mounted, the two continued on in the midmorning sunlight, staying back far enough to keep from being seen, yet following close enough to keep an eye on the three lumbering freight wagons.

They had crossed the border in the late afternoon when Sam saw the dust from the riders and the wagons settle. But instead of making camp right there, he rested their horses and donkey until darkness set in. "We're going to get in front of them," he said to Jefferies, who sat on the ground with his wrists cuffed around a smaller pine.

"Good," said Jefferies. "Tomorrow afternoon we'll reach the bridge crossing Cala del Rescate. We've got to get ahead and wire it. That's where they'll meet Murella."

"Redemption Creek, eh?" said Sam, considering it as he unlocked the cuffs. Jefferies stood up and stretched his arms before Sam cuffed him again. "What makes you so sure they'll meet there?"

"They always do," said Jefferies. "Keough told me that much before he decided to try and kill me." Walking to the horses, Jefferies continued. "Prew knows he can't trust

Murella, not out on the open land. They meet on that narrow bridge, Prew gets his money, Murella gets his munitions. By the time his *federales* got across the bridge and around those wagons Prew and his men would be long gone."

"Makes sense to me," said Sam, giving him a hand up into his saddle. "What makes you think Murella won't send one of his men to deliver the money?"

"He never does," said Jefferies. "Would you if you were him—trust one of the troops to carry forty, fifty thousand dollars?"

"No." Sam stepped up into his saddle, the lead rope to the donkey in hand. "I expect I wouldn't." Before nudging the stallion forward, he reached into his shirt pocket and took out one of the cigars he'd taken from the leather supply bag. He lit it and blew a long stream of blue-gray smoke.

"You're not a cigar smoker, are you?" Jefferies asked.

"On occasion I am," Sam said. "I thought I'd better try one of these, make sure they'll stay lit when I need them to."

"Are you going to offer me one?" Jefferies asked.

Considering it for a moment, Sam pulled one of the black cigars from his shirt pocket and handed it to Jefferies. He struck a match and held it cupped in his hands until Jefferies got the cigar burning. "*El capitán* might have some hard feelings toward Prew when they meet," he said.

"Oh?" Jefferies looked curious.

"That *was* no dry run," said the ranger. "Murella and Prew set up the bank at Plaza Fuerte. I followed Prew and left a small amount of money for Murella to find and think it was his share. So, there's no telling what we should expect out on the bridge at Redemption Creek."

A thin smile came to Jefferies' sore lips. "That's pretty good, Ranger."

"I try," said Sam, shaking out the match and gesturing Jefferies forward. "Let's go."

Circling wide around Prew's dark camp, they rode on

throughout the night until they reached the high wood and stone bridge at Cala del Rescate. There they dismounted and hitched the animals to the bridge railing. The ranger swung the supply bag over his shoulder and kept Jefferies in front of him as they walked down under the bridge out into the crossstructure of thick wooden support beams.

Two hundred feet below them the creek lay black as coal.

"So you are going to let me help," Jefferies said, sounding confident. "Good. Believe me, I want these men as bad as you do—"

"Talk to the post," the ranger said, motioning toward the thick wooden support post.

"Ranger, you've got to let me do this," Jefferies insisted, even as he held out his handcuffs for the ranger to unlock and relock around the post.

"Why?" said Sam. "You told me not long ago how easy it was going to be if I had to do it without you." Snapping the cuffs he said, "I'm having to do it without you."

"But you don't have to," said Jefferies. "I'm right here. Let me do it!"

"Anything I need to know, you can tell me from here," Sam said.

"In the dark?" said Jefferies. "This is crazy. It's never going to work. Turn me loose. Let me help."

"I can't trust you, Jefferies. Now shut up," Sam said. Setting the leather supply bag down at his feet, he stooped down and opened it.

Before dawn the ranger led Jefferies back to where they'd left the horses and the donkey. The leather supply bag on the ranger's shoulder was much lighter, with nothing in it now but the hand grenades and a short coil of fuse. As Jefferies swung up onto his saddle, Sam tied down the supply bag.

"Let's hope you got it all wired just right," Jefferies said, his hands still cuffed in front of him. "How much fuse did you leave?"

"Six feet," Sam replied, swinging up onto his saddle, the donkey's lead rope in hand. "That should give me time to light it and get at least a hundred yards away before it goes off."

"I'd feel better if was me lighting it," Jefferies commented under his breath.

"I bet you would," said Sam. He nudged his stallion toward a long stretch of woodlands whose outline stood black against a purple sky.

"What about me?" Jefferies asked. "Where are you going to leave me when you slip back to light it?"

Nodding toward the dark stretch of woodlands lying ahead of them, Sam said, "There are plenty of trees there. We'll find one that fits."

"You can't leave me cuffed around a tree, Ranger," Jefferies protested. "What if something goes wrong and you don't come back?"

"I suppose you better be rooting for me."

They rode thirty yards into the dark woods and stopped at a small clearing. In the east, a thin sliver of daylight seeped up over the horizon. "Now we wait until I know Prew and his wagons are close by." He stepped down from the saddle and gestured for Jefferies to do the same.

Once he had him cuffed around a tree, Sam untied Jefferies' bandanna from around his neck, looked at it and said, "This will have to do."

"Ranger, you can't leave me here tied and gagged—"

"Shhh," the ranger said, cutting him off.

They both listened to the sound of something or someone slipping in closer on their right, then on their left. Sam stepped over and lifted his Winchester from his saddle boot, realizing even as he did so that they were slowly being surrounded. He started to step forward, unlock Jefferies' cuffs and make a run for it. But before he could take a step, Sway Loden called out from within the trees, "Drop that rifle, lawdog. We've got you circled."

Sam stalled, trying to get an idea of how many guns pointed at him from within the predawn darkness. "I don't drop my firearms unless there's an awfully good reason," he said, his eyes cutting around, seeing no one.

"Let's see if these are reasons enough," Loden said.

After a moment of silence, Caridad called out to Jefferies in a frightened tone, "William, they have me and Sabio. But do not do something to endanger your own life—"

"That's plenty, little lady," Loden said. "Ranger, you're the one holding the gun. What say you now? You want to drop it, or you want me to pitch one of these Mexicans in there with their throat cut?"

"Do what he says, please, Ranger!" Jefferies said from his tree. "He'll kill them both without batting an eye!"

Hearing Jefferies, Loden chuckled and said, "Sounds like he knows me well enough, Ranger. Now what's it going to be?"

Sam took a deep breath and let it out slowly. "Don't hurt them. Here's the rifle." He gave the rifle a slight pitch away from him.

"Toss the Colt away too," said Loden. "Lift it easy like."

Sam raised his Colt with two fingers and threw it over beside the rifle.

"Now pull your hands up and keep them where we can see them," Loden said, starting to step closer out of the darker woods into the grainy light in the small clearing.

Glancing around, Sam saw other figures emerging slowly from the darkness like phantoms from some lower world. In front of him, Loden held Caridad against his chest with his right arm, his gun hand swollen from the beating he'd given Jefferies. Holding his revolver in his left hand, he raised a boot and gave Sabio a hard shove in the rear, launching him forward.

The former priest fell at the ranger's feet. When Sam instinctively started to reach down and give Sabio a hand up,

Loden called out, "Uh-uh, Ranger. He gets up on his own, or else lays there. Keep your hands high."

Sam straightened and watched Loden walk closer. When he stopped and kept Caridad against his chest, Jefferies tugged at his cuffs as if he might pull them loose. "If you hurt her, Loden," he growled.

"Shut up, Kid," Loden snapped, "or I'll kill her just for the fun of it." He eyed Jefferies warily, his arms cuffed around the tree. Looking at the ranger, he said, "What's this all about, a lovers' spat?"

Sam didn't answer. He wondered how much Loden and these men had seen and heard as they'd crept in.

"Why's the Kid cuffed, Ranger?" Loden asked. "Don't make me ask you something twice." He shook Caridad roughly against him.

"We disagreed on how to take you mercenaries down this morning," Sam said flatly.

"Take us down?" Loden chuckled again. "Hear that, men? We was about to be taken down this morning. Lucky for us we had a good hearty breakfast after a good night's sleep." Dark laughter rose and fell from the other three men. They stepped in close enough for Sam to see their faces.

Sam breathed a silent sigh of relief, realizing they had no idea that he had just wired the bridge.

"Here's why they feel so confident," said Elmsly. He held open the untied supply bag and pulled out two grenades and the remaining coil of fuse.

"Oh, I see," said Loden. He lowered his arm from around Caridad's neck and took one of the grenades in his free hand. "You were going to throw these at us?" He made a *tsk-tsk* sound. "Now that would have been plumb unfriendly." He passed the grenade back to Elmsly.

In the darkness, Sam watched Elmsly cut two six-inch lengths from the coil of fuse and stick one into each of the grenades. "There you are," he said, "just like the French do it."

"I'll be damned," Loden said in mock surprise. "You know something after all."

Elmsly dropped the two grenades and stepped back from them. Cocking his gun he said, "All right, let's kill them all and get it over with."

"Don't get stupid on me," Loden said to him. "We can't take a chance firing guns, maybe scare away *el capitán* before we transact with him."

"All right then, let's stab them," said Elmsly, staring hard at the Ranger in the grainy light.

"I can see you're not the man to leave here guarding them while the rest of us ride back to help Prew with the wagons." As he spoke, he worked his stiff, swollen hand open and closed, trying to loosen it.

Noting Loden's hand, Elmsly said, "Then why don't you stay here and guard them? You're going to take credit for capturing them anyways."

Loden stared at him for a moment, then said, "Hell, why not? Get a rope. Tie the ranger hand and foot over here by his pal for me. Then all of yas go help Prew bring the wagons forward. I'll wait here until the exchange is made." He grinned as he searched the ranger and pulled the handcuff key out of his vest pocket. He dropped the key into his trouser pocket and said, "I've got to practice taking it easy. We're about to become rich men."

CHAPTER 26

No sooner had the men left than Loden seated himself on a downed tree trunk closer to the edge of the woods, where he could alternate his time between watching his four captives and keeping an eye on the trail in both directions. Caridad sat down beside Jefferies and, while Loden looked off toward the bridge, whispered, "Why does the ranger have you cuffed here?"

"It's a long story," said Jefferies, his arms still wrapped around the tree.

"But perhaps a story we should both hear," Sabio said, giving Jefferies a wary look, "if we are to ever trust you."

"You're right. It's time I tell both of you everything about myself. Keeping the truth from the ranger is what landed me in these cuffs.

"But the important thing now is to get you and Sabio out of harm's way. Once Prew and his men are finished here, they're not about to leave any living witnesses."

The two listened while Jefferies explained who he was and what he was doing in Mexico. Twice he had to stop abruptly and wait until Loden looked away from them again before continuing.

When he'd finished telling them, Sabio looked at the ranger, but did not ask him whether or not Jefferies was telling the truth. Instead he whispered to Sam, "If you turn away from me I will untie your hands."

Sam waited until the next time Loden looked off toward the bridge. Scooting around quickly to Sabio, he felt the old

235

priest's thin fingers move across the ropes before untying them. "You must give me your word that before you leave you will give me the keys to the handcuffs."

"I'll give you my word," Sam whispered, "but only if you give me your word you won't turn him loose unless something happens to me."

"You have my word," Sabio said, his fingers going to work quickly.

"The word of a holy man?" Sam asked.

Sabio stopped and hesitated as if having to get something clear in his mind. Finally, as if grateful for the ranger's reminding him, he glanced at Caridad and Jefferies, then said softly to the ranger, "*Sí*, it is the word of a holy man."

After Sabio freed Sam's hands the ranger scooted away and turned quickly, without a second to spare before Loden took another look at them. In the near distance came the faint sound of creaking freight wagons. When Loden looked away again, Sam loosened the rope from around his boots, but left it lying there for the time being.

Near the edge of the trees, Loden stood up, his rifle propped against the downed tree trunk. "Here come the wagons," he said, more to himself than to his prisoners. Turning toward them, opening and closing his stiff fingers, he gave them a grim smile, one that fully revealed his intention as soon as the exchange had been made.

Sam had planned on waiting until Loden walked over closer, then jerk the loose ropes from his boots, spring up onto the man, take his rifle and knock him senseless. But as soon as he saw Loden look at the rope lying loose across his boots and heard him say, "What the—?" Sam knew he had to make his move right away.

Shaking the rope away Sam raced forward. Loden stooped quickly and made a grab for the rifle, but in his haste, the rifle slipped from his swollen hand and fell to the ground. As Sam charged toward him, Loden let the rifle go and went for the gun in his holster. Again his swollen hand failed him. He brought the gun up from his holster, but as his thumb tried to go across the hammer and cock it, the gun tumbled from his grasp and fell to his feet. He managed to grab a knife from his belt with his left hand, but Sam was upon him before he could put it to use. Thrashing about, the ranger with a firm hold on his wrist, Loden tried to cry out for help from the three wagons rolling across the flatlands. But Sam clasped his throat, silencing him.

From against the tree, Sabio pulled Caridad to him and held a hand over her eyes as he and Jefferies watched the big knife come down hard. Guiding Loden's hand the ranger plunged the blade deep into the outlaw's chest, then rolled off his body and pulled his own Colt from Loden's waistband.

"Hurry, Ranger. They'll see you," Jefferies called out in a lowered voice.

Sam rolled Loden out of his coat and snatched his hat from the ground before turning and crawling quickly back to the tree. He pulled cigars and matches from his shirt pocket, lit one and dropped the others on the ground. Seeing the curious look on Sabio's face he said, "For me to light the dynamite fuse."

"Oh," said Sabio, watching intently.

Looking off through the trees toward the bridge, Jefferies said, "Here comes Murella, right on time. You'll never get to the bridge and light the fuse now without getting shot."

"I can if they think it's Loden riding in," said Sam.

"They'll know it's not Loden once you get on the bridge," said Jefferies.

"Then I won't get on the bridge," said Sam. "I'll get under the bridge, cut the fuse and light it from under there."

"But you'll never get away in time, Ranger!" said Jefferies.

"I'll get away in time," Sam said confidently. "It'll go off before they figure out what I've done." As Sam spoke he took off his own hat and shoved Loden's down onto his head. He stripped off his duster and put on Loden's rawhide fringed jacket. Seeing Jefferies shake the handcuffs on his wrists, Sam said to Sabio, "Keep him here." He walked over to Loden's horse and picked up its reins.

"Ranger, this is crazy!" said Jefferies. "You're going to get yourself killed!"

Ignoring him, Sam stepped up onto Loden's California saddle and rode away as the wagons drew closer to the bridge.

* * *

The first wagon followed Prew and Cherokee out onto the bridge where Captain Murella and his men sat waiting atop their horses. A few yards behind the first wagon, three of Prew's men escorted the second wagon up onto the bridge. The third had just started to roll up when Murella pointed at the fast-approaching rider and said with his hand on his pistol butt, "Who is this? What kind of treachery are you trying to pull?"

"Easy, *Capitán*. That's one of my men," said Prew. But craning his neck for a better look, he said angrily to Cherokee, "What does Loden think he's doing! He's supposed to be watching the ranger and the Kid over in the woods!"

"I'll go meet him," said Cherokee.

"No, you wait here," said Prew. "I'll go see." A suspicious look came over Prew's face as he stared at the oncoming rider. He gigged his horse hard and raced back to the end of the bridge.

Giving the captain a puzzled look, Cherokee said, "I don't know what that's all about."

"Perhaps he leaves you to explain where my share of the gold from the bank is," the captain said bitterly.

"The what?" Cherokee looked stunned.

"Oh, you do not know what I am talking about?" said the captain. "Perhaps a bullet in your belly will help you remember."

"*Capitán*, wait!" said Cherokee. "I was with him when he buried the bank gold. It's waiting for you, just like always!"

"You lying pig!" shouted Murella. His pistol bucked in his hand. Cherokee fell from his saddle clutching his lower belly.

The two men in the first wagon went for their guns as Cherokee staggered to his feet, his revolver out, cocked and pointed at the Mexican captain. Shots erupted back and forth between the *federales* and the mercenaries. Prew spun toward the sound of gunshots. His horse reared as he turned it back toward the oncoming rider. He drew his Colt and shouted at his men, "It's a setup! Loden has sold us out! Kill him!"

Pounding toward the bridge, the ranger saw the fight break out between the *federales* and the mercenaries. Colt in hand, he returned fire as Prew and the men around the wagons fired an endless volley of pistol and rifle shots at him. Watching from the edge of the woods, Sabio threw his hand to his mouth and shouted back to Jefferies and Caridad, "The ranger is in trouble!"

"Hurry, Sabio!" Jefferies shouted. "Get these cuffs off me!"

"No, I gave my word!" Sabio said. "The word of a holy man!"

Even as he spoke, he saw Loden's big horse go down beneath the ranger, sending Sam tumbling head over heels across the ground. Sabio watched breathless for a second, not seeing the ranger move. "He has gone down!" he cried. "I fear he is dead."

"Oh, no, Sam . . ." Jefferies winced, but he had no time to dwell on the ranger's death. "Sabio, he's dead. You kept your word. Now set me free."

"No, Sabio, do not set him free," Caridad shouted. "He will be killed too!"

"Caridad, I've got to go," Jefferies said. "Sabio, don't

listen to her!"

"I will not send you out there to die," said Sabio. "They will kill anyone who rides toward them!"

"I have to go. Don't you understand?" Jefferies shouted, jerking at the cuffs around the tree.

Jefferies and Caridad watched a strange look of revelation come to the old priest's face as he dropped to his knees and picked up a hand grenade in either hand. "Ah, yes, they will kill anyone—except *me!*" he said, as if a tremendous puzzle had suddenly fallen into place before his eyes. "Their bullets will not kill me! My power is back. My gift will take me through their bullets unharmed!"

"No, Sabio, you're wrong!" said Jefferies. "Caridad, tell him he's wrong! Please, before he gets himself killed too!"

Caridad asked him calmly, "Sabio, are you certain your power is with you?"

"At a moment like this, my dear Caridad," Sabio said, reaching his hand out and cupping her cheek, "I am certain my power has *never* forsaken me. I have had times when my faith has been lacking. But today my eyes are cleared. Nothing can harm me . . . ever again." He turned and threw the key into the woods. "Step into the woods and find the key, Caridad. It is time for me to leave you."

From the end of the bridge, Prew fired behind him at the Mexicans as their bullets whizzed past him. But upon seeing the old priest charging out of the woods, he shouted at his men, "Here comes that old *brujo*. Shoot him!" As he shouted, he looked all around for the Kid and the ranger, knowing Loden had taken them captive along with the old priest and the cleaning girl.

Prew fired two shots at Sabio, but as his men set up a deadly barrage of fire toward the old priest, the gunman leader turned his horse and began firing at Murella and his men, seeing them about to overtake the first wagon. "What the hell has gone wrong?" he shouted. But shots from the *federales* shifted their focus up away from the first wagon and sliced past his head like angry hornets.

Prew could do nothing but race away from the deadly Mexican gunfire and veer wide of his own men as they fired on Sabio. Seeing the cigar in Sabio's teeth and the grenades in his hands, Prew shouted as he rode, "Kill him! He's gone crazy!"

On the flatlands, Sam came to and shoved himself up on his knees, still wobbly from the fall that knocked his breath out of him. Looking toward the sound of pounding hoofbeats he saw Sabio racing toward him, cigar, grenades and all. "Stop, *Padre!*" Sam shouted, struggling to his feet, but only in time to see Sabio streak past him.

Sabio neither heard nor saw him as he raced on through the heavy gunfire, wearing a glazed look and a radiant smile on his face. "Stop him!" Prew screamed. "Get those grenades!"

But it was impossible to be heard now in the steady hammering of gunfire. Prew saw that things had gotten out of his control. Looking all around for a way out, he suddenly saw the ranger standing on unsteady feet. "That blasted ranger! This is all his doing," Prew said aloud to himself. Batting his boots to his horse's sides, he raced straight toward the ranger, his Colt blazing.

Fifty yards to Prew's left, Sabio sped past, bullets flying all around him. "The fool won't die!" shouted Indian Frank. He emptied his six-shooter toward the old priest, then reached down and picked up a rifle that another man had dropped when one of the bullets from the *federales* had knocked him dead. Round after round, Frank fired, shouting, "Die! Die! Die!" But he began backing up quickly, seeing the old priest draw closer to the bridge. "Oh, hell!" he shouted.

The first explosions were the hand grenades going off simultaneously in Sabio's outstretched hands. The fire and fury of the blasts ignited the fuse running down the side of the bridge to the strategically placed sticks of dynamite tied into the beams and pillars. From the far end of the bridge *Capitán* Murella stood in his stirrups, looking into the gray cloud of smoke from the grenades.

Realizing that the sizzling fire running through the smoke was that of a dynamite fuse, he shouted to his men spread out over the first two wagons, "Retreat! Everybody retreat!"

He turned his horse and spurred it hard. Yet, before his horse could get a start, the bundles of dynamite sticks went off, one after another, less than a second apart.

On the flatlands, the ranger staggered and dove to the ground, feeling the jarring of the earth beneath him. He watched a large fiery ball of man, animal, bridgework and iron roll and sail high in the air. On the flatlands before him he saw Desmond Prew tumble, horse and all, and flatten as the blast of fire and debris skimmed over his back.

Sam covered his head with both hands and felt a hot wave sweep past him, pressing him against the ground. He knew the dynamite had gone off, but he expected the wagons themselves to explode any second. Yet, after a moment had passed he began to realize that the army wasn't going to ship real explosives, knowing how easily they could be taken by a gang like Prew and his mercenaries.

Standing in the passing smoke and falling bits of splinters and dirt, he looked at Prew, who'd also stood up, smoke curling from his scorched hat and riding duster. "You had to butt in where you don't belong, didn't you, Ranger?" he said, his voice sounding thick and distant in the ranger's throbbing ears.

"What?" Sam said, not hearing him.

Seeing the ranger's lips move but not hearing either, Prew said, "Huh? What's that?" He lifted his Colt and cocked it toward the ranger.

Sam didn't have to hear to know when somebody meant to kill him. He raised his Colt from his holster and fired. To Sam it was almost soundless, the shot echoing like a short distant clap of thunder. He watched the shot knock Prew flat on his back, one knee cocking up for a moment, then sliding to the ground.

Sam slumped and looked toward the woods. Caridad and Jefferies rode toward him on the Appaloosa. Staggering in place, he looked away toward the border and saw a column of cavalry riding up onto the flatlands, a civilian in a dark suit sharing the lead with an army colonel.

Feeling the throbbing in his head begin to subside, Sam heard Jefferies as he and Caridad slipped down from the saddle. "You did it, Ranger! You brought them all down!"

His head still feeling spongy, Sam said in a voice that sounded strange to him, "No, Sabio Tonto did it. He did it for her." Sam turned and nodded toward Caridad, who'd walked past them and stood looking at the high rolling smoke above Redemption Creek.

"Yeah," Jefferies said quietly. He looked at Sam. "She needs me over there with her."

"Then get over there," Sam replied.

But before going, Jefferies said, "Ranger, the man coming here in the black suit?"

"Yeah, what about him?" Sam asked, picking up the reins to the Appaloosa where Jefferies had left them dangling on the ground.

"He's going to verify everything I told you. He's going to tell you that I am with the army, and that my hands are clean in all this. He's going to say this is my job I've been doing."

"That you're one of the good guys?" Sam asked with a flat expression.

"Yes, as a matter of fact," said Jefferies, tilting his chin up a bit with pride, "he *is* going to say that."

"Not to me he's not," Sam said.

"Oh, and why's that?" Jefferies asked.

"Because I won't be here," Sam said. "This is army business now." He swung up onto his stallion and looked down at Jefferies. "Anyway, I already know it."

"You do?" Jefferies looked surprised. "Then why . . . ? I mean, what was all . . . ?" He looked confused.

"Take care of that good woman, Captain," said Sam. "You two sure went through a lot to find each other." He gazed off toward the smoke where Sabio Tonto had disappeared—*simply risen and vanished into the sky,* he told himself. *Yes, that's one way of putting it,* he decided. He turned the stallion, touched his boots to its sides and rode away. He liked thinking of the old holy man leaving that way.

Chapter 1

Gunfight at Cold Devil

*Here are preview chapters from Ralph Cotton's **Gunfight at Cold Devil**, the 16th book in the popular **Arizona Ranger Sam Burrack** series. Available soon in paperback and ebook editions.*

Ranger Sam Burrack stepped back from the crowded bar and left as quietly as he'd entered, through the rear door of Texas Jack Spain's Gay Lady Saloon. A cold gust of air swirled in and dissipated behind him. Save for the bartender, Ned Rose, who'd poured him a shot of whiskey, and one of the old miners standing beside him, who had picked up the half-full shot glass and drained it when he'd left, no one had noticed the ranger among the early drinking and gambling crowd.

"Didn't say much, did he?" the old miner, Scratch Ebbons, commented to the bartender, wiping the back of his hand across his wiry gray mustache. Five feet away a potbellied stove glowed and crackled in the dim smoky light.

"No, he didn't," said the bartender, having noted the sizable amount of whiskey the stranger had left, here in this cold land where whiskey and gold were held in equal reverence. Staring warily toward the rear door, he also noted to himself the way the pearl gray sombrero had remained tipped a bit more forward than was customary. *Hiding his face . . . ?* Ned asked himself. "Who was he? Did you know him, Scratch?" he asked the miner.

Scratch gave a crafty grin and said, "It might be I could come up with his name, over a drink or two."

"I see, then," said Ned, returning the grin good-naturedly. His hand closed around a bottle of rye as if ready to pour. Yet, instead of holding the bottle toward the old man's glass, he drew it back slightly and said in a quickly changing tone, "What say instead of me pouring you a drink, I knock what few teeth you've got out the side of your gawddamn head?"

Before old Scratch could duck away, Ned Rose's free hand reached out and grabbed him by his shirt, not letting him move. "Pl-please, Ned!" Scratch whimpered. "I was only funning! I meant no harm! If I knew who that feller was, I would've told you, *for free!* No drink needed!"

"Yeah, I figured you didn't know his name, you worthless old son of a bitch," Ned growled, turning Scratch loose. "Get out of my sight!"

As the old miner scurried away, Ned straightened his short black necktie and straightened the garters on his white shirtsleeves. He gave the drinkers across the bar from him a hard stare. "Any of you other old dolts ever seen that man before?"

"The sombrero?" said an older miner called Rags Stiles.

"Yeah, the sombrero, gawddamn it," said Ned, sounding impatient. "Who the hell do you think we're talking about here?"

"Easy, Mr. Ned," said Rags, not caring about Ned Rose's growing reputation for having a white-hot temper and a fast gun hand. "You draw more flies with sugar than you can with . . ." He stalled for a second as if to recall what else drew flies. "Well, more than you can with . . . stuff not as sweet . . . as sugar that is," he said weakly.

"Jesus," Ned muttered, shaking his head. "No wonder I'd

like to strangle all you old bastards to death!"

"As *gray sombreros* go," said Rags, unmoved by Ned Rose's attitude and insults, "there's two from these parts I can think of. One is Whitey Stone, runs a big herd for some Englishmen north of the territory. The other is a ranger named Sam something or other. But this is too far up country for the ranger. He'd be way off his graze."

"Whitey Stone died of snake bite, is what I heard," said one of the old men.

"Me too," another replied.

"Sam Burrack!" said Ned Rose, ignoring the others' comments, his senses seeming to pique suddenly. His right hand instinctively slipped behind the bib of his bartender's apron and touched the bone handle of his Remington .45 caliber revolver. His voice lowered to a whisper to himself. "Christ, that's him."

The old men looked back and forth at one another as the bartender walked away along the bar, not in a big hurry, yet not taking his time either. "After a *drink or two?*" Rags said, mocking Scratch with a critical look. "What the hell was you thinking?"

"Me?" said Scratch. "What the hell about *you? Something not as sweet as sugar* . . ." he said with equal contempt, all of them watching Ned Rose flip up a hinged flap at the far end of the bar.

Rose walked across the hard-packed dirt floor and pushed his way through a collection of men gathered beneath a halo of cigar smoke. "I think you're bluffing, mister," he heard a voice say from amid the onlookers. "I think you've been bluffing all night and all day."

At the edge of a battered, round-topped gaming table, Texas Jack Spain looked up and saw Rose step into sight as he dropped stack after stack of twenty-dollar gold pieces into the center of the table. "It'll only cost you another two thousand to find out, my friend," he replied, speaking above the ring and jingle of newly minted gold. A cigar stood loosely cocked in the corner of his mouth.

"That's what I figured," the cattleman sitting across the table from him said in a bitter tone. Inches from his right hand a LeMat horse pistol lay, its big bore agape, like some sleeping demon.

Paying the cattleman little regard, Jack Spain motioned impatiently for Ned Rose to step over to him. "What is it, bartender?" he asked, sounding just a bit annoyed by Ned's presence. "You know I don't like being disturbed in a poker game."

"You told me to keep you informed of all strangers coming in," said Ned, bending slightly and speaking up close, to keep the conversation between the two of them.

Jack Spain pulled his face away from the persistent bartender. "Yeah, but use some good judgment, Rose!" he said. "This whole mountain range is made up of *strangers*. I don't need to hear about one in the midst of a card game, do I?" He gave an annoyed smile and pulled back farther, as Rose tried leaning in closer.

"This one I thought you *might* need to," said the bartender, getting irritated himself. "He wore a gray sombrero—"

"Jesus, Rose, back off!" said Spain, pulling his face farther away, this time with a wince, fanning a hand in front of his face. "Your breath smells like you've been chewing rabbit guts."

Rose's face reddened; a chuckle arose among the bystanders. The cattleman gave a short grin beneath a thick mustache and commented idly, "I call you, Spain." Adding his bid to the already large pile of chips, cash and gold coin lying in the middle of the table, he said, "That is, if it's all right with your bartender here."

Before Jack Spain could answer, Ned Rose cut the cattleman a sharp stare. "Did anybody say a gawddamn word to you, Whitfield?"

"Hey," the cattleman replied, the grin gone from his face, his right hand tensing a bit, "there was no harm intended in my remark . . . nothing to get nervous about."

Rose took a step back and replied, "*Nervous*, am I?" His hand raised an inch, then streaked to the handle of the revolver beneath the bib of his apron. "Here's *nervous* for you, you cow-sucking son of a bitch!"

Leonard Whitfield saw the bartender's move, but was too late to make a play of his own. Before he could even start to reach toward his big LeMat, Rose's Remington came out, cocked and pointed, only inches from his face. "Who's nervous now?" Rose shouted. The onlookers around the table stepped back warily.

"Looks like you got the drop on me, bartender," said Leonard Whitfield, no longer attempting to grab his gun, his hand slumping. Yet defiance shined in his narrowed eyes. "Now either *pull* that trigger or else stop wasting my time."

Rose's gun hand stiffened. "My pleasur—"

"Whoa, whoa, *whoa!*" shouted Jack Spain, cutting Ned Rose off. Half rising from his chair, he said, "Put that gun away, Rose! Jesus! This is nothing worth killing over! You know Whitfield! He's never showed you anything but respect! Ain't that right, Leonard?" he asked Whitfield, hoping for support.

"I'm still sitting here," the cattleman commented, staring straight into Rose's eyes. "Where's all your guts, bartender?"

"Well, hell, then." Spain shrugged. He stood the rest of the way up and took a step back from the table. "Let 'er fly, if you two can't stand living!" He stared at Whitfield. "But he'll kill you, deader than hell, Leonard." He turned his stare to the angry bartender, adding, "And they'll *hang* you for murder before Leonard's washed and stuck underground."

Rose considered something for a second, something that didn't appear to be a fear of hanging. At the end of his thought, he let out a breath, tipped the gun barrel up quickly and let the hammer down with a flick of his thumb and trigger finger. All the while his eyes never left Whitfield's. In a lowered voice, he said to the unshaken cattleman, "You ever need to talk more about *nervous*, come let me know."

The whole barroom crowd watched in silence as Rose turned and walked away, showing his back to Leonard Whitfield. Only when he'd walked back behind the bar and lowered the flap on the bar top did the silence lift slowly like some unseen vapor. Then, in an even tone, as if nothing had happened, Whitfield said to Jack Spain, "Well, are you going to show me them cards? I damn sure paid enough to see them."

Spain took the cigar from between his teeth and shook his head. "Ned's got a temper a mile wide but only a hair thick. I ought to fire his ass for pulling that kind of shenanigan." As he spoke, he snapped his cards onto the green felt and spread them, a diamond ring glittering on his hand. "Two pair, aces over sevens."

"Damn it to hell," Whitfield growled, flipping his cards away. "I wish he *had* shot me."

As he stood back behind the bar waiting on the drinkers, Ned Rose's temper simmered, under control. But he had not forgotten Spain's remark about his breath. When Spain had gathered all of his winnings and stopped long enough to take his big wool greatcoat from a peg on the wall on his way to the side door, he gave Rose a flat, smug grin and said, "Now, then, Rose, what was it you wanted to tell me about a stranger wearing a derby?" He threw the big coat around him and pointed toward the door. "Make it quick, I'm headed for the jake."

"It wasn't a derby," Rose said in a tight voice, gazing toward the door.

"Well, whatever it was, you need to calm down, not to let things rile you so easily," said Spain. He spread his arms in a grand manner, stopping long enough at the door to turn and say to the bartender, "Enjoy life. Learn not to take everything so serious!"

Rose grumbled under his breath, watching Spain throw open the door and stride through it with a bounce in his step. No sooner than Spain walked out, Rose heard the deep thump of a metal gun barrel hitting human skull bone. Then, as quickly as Spain had left, he came staggering backward in three loose-legged steps, sinking lower with each step until he collapsed flat on his back and lay staring at the ceiling, knocked senseless. A blast of cold swirled in the open doorway.

"Sombrero, is what I said," Rose murmured to himself, a look of satisfaction on his face.

The ranger stepped inside the door, his big Colt in hand, his eyes making a quick sweep across the room. "I'm acting Federal Marshal Sam Burrack," he said, loud enough to be heard, but in a calm even voice. "I'm arresting Jack Spain for participating in a stagecoach robbery in Arizona Territory last fall." He paused, his thumb across the hammer of his Colt, ready to cock it.

"And I'm U.S. Marshal Pete Summers," said a voice. From against the bar, a young man stepped back to the middle of the floor, swinging a sawed-off shotgun up from under his long riding duster. Looking straight at Ned Rose, Summers asked, "Does everybody understand us?"

Rose shrugged. "I just tend bar here, fellows. I've got no fight with you two . . . unless *you* pick it."

"That's a good attitude," said the ranger, even though he noted a harsh tone in the bartender's voice. Stepping in closer, stooping down over Spain as Spain moaned and tried to rise up onto his haunches, the ranger pulled out a pair of handcuffs, flipped Spain over his belly and pulled his arms behind his back. Marshal Summers held the crowd covered with the cocked shotgun.

"Jesus!" said Spain, shaking his head in attempt to clear it. "What the hell is this?" His voice sounded thick. "You can't just crack a man's head with no word of warning!"

"I decided it was better than having to kill you," Sam said, clicking the cuffs snug around Spain's wrists and dragging him to his feet.

Staggering on wobbly legs, Spain tried to focus his swimming eyes on his bartender. "Damn it, Rose, are you just going to *stand* there?" he shouted in a strained and groggy voice. "Grab up that scattergun and let him have both barrels! These men are Arizona Rangers! They've got no jurisdiction here!"

"I've never been a ranger in my life," Summers called out, still keeping an eye on the crowd. "But I am a United Sates marshal—you can count on it.

"See? That's good enough for me." Rose raised his hands chest high, showing the two lawmen that he had no intention of trying any such thing. "No trouble out of me," he said, stepping backward away from the bar.

"You damn coward!" Spain said. "Don't let them take me out of here! I can't go to prison! I've got responsibilities! I won't last a week in prison!"

"You'll do just fine, Texas Jack," said Rose, concealing a smile. "Learn not to take it all so serious."

Spain stared coldly at him, his eyes starting to settle down and focus. "I'll get a lawyer and I'll beat this charge. I'm coming back, and I better find everything here just the way I left it, Rose. Or you'll wish to God you was never born."

"I don't want you to worry about a thing," Rose said, grinning, ignoring Spain's threat. He picked up a shot glass, inspected it and poured himself a drink. "Here's to *breaking rocks with hammers*, Spain," he said, raising the glass. "Don't you worry about a thing. I'll keep a close watch on the Gay Lady."

"You better, gawddamn it!" Spain bellowed as the ranger pulled him to the side door, opening it with his free hand. Toward the crowd that had left the gaming table and ventured closer for a better look, Spain shouted, "Ten thousand dollars, boys! Hard cash to whoever kills these lawdogs and sets me free!"

"That's enough of that," the ranger said, shaking Spain by his handcuffs and pulling him toward the open door. To the crowd, he called out, "Put it out of your minds. We're both lawmen in the pursuit of our duty. Don't try to stop us. Don't get yourself killed for Texas Jack Spain."

Stepping forward from the crowd with his hands chest high in a show of peace, Leonard Whitfield said, "Ranger, not to butt into your business, but you're not going to get much support from our *part-time* sheriff, especially when it comes to this man." He pointed a rough crooked finger toward Spain.

"Shut your mouth, Whitfield, you sore loser son of a bitch!" shouted Spain, trying to lean back inside the door. The ranger had to give him a strong shove. Summers stepped out behind him and closed the door.

"There was no reason for you to pull a stunt like that, Spain," Sam said to Spain, his breath steaming in the cold. He shoved him along the boardwalk in the direction of a small cabin and stone framed building with a sign reading SHERIFF'S OFFICE above the door. "This is no hanging offense we're taking you in for."

"What do you know about anything, Ranger!" Spain bellowed at him. "I've spent the whole past year and every dollar to my name getting this business up and running! Now I'll lose it all before I get back to look after things! Ned Rose is in there right now, stealing from me with both hands!"

"You built this business with the money you made robbing the Cottonwood stage," Sam replied. "So don't look to me for sympathy." He ushered Spain on, taking a firm grip on his upper arm.

"Then to hell with *sympathy*," Spain said in a lowered voice, sounding desperate. "Let's talk about some hard cash!" He stumbled along the boardwalk, half-turned toward the ranger and the marshal, his hands cuffed behind his back. A thin trickle of blood ran down from the swollen welt at his hairline. "I'm on the spot, fellows! What will it cost to get these cuffs off me?"

"Save your breath, Spain," Sam said, starting straight ahead.

"All right then, you hardheaded, stiff-necked lawdog son of a—"

"Easy, Spain," Summers cautioned him. "Don't think I won't knock you cold and carry you over my shoulder."

Spain settled himself and walked along, still a bit blurry from the blow to his forehead. At the door to the sheriff's office, he tried one more play, saying, "You two best consider taking my offer. You're going to find Whitfield is right. This sheriff and me are friends. He won't stand for you dragging me out of here. . . ."

Spain's voice trailed away as Sam shoved the wooden door open. On the other side of the office, inside a single cell, Sheriff Max Denton stood facing them with a stoic look on his face. A welt on his forehead matched the one on Spain's.

"I'll be damned," said Spain. "You've arrested the sheriff too?"

"Yep," said the ranger. "Max here had a pretty long run at robbing and killing before he ever pinned on a badge. The federal judge figured we might as well gather you both up since I was coming this way."

"Federal judge?" Spain asked. "What's a federal judge got to do with this? You're a territory ranger."

On the way across the floor to the cell, Sam took a U.S. marshal's badge from his vest pocket and said, "I'm working with Marshal Summers for a while. I have an appointment as a U.S. marshal for as long as I need it."

"Jesus," Spain moaned. "This country is going straight to hell. It's getting to where a man don't stand a chance."

Chapter 2

Gunfight at Cold Devil

Within a minute after the ranger had closed the side door behind him at the Gay Lady, Ned Rose poured himself a shot of whiskey and downed it in one gulp, as the customers milled and drank and talked among themselves about what they had just witnessed. All right, here was just the chance he'd always dreamed of, he told himself. It was time to make himself some real money and get out of Cold Devil. No good gunman could make a reputation for himself in a place like this.

Across the bar top from Rose stood a short, powerfully built teamster named James Earl Coots. Water dripped from the lower edge of his ragged buffalo fur greatcoat, where a thin layer of ice had melted from the heat inside the warm building. "I don't know what just went on here," he said to Rose, holding a delivery order in a thick glove. "But I've got seven barrels of beer out back that's going to be seven chunks of ice if we don't get them inside before long. "

"So? Get them on in here, James Earl, gawddamn it," said Rose, snapping out of his deep thoughts.

"Mr. Rudiheil says no more beer unless I collect for this load this trip," said the teamster. "I don't unload till I collect forty-eight dollars for this trip and at least ten dollars on the balance that Mr. Spain already owes on his account."

"Spain owes money for beer?" said Rose. "How much?"

"Close to two hundred, according to the old German," said the teamster, "and he says he's tired of waiting on it."

"Two hundred gawddamn dollars," Rose growled to himself. "Spain, you cheap turd." He turned to the metal cash box just beneath the bar and flipped it open. "Just one minute. Let me see what I've got here."

Walking up beside the waiting teamster and leaning on the bar, Stanley Woods, who worked as a pimp for the Gay Lady's two prostitutes, stood watching Rose in silence.

"Damn it to hell!" Rose cursed after a moment of counting money from one hand to the other. Snapping the metal lid shut, he turned, took off his bartender's apron, wadded it up and tossed it under the bar. He raised the Remington from his waist, checked it and shoved it back down behind his red waist sash.

"I know what you're thinking. You're thinking about collecting that ten thousand dollars, ain't you?" Stanley Woods asked, staring at Rose from beneath the brim of a frayed bowler hat drawn low on his forehead.

"Not me. But point out one other sumbitch here who's not," Rose said, a serious look in his eyes. "Ten thousand dollars is a hell of lot of money."

"Yeah, all these mules thought about it as soon as Spain said it," said Woods, sliding an uninterested glance over his shoulder, then back to Ned Rose. "But thinking about it's one thing. Acting on it is another." He picked up the bottle sitting on the bar and poured himself a drink as he spoke. "You're about on the verge of acting on it. I see it in your eyes."

"Yeah?" said Rose, staring at him. "Do you see anything in my eyes that tells you I give a damn what you think about *anything* . . . anything at all?"

Paying little attention to their conversation as he looked all about the saloon, the teamster finally said, "What about that beer, Rose?"

"Yeah, just a minute," said Rose, raising a finger toward

him to keep him waiting.

"It'll freeze sure as hell," the teamster said in a lowered tone.

"I'm getting your money, James Earl," said Rose, sounding irritated.

"I'm trying to talk business with you, Ned," said Woods, returning Rose's hard stare. "I know you and me ain't been on friendly terms ever since I started running whores for Spain. But we don't have to like one another in order to team up and make ourselves a fast five thousand each." He shrugged a shoulder. "What's your problem with that?"

"My problem? Well, let me see. . . ." Snatching the whiskey bottle from the bar top, Rose appeared to give the matter serious thought while he jammed a cork into the bottle and set it out of arm's reach. "If I *was* interested, which I'm not, my *problem* is, as soon as you opened your mouth, *ten* thousand dollars dropped to *five* thousand dollars."

"But your risk of getting killed by that ranger dropped in half, *too*," Woods said in defense of the two forming an alliance. "Sam Burrack is not a light piece of work, in case you haven't heard."

"Neither am I, in case *you* haven't noticed." Rose rapped his knuckle on the bar and added, "That'll be two bits for the whiskey. You just stick with the whores. It better suits your nature."

Woods' face reddened in anger and embarrassment. "You've got no reason to insult me like that, Rose," he said. "I came to you in an offer of partnership for both our own good."

"I told you I'm not interested. But if you demand satisfaction for anything I've said, I'll gladly oblige you, Woods," Rose replied with a smug grin. "You're packing a gun. We can go settle up in the street right now."

"I don't want a gunfight with you, Rose," said Woods, feeling things start to get out of hand.

"You're damn right, you don't," Rose said with all the

confidence in the world, "because we both know I. could nail your shirt buttons into your belly before you could get a hand wrapped around your Colt. Now does that give you any idea why I don't *need you* as a partner?"

Humiliated, Woods said, "I shouldn't have brought it up. I'll collect that money without you. Me and Carney will take care of the ranger."

"Carney Blake? Don't make me laugh." Rose chuckled, his hand still extended for payment. "He's been down drunk all summer. He'll be lucky if he doesn't shoot *himself.*"

"He used to be a hell of a gunman," said Woods, trying to save face. "All he needs is a—"

"Yeah, yeah, whatever you say," Rose said, cutting him off. "Now pay me two bits for the drink. Don't make me tell you again."

"Two bits?" Woods gave him a skeptical look. "Since when did a shot of rye cost two bits here?"

"The rye only costs a dime," Rose said, motioning with a finger for Woods to hand over the money. "The other fifteen cents is for me having to listen to your mouth. Now come up with it."

"Here's your two bits," said Woods, giving Rose a disgruntled look. He pulled a silver dollar from his pocket and laid it on the bar. "I said my piece. Now I'm going on with my plans. If you don't want to join me, that's your choice. Me and Carney Blake will do just fine without you."

"That's good to hear," Rose said sarcastically. "Don't try sobering ole Carney up too fast, or he'll start seeing lights flying around in the sky again."

"There were other people up around Benton who claim they saw the same damn thing," said Woods in Carney Blake's defense. "Some of them were sober as a judge."

"Then they must've been standing too close to Carney and it rubbed off on them," Rose said. "Stick around that drunken old gunslinger long enough, he'll have you seeing angels riding alligators."

"I'll take my chances with him," said Woods.

"Good for you." Rose made change from his pocket and dropped the silver dollar into his trousers instead of placing it in the big metal cash box lying just below the bar top. Seeing the curious look on Woods's face, he said bluntly, "As long as I'm having to run this joint by myself, I'm paying myself top wages."

At the top of a steep stairs, a young woman stepped out of a room, straightening her dress. Right behind her a young man named Riley Padgett swaggered along, buttoning his shirt, a drunken glow on his face. Rose raised a hand and motioned the woman down to him as he said to Woods, "You keep on running these whores. Only now you're answering to me instead of Spain. It's that simple. Any questions?"

"Spain didn't put you in charge," Woods ventured. "Until I hear from him, I'm going to—"

"Do as you're gawddamn told," Rose interrupted, finishing Woods' words for him. "I don't have to be put in charge. I took charge." He thumbed himself on the chest. "You'll either do like you're told, or else get the hell out of here."

He stared hard at Woods as the young woman came down the stairs and over to the bar. Behind her Riley Padgett smoothed back his hair, placed his hat down atop his head and drifted away toward a gaming table. "Any *other* questions?" Rose asked.

"Whoa!" said the young woman, hearing Rose's harsh tone of voice. "What's got your bowels in an uproar?" She reached out to Woods and put three folded dollars into his hand. Woods took the money and put it away.

Without answering her, Rose said bluntly, "Trixie, you're going to tend bar for me."

"Tend bar?" Trixie Minton gave Woods a startled look, then looked quickly back at Rose. "I don't know nothing about tending bar!" She looked all around. "Where's Jack?"

"Forget Spain. He's gotten his sorry ass arrested," said Rose. "Can you count—at least enough to *look like* you know what you're doing?"

"I can count some, sure," said Trixie, giving a slight shrug. "But not real good. Hell, not enough to make change . . . without getting us all in trouble."

"Then don't make change unless they ask for it," said Rose, dismissing the matter. "Keep them drunk and staring at your teats. I've got some business to take care of. Get on back here." He nodded toward the wooden flap at the far end of the bar.

"Is he serious?" Trixie asked Woods. "Margo has two miners waiting up in her room. She needs me to help her. Two miners at once is more than just a handful."

"Hey, whore!" Rose shouted, slapping a loud palm down on the bar top before Woods could answer. "Am I going to have to slap you cross-eyed before you start doing like I tell you?"

"Yeah, he's serious, Trixie," Woods said quietly. "You go on, do what he says. Margo can handle both miners on her own just this once."

Trixie walked to the far end of the bar, cursing under her breath as she lifted the hinged wooden flap. Rose swung himself up over the bar and landed beside Woods. Trixie picked up the wadded apron, put it on and tied the string behind her. On the other side of the bar, Rose straightened his vest and his tie and held out a hand to Woods.

"What now?" Woods asked.

"The whore's money, that's what," said Rose, snapping his fingers to hurry Woods. "She just gave it you. Don't start acting dumb on me."

"Spain always let me hold on to the money and turn it in twice a day."

"That was his way of making you feel important, going around with a roll of cash in your pocket," said Rose. "But not me. I don't give a damn how little you think of yourself—you deserve it. Now give me the damn money before I lose my temper with you."

"All right." Woods handed him the money Trixie had just given him, along with another thicker roll of bills and a leather bag of coins he'd collected from the two women since the night before. "Does this mean I'm supposed to hand the money over as soon as the girls earn it?"

"No, but be prepared to hand it over anytime I ask for it," said Rose, offering a slight grin. "It'll keep you paying attention." He quickly counted the bills from one hand to another.

Seeing the money caused the teamster to say, "I need to get moving. I need some money here."

"I hear you, James Earl." Rose shot him a sharp dark glance, nodded and finished counting.

"Divide what you've got there by two, and you'll know how many customers they've taken upstairs this morning," said Woods.

Rose cut Woods the same sharp glance. "I know how to count money, Woods," he said. "From now on make sure these whores turn in any extra money the men give them. I want a full count on every dollar coming through the doors."

"Damn, that's their money, Rose," said Woods. "How will I even know they're getting any extra? They'll just lie about it. They'll be hard to handle if we start messing with their tips."

"Search them for it, gawddamn it!" said Rose. "If you can't search whores and keep them under control, what do I need you for? I can have them turn money in to me, if that's all *you're* doing."

"There's lots more to running whores than that," said Woods. "You have to—"

"I don't want to hear it," said Rose. "Just do like I'm telling you." He reached over the bar, pulled up a heavy wool coat and put it on. "Search them for money each time as soon as they're finished, while they're still naked, before they hide it," he said, buttoning the coat. "Another thing. I want them telling us about anybody who's carrying lots of money."

"You mean . . . ?" Woods let his words trail. "Yeah, I want it," said Rose. "There's too much money getting through this place without us getting it." He paused for a moment, then said, "If you can sober Carney Blake up, and you really want to make some money, you ought to both be out there every night, knocking these old goats in the head and robbing them when they leave here."

"That's quick money, but it's bad for business in the long run," said Woods. "We'll get a bad reputation for people getting robbed here, and you'll see business go to hell. Spain would never stood for nothing like that."

"I know you're stupid, Woods, so let me make sure you understand what's going on," Rose said, getting impatient with him. "Texas Jack Spain is gone! The ranger has him. I don't know how long I'll get the chance to make myself some money here, but for as long as I can, I'm going to squeeze the settlement of Cold Devil for every dollar I can get my hand around. Is that clear enough for you?"

"I need to get paid here," said the teamster. "The beer's freezing."

Rose snapped round toward him. "Mention that gawddamn beer freezing one more gawddamn time, James Earl," he said in a tense but even tone, "and I will shoot you dead on the very spot where you're now standing!"

The teamster snarled, but backed away a step and fell silent.

"Yeah, you've made yourself clear enough," Woods said grudgingly, ignoring what had happened with the teamster.

"If you had any sense, you'd do the same," said Rose. Backing away to turn and leave, Rose pointed a finger at Woods and added, "But don't let me catch you stealing from me. This is my game now."

"Stealing from *him*, is it?" Trixie Minton said to Woods when Rose was safely across the floor and out of hearing range. "Since when did Jack Spain let this gunslinging bully start running the Gay Lady?"

"Have you not heard a damn thing that's been said here, Trixie?" Woods asked, getting cross and impatient himself now that Rose had walked out the front door.

"Yeah, I heard that Spain is in jail," said Trixie. "That's about as much as I could make out of it. What's he in jail for?"

"Jesus." Woods sighed, not wanting to have to repeat the story. From one of the rooms on the upstairs landing came a hard rapid thumping sound. Dismissing her question, he nodded toward the room and said, "Go on up there and help Margo. I've got the bar covered."

"But he told me to tend bar," Trixie offered.

"And now *I'm* telling you to do otherwise," Woods said in a stronger tone.

"If he gets mad . . ." Trixie said, hesitating.

"Don't worry. I'll take care of it," said Woods. "I'm as much a part of this place as he is."

Trixie Minton shook her head. "I hate thinking what's going to happen to the Gay Lady with Spain gone." She picked up a damp rag and began idly wiping the bar top.

"Me too," Woods said to himself, tapping his fingers on a Colt he carried holstered on his hip. "But I'm starting to get some ideas of my own."

"If you're thinking about that ten thousand Spain promised, it'll only get you killed. I've heard of that ranger. He's a tough one."

Looking all around the large saloon, Woods said almost to himself, "Forget the ten thousand. Maybe there's bigger, money right here just waiting for the taking."

Chapter 3

Gunfight at Cold Devil

Inside the single cell, Jack Spain sat on the side of a cot with a damp cloth pressed to his forehead. He cut a sidelong glance to Max Denton, who slouched on the far end of the cot, and said, "You told me nobody was looking for you when I offered to make you sheriff."

"Far as I knew they *wasn't*," Denton replied, holding a wet cloth to his own head. "The law seldom comes this far north. They must figure if a man makes it up this high into the mountain range, he'd most likely go on over into the Canadians."

"The law has gone crazy," Spain offered. "You can't put nothing past them anymore. I always figured one really big haul from a robbery and I could go legitimate the rest of my life. But *no-ooo*," he growled. "These sonsabitches won't leave you alone. Whatever happened to forgive and *forget*—to live and *let* live?"

The two leered with hatred toward the lawmen, who stood putting Spain's personal property into a canvas bag for safekeeping. He watched Sam drop his pocket watch, a large brass key, a roll of bills and a leather pouch full of gold coins into a canvas bag. "I offered ten thousand dollars to anybody who will kill these two bastards and set me free," Spain whispered to Denton.

"Was any of Morgan Waite's boys there when you made the offer?" Denton asked, watching the ranger fold the canvas bag and place it into an open saddlebag hanging over a chair back. "If they were, Waite is one son of a bitch who'll take you up on the offer."

"Riley Padgett might have still been there," Spain whispered. "He'd been there all morning, bucking back and forth between Trixie's and Margo's rooms like a stag elk. I hope to God he'll tell Waite."

"Me, too. Waite hates lawmen as bad as we do," said Denton. "There's times I felt a little tense being around him *myself*, that tin star pinned on my chest. I never knew when he might get drunk, start recalling some bitter memories and shoot the hell out of me."

"I hope he hears about it," Spain whispered. "Raymond Curly and his boys are coming any day. I've got to be here when they arrive. I expect you realize that I *don't* want to disappoint Raymond Curly."

Denton shook his head slowly with a troubled look and said, "Not if you want to go on living, you don't."

The two sat in silent contemplation for a moment. Then Spain said, "That same offer goes out to you, Max. If you see a chance for us to kill these two and make a break, I'll pay you the same as I would anybody else." He reconsidered and said, "Well, not ten thousand, not with you needing to get away as bad as I do. But you'll be well paid—you can count on that."

"How much then?" Denton asked in a hushed tone of voice.

"Enough," said Spain.

"How much is that?" Denton persisted.

Before Spain could reply, Sam called out to them from the battered sheriff's desk, "Where's the best place in Cold Devil to order in some hot food? This might be our last hot meal for a week, so pick wisely."

"Bracket's," Denton and Spain both said without hesitation.

"Look for the sign at the north end of town, if the whole place hasn't fallen over the edge of the cliffs," Denton added. "The Brackets was among the first to come up here, followed the miners. George Bracket fell over the cliffs building their place. Widow Claire Bracket stayed on, cooking and darning for the miners."

Gigging Denton in his ribs, Spain said, "Don't tell these sonsabitches all that. To hell with them." Denton fell silent.

"I'll go find the place while you fix us a pot of coffee," Pete Summers offered.

"All right," Sam replied. "I'll watch your back from the boardwalk, in case anybody from the saloon decides to take up Spain's offer."

From the cell, Spain called out, "You said *last hot meal for a week*. Does that mean we're leaving here soon?"

"You'll know when we're leaving, Spain," the ranger said flatly. "You'll see the town start getting smaller behind you."

Spain gritted his teeth. "There's no call for being rude, lawman. A man has a right to know where he's being taken and when he's being taken there."

"Any right you think you had went out the window the minute you made an offer to have us killed, Spain," Sam said, turning toward the cell. "The smartest thing you can do for yourself is try to keep your mouth shut as much as possible this whole trip."

Before Spain could offer a reply, the sound of boots walking up onto the boardwalk caused both lawmen to turn quickly toward the front door. Their guns came up from their holsters, cocked and ready. Upon hearing a knock, Sam gave Summers a calm look, both men knowing that, when trouble came, it seldom knocked.

"Who's there?" Summers asked, as Sam and he both listened for the sound of any more boots, either near the front door or around the side of the building.

"It's Ned Rose, bartender from the Gay Lady," the voice

said through the rough pine door. "Can I come in?"

"Yes, come on in, but make it slow and easy," Sam called out.

The door creaked open slowly and Rose stepped cautiously inside. Seeing the two big revolvers pointed at him, he raised his hands chest high in a show of peace and said with a cordial smile, "Damn, I'm glad I showed good manners instead of just barging on in."

Without returning his smile, Sam stepped forward, his and Summers' Colts still pointed, and flipped the front of Rose's coat open. He saw the Remington standing behind the waist sash, but didn't reach out for it. Knowing its whereabouts was good enough.

"I always wear it, Ranger, even to church," Rose said in explanation. "No offense."

"It's all right with me if it's all right with your preacher," Sam said. "What can we do for you?"

"I'm hoping you'll allow me to speak to Jack Spain. I'm running the Gay Lady. I need him to tell me how to get some cash for operating expenses and whatnot."

"And *whatnot?*" Summers asked warily. "You mean like the ten thousand dollars he's offering to pay somebody to kill us?"

Behind them, Spain and Denton stood up from the edge of the cot, taking interest in Ned Rose being there.

"No, you've got me pegged all wrong, Marshal," said Rose. "I've got nothing to do with that. And I don't condone hired killing." He gave a narrowed gaze past the two lawmen to Jack Spain. "Far as I'm concerned, a man with big nuts ought to be able to defend himself, or else keep his mouth shut and take what's handed him."

"Damn you, Rose," Spain growled, gripping the bars tightly with both hands.

Ignoring Spain, Rose continued. "The fact is, I need operating cash, if I'm to keep his business from going bust."

The two lawmen looked at each other for a moment. Finally Sam said, "You can talk to him from here, bartender, but don't try going near the cell."

"Obliged, lawman," said Rose. Turning to face Spain across the room, he said, "Seven barrels of beer is sitting out in the alley freezing. Rudiheil gave Earl strict orders not to unload it until he's paid fifty-six dollars for the load and a hundred dollars on the account you've been shirking on," he lied.

"Fifty-six dollars!" Spain turned red. "For seven barrels of *beer?* That's eight dollars a barrel! It's more than I've ever paid!"

"Then I'll tell him to take them back because we've quit selling beer at the Gay Lady." Rose said, unconcerned, as if dismissing the matter. He started to turn toward the door.

"Wait!" said Spain, stopping him from leaving. He stood staring at Rose with a smoldering look of hatred on his face. "Ranger, can I give this man some money out of my personal roll?" he asked Sam.

Rose held back a smile of satisfaction.

Sam looked Rose up and down and said, "I don't see why not, do you, Marshal Summers, to keep a saloon from running out of beer?"

"Sure. Why not?" said Summers.

As Sam reached down inside his saddlebags and pulled up the canvas bag containing Spain's personal items, Rose said to Spain and the lawmen, "What I really need is the key to the office safe." His words turned toward Spain. "I'll need operating cash to keep the saloon afloat."

"Like hell," said Spain. "Nobody gets the key to my safe, or to my office!"

"You forgot to lock your office door," said Rose, "so that's not a problem."

"I never forget to lock my office door!" said Spain, but he gave a puzzled look as he questioned himself. "You broke in!"

"It wasn't locked, Spain," Rose said firmly. He paused for a moment, then said, "Look, you could be gone a long time even if you get a lawyer and beat this thing. How long do you think that safe will sit there once the Gay Lady goes broke and the building is standing there empty? I'll run the saloon for you, but I'll need money to do it."

Spain knew Rose was right, but he couldn't make himself turn everything he owned over to a man he was convinced was out to rob him. Swallowing a hard knot in his throat, Spain said, "All right. The truth is, I lost the key to that safe a long time ago. There's no money in it anyway—maybe a few dollars is all."

"Then you won't mind if I go through your personal stuff, make sure it's not there. Maybe you overlooked it somehow?" said Rose.

Before Spain could answer, Sam cut in, saying, "Nobody can go through a prisoner's personal items without the prisoner's permission."

Rose turned to Spain. "Are you going to tell him it's okay to let me search your stuff?"

"Hell, no," said Spain. "It's the same as you calling me a liar, Rose."

"Is there a key there?" Rose turned and asked the ranger. He studied Sam's eyes closely, seeing if he could detect anything.

"I won't talk about a prisoner's personal items," Sam said, eyes giving up nothing.

Rose looked back at Spain. "All right, then, the key is lost," he said. "I'll have to make do on what cash there is in the till, and what the whores bring in." He paused as if considering everything, then said to Spain, "I'm only running this place for your benefit, Spain, thinking maybe you *will* get off easy and get back here real quick. If you want somebody else to run things, you say the word right now before I even take the hundred and fifty-six dollars for the beer."

Spain gritted his teeth and gripped the bars even tighter. "Take the money, Rose, gawddamn you!"

Rose ignored the cursing and asked, "Then you *do* want me to run the Gay Lady until you come back?"

"I said take the money, didn't I?" Spain rasped, barely holding on to his temper.

"Because if you'd rather get Woods, or Trixie, or Margo to run things, I'll gladly step aside—"

"Ranger!" Spain shouted. "*Please* give him the gawddamn beer money!"

Rose relaxed and watched the ranger turn away from him and began to count money from Spain's roll of cash.

"I'm warning you, Rose," Spain called, sticking his arm out through the bars and pointing a stiffened finger at his bartender, "I better not come back here and find you've been stealing from the saloon! I won't stand for it! Do you hear me? I won't stand for it!"

"Neither will I, Spain," said Rose, a slight smile on his face. "Anybody stealing from the Gay Lady will answer to me, as long as I'm running things. I already told Woods as much, in case he decides to try something. The main thing is, you get yourself a good lawyer and get on back to us." His smile widened. "That's what I'll be praying for."

"Son of a bitch," Spain growled under his breath.

Sam placed the roll of cash back into the canvas bag, and placed the canvas bag in his saddlebags. Turning to Rose, he counted the money aloud into his palm, making sure Spain saw and heard him do it. When he'd finished, he said to Rose, "I expect this will be the last we see of you while we're in Cold Devil?"

"That would suit me, Ranger," said Rose, seeming less cordial now that he'd gotten what he came for. He folded the bills and put them away inside his coat. But before he could turn to leave, a shot rang out in the street and splinters exploded from the pine door. "Jesus!" Rose shouted, ducking away and reaching instinctively for the Remington in his sash. In the cell, Spain and Denton both dropped to the floor for cover.

Sam and Summers both jumped a step away from the splintered door; but even as they did so, Sam's cocked Colt leveled toward Rose, causing the bartender to jerk his hand away from his gun. "It's not my doing, Ranger!" Rose said quickly. "I came here alone. I swear it."

"Then you won't mind giving this up," said Summers, reaching in and snatching Rose's gun from his waist.

Before Rose could respond, a drunken voice called out from the street, "Lawdogs! Get out here and face me! I come to set Texas Jack Spain free as the wind! Hear me, Jack? I'm here to free ya! Get my money ready!"

"Damn it," said Rose, "that's Riley Padgett. He's been drunk and randy as hell the past three days."

"Jesus!" Spain cried out from the cell. "I'm bleeding! I'm shot here!"

"How bad?" Summers asked, Sam and him both wary of a trick.

"A graze above my ear," said Spain, "but damn it, I'm hit!"

"Hang on, Spain," said Sam. While Marshal Summers kept watch on Ned Rose, Sam stepped to the front wall and peeped out from the edge of a window. Giving the staggering gunman only a once-over glance, Sam searched the roof lines, doorways and alleyways along the street. "Who's been drinking with him?" he asked Rose over his shoulder.

"Nobody in particular," said Rose. "He's spent most of his time with the whores, Margo and Trixie." Giving Spain a quick disdainful glance, he added, "I guess he heard about the ten thousand dollars and couldn't pass it up."

"Don't give me that look, Rose!" Spain shouted. "I'm the one bleeding here!"

"You're lucky to be alive," Rose called out. "Only a fool

would offer that kind of money. You'll draw every drunk and lunatic west of the Mississippi. They'll all be shooting in *your* direction."

"I was desperate," Spain shouted. "I wasn't thinking straight! Look at me! I'm shot!"

"And you deserve it," Rose shouted back at him.

"Rose, listen to me," Spain pleaded. "Tell everybody I didn't mean it! Tell them the deal is off, will you? Will you, please? Just tell Waite to come get me out. Just him, nobody else!"

"Shut up over there," said Summers, hearing Spain's message.

"Yeah, sure thing," Rose replied to Spain, sounding skeptical of the idea. "Why don't I put a sign up over the bar, saying, 'Spain didn't mean it'? Would that do it for you?"

"Both of you shut up," said Summers. He took a threatening step closer to Rose.

The bartender stopped talking to Spain. But he said to Summers and the ranger, "What about you two? Want me to put up a sign saying no reward for killing yas?"

From the street, the drunken gunman called out, "Are you coming out, or am I coming in blazing?"

Sam let out a breath. He gave Summers a nod and walked to the front door. "Keep an eye on my back," the ranger said over his shoulder. "When I give a signal open the window and let Spain talk some sense to his man."

"You're covered, Sam," said Summers, seeing Sam reach for the door handle. Then to Rose, he said, "Do what suits you after you leave here. But right now, keep still and keep your hands up. We don't know where you stand in this."

"I understand," said Rose, hiking his hands a little higher and away from his coat. "I came here for the beer money. I've got it. That's all I wanted. Let me know when I can leave." He tossed Spain a glance and said, "I left a *whore* tending bar. She says she can't count worth a damn."

Gunfight at Cold Devil

"Jesus!" Spain moaned, blood running beneath the hand he held to his grazed head.

Other Books by Ralph Cotton

The Gun Culture Series

1. Friend of a Friend   *2015*
2. Season of the Wind
...More to Come...

Western Classics

The Life and Times of Jeston Nash

1. While Angels Dance*	*1994*
2. Powder River	*1995*
3. Price of a Horse	*1996*
4. Cost of a Killing	*1996*
5. Killers of Man	*1997*
6. Trick of the Trade	*1997*

** **While Angels Dance** was a candidate for the **Pulitzer Prize** in fiction in 1994. This entire **Western Classic** series has been released and is available from Amazon.com and other retailers, as well as Kindle and other ebook formats.*

Dead or Alive Trilogy

1. Hangman's Choice	*2000*
2. Devil's Due	*2001*
3. Blood Money	*2002*

*The **Dead or Alive Trilogy** is available from Amazon.com and other retailers, as well as Kindle and other ebook formats, as part of **Ralph Cotton's Western Classics**.*

Other Books by Ralph Cotton

Danny Duggin (Written for the Estate of Ralph Compton)

1. The Shadow of a Noose	*2000*
2. Riders of Judgement	*2001*
3. Death Along the Cimarron	*2003*

Gunman's Reputation (Lawrence Shaw)

1. Gunman's Song	*2004*
2. Between Hell and Texas	*2004*
3. The Law in Somos Santos	*2005*
4. Bad Day at Willow Creek	*2006*
5. Fast Guns Out of Texas	*2007*
6. Gunmen of the Desert Sands	*2008*
7. Ride to Hell's Gate	*2008*
8. Crossing Fire River	*2009*
9. Escape From Fire River	*2009*
10. Gun Country	*2010*
11. City of Bad Men	*2011*

Spin-Off Novels

1. Webb's Posse	*2003*
2. Fighting Men (Sherman Dahl)	*2010*
3. Gun Law (Sherman Dahl)	*2011*
4. Summer's Horses (Will Summers)	*2011*
5. Incident at Gunn Point (Will Summers)	*2012*
6. Midnight Rider (Will Summers)	*2012*

Other Books by Ralph Cotton

Ranger Sam Burrack (Big Iron Series)

1. *Montana Red*	*1998*
2. *The Badlands*	*1998*
3. *Justice*	*1999*
4. *Border Dogs*	*1999*
5. *Blue Star Tattoo*	*2000*
6. *Blood Rock*	*2001*
7. *Jurisdiction*	*2002*
8. *Vengence*	*2003*
9. *Sabre's Edge*	*2003*
10. *Hell's Riders*	*2004*
11. *Showdown at Rio Sagrado*	*2004*
12. *Dead Man's Canyon*	*2004*
13. *Killing Plain*	*2005*
14. *Black Mesa*	*2005*
15. *Trouble Creek*	*2006*
16. *Gunfight at Cold Devil*	*2006*
17. *Sabio's Redemption*	*2007*
18. *Killing Texas Bob*	*2007*
19. *Nightfall at Little Aces*	*2008*
20. *Ambush at Shadow Valley*	*2008*
21. *Showdown at Hole-In-The-Wall*	*2009*
22. *Riders from Long Pines*	*2009*
23. *A Hanging in Wild Wind*	*2010*
24. *Black Valley Riders*	*2010*
25. *Lawman from Nogales*	*2011*
26. *Wildfire*	*2012*
27. *Lookout Hill*	*2012*

Other Books by Ralph Cotton

Ranger Sam Burrack (Big Iron Series), *cont.*

28. Valley of the Gun	*2012*
29. High Wild Desert	*2013*
30. Red Moon	*2013*
31. Lawless Trail	*2013*
32. Twisted Hills	*2014*
33. Shadow River	*2014*
34. Golden Riders	*2014*
35. Mesa Grande	*2015*
36. Scalpers	*2015*
37. Showdown at Gun Hill	*2015*

Stand Alone Novels

1. Jackpot Ridge	*2003*
2. Wolf Valley	*2004*
3. Blood Lands	*2006*
4. Midnight Rider	*2012*

Author Ralph Cotton

Ralph Cotton is a *Best Selling Author* with over *Seventy* books to his credit and millions of books in print. Ralph's books are top sellers in the Western and Civil War/Western genres, and in 2015 he debuted his new **Gun Culture** series with **Friend of a Friend**. Known for fast-paced narrative and wry dark humor, Ralph's introduction to the Florida crime fiction genre has been well received.

Sabio's Redemption is the 17th novel in the **Ranger Sam Burrack (Big Iron) series**, previously titled *Guns on the Border*, written in 2007 and reissued in 2016 in Ralph's Western Classics group of books, as well as an ebook.

Ralph lives on the Florida coast with his wife Mary Lynn. He writes prodigiously, but also enjoys painting, photography, sailing and playing guitar.

CPSIA information can be obtained
at www.ICGtesting.com
Printed in the USA
LVOW07s1500050217
523247LV00001B/25/P